DEEP IN THE HEART

AN AUSTIN AFTER DARK BOOK

Alexa Padgett

ISBN-13: 978-1-945090-24-0

Edited by Deborah Nemeth and Sarah Allen
Cover Design by Covers by Combs

For Deborah, my sharp-eyed editor,
who makes it all happen just as it should.

CHAPTER ONE | Jenna

The shop's outdated brass doorbell tinkled, and I froze, hands hovering over the small black keys of my laptop. Like most of the rest of the shop, the bell was a holdover from the mid-century remodeling done when Austin was just a small town with country music roots. Before South by Southwest—and most of the hot live-music venues—lined Sixth Street, located a mere block from the store.

I strained for another sound. My body tensed further in my seat, unwilling to move, much like a rabbit who'd scented a coyote.

That stupid little bell. Its sweet, tinkling chime remained an unusual occurrence, and one of the reasons I'd agreed to work with my Pop-pop. Interacting for hours on end with people exhausted me still. Even years after I'd been the unwitting—and unhappy—star witness in one of the most significant trials in the country's history.

Good news: bad people went to jail. I survived. Now, I even flourished. I sighed, still slightly annoyed I'd run back to Austin, a town I'd left, never planning to return.

Footsteps echoed through the front room, tapping a leisurely pace across the hardwood floors. Unfrozen muscles eased. My heart rate sped up as I rose and rounded my desk, cursing

Pop-pop's dental appointment. I was even worse at customer service than I was at idle chitchat. But as the sole employee—correction, co-owner—in the building, my responsibility was to the customer. Didn't mean I had to like it.

I grabbed one of Pop-pop's faded red flannel squares and gripped it in my palm. A throwback to the Depression, he said, though why I wasn't quite sure. Pop-pop was born at the start of World War II, so it wasn't like the man lived through those days. Yet, even now, the man wouldn't toss anything—and I mean one little wrapper—if he thought he could reuse it.

I stumbled to a stop and squeezed the cloth, trying hard not to hyperventilate. Of all the days… Of all the people… Dammit, *this* was why I'd attended college in Seattle. That, and to prove to my family I was strong enough to be on my own.

"Ben," I said, my voice small. My shoulders folded in.

The look Ben gave me now caused shudders to roll up my spine. He swiveled around to face me, his whiskey-brown eyes widening then narrowing as a smirk drifted over those perfect, sculpted lips.

"Hey, there, little girl," he said. I hated his drawl near as much as the fact he'd called me "little girl" since high school. "Heard tell you were in some music magazine."

"Not the first time," I shot back. The thing about Ben was never to show fear. Never back down. He craved the rush of overpowering me emotionally, physically.

He leaned in. "So I was told. But, see, none of the old crowd knew you were back."

My heart thumped in a painful, erratic rhythm against my

ribs. That was intentional. I didn't want to hang around Ben or Robbie or any of the other shallow people I'd surrounded myself with all those years before.

I gripped the piece of flannel even tighter in my fist as I threw my shoulders back, giving him my haughtiest stare-down. Not easy to do when he had a good six inches on me.

"Well, here I am. Now, will you please leave?" I asked.

His eyes darkened, and his expression collapsed into an angry sneer. There's the Ben I remembered.

He missed my glare because he glanced around, his lip curling as he eyed the small shop. Of course, Ben, being the preppy baseball player he was—wanted to believe he still was if the gossip I'd heard was true—wouldn't recognize the quality or value of the instruments surrounding him, either in monetary value or prestige. Just walking into this shop was a privilege many musicians longed for but couldn't afford.

Ben, like Robbie and the rest of the people I used to hang out with who I used to consider relevant, knew nothing of this world. He lived baseball. Had all through high school and college, too. Both boys' dedication to the sport meant I spent little time with Robbie, my boyfriend during our senior year.

Robbie's hard work earned him the starting position at second base at the University of Texas while Ben typically rode the bench. I'd heard through a convoluted grapevine that Ben was cut from his minor league team this year, which explained his sudden interest in me.

He'd always needed someone else to beat up on to feel good.

Why had I ever hung out with this guy?

Because he was best friends with my boyfriend—the only boy I could see, would ever love—all that lame shit so common in seventeen-year-old girls who hadn't lived enough to know better. Know anything, really.

The years I'd put into this shop, my reputation, mattered. I was proud to work here, proud that people wanted one of my guitars. Proud to be written up in some of the top industry magazines and of the shelf of awards I accrued.

"I can't believe I once screwed someone who works in a guitar shop," Ben said, pulling me out of my daydream where I kicked him in the crotch. "I thought, with your parents and your looks, you'd accomplish something with your life, Jenna. These are nice, for instruments. I should get one."

Ben peered around, then raised his eyebrows and gestured at it. "Why isn't there a price tag?"

I swallowed back the snort. "Because it's a custom-made guitar that took six months to build."

"Are you saying I can't afford it?" he said. Yeah. That, and, more importantly, my grandfather would never sell one to him.

"Most of these are spoken for," I said, refusing to be drawn into a verbal sparring match. Those exhausted me almost as much as being friendly to Ben.

The bell tinkled again.

Really?

Twice in less than ten minutes. This barrage of people was *not* okay.

I needed to hire someone to handle all this.

I blinked away the dizziness. I needed to eat. I needed my

pills. I needed to get into my workshop and away from Ben and the ugly memories he evoked.

"Look, we don't have anything in common anymore," I said. "As you just pointed out. I make guitars, and you want to play pro ball." Best to pretend I didn't know he'd been removed from the roster, thanks to his bad attitude and escalating violence toward his teammates. That would just make him meaner. And harder to get rid of.

"We're like…corn and toads," I finished. That didn't make much sense. Half of what I said didn't make sense, especially when I was stressed.

I finally caught a glimpse of the new customer. Tall. Taller than Ben, and broader, too. His dark hair was short on the sides but tousled on top. His slightly ratty T-shirt hugged him tighter than a jealous lover. Most of the time, tight tees meant men with big egos. Not my thing.

He turned toward me, and I sucked in a breath, squeezing that piece of flannel as if it alone would keep me upright. Holy shit on sugar toast, this man was *pretty*.

No. That was the wrong word. This man's eyes, much warmer and a lighter brown than Ben's, caught mine and held. I'd already cataloged the rest of his face: a couple days of scruff shadowed his firm chin and square jaw, full lips—not as full as Ben's bee-stung ones, slashing dark brows, and warm tanned skin. The bridge of his nose thickened in the same way my older brother Jude's had after he'd broken it in a football accident ten years ago.

"Hey. I'm talking to you." Ben grabbed my wrist.

"I'm done listening." I twisted my arm, trying to wriggle from his hold. Ben's fingers tightened to the point of numbing my fingers. He leaned into my personal space and used my captured hand to pull me forward until my chest was practically laying on the wood counter.

Nope, nope, nope.

I gripped the bat—I called him Gerald because…well, no good reason. I just thought my bat needed a name. I'd leaned my bat buddy against the cabinets earlier, and now I hefted the substantial weight as I brought it up, the end shoving hard against Ben's chest.

"I said I'm done."

He squeezed my wrist tighter and leaned into the bat. "We're finished when *I* say—"

Sweet baby Jesus in a peach tree. I regripped the bat, planning to take a swing.

"What's going on here?" the newcomer asked. His voice, all gravelly and rich, washed over me. "You all right there, miss?"

I yanked my arm, twisting, as I shoved the bat harder into Ben's chest. Ben let go of me, and I stumbled back. My piece of flannel dropped to the counter.

"You need to leave," I said.

Ben scowled at my look, so I turned my attention to the second man. My gaze locked on my new customer, trying to place him. He was older than me by a few years—late twenties, early thirties, I'd bet—and his jeans were worn in that sexy, I-work-hard way no type of washing could replicate. Now that he faced me, I saw his T-shirt said ARMY. An *excellent* look for him, especially when paired with—swoon!—scuffed motorcycle boots.

Who was he? I should know him; I knew I should.

His gaze never wavered from mine but, somehow, I knew he was keeping tabs on the rest of the store at the same time. He stepped forward again, getting between Ben and me.

His gait hitched as if he had a stiff leg. While uneven, he had the tread of a predator. Too young for the arthritis Pop-pop fought off each morning. I shivered with delicious anticipation for his voice.

"Y'all good here?" the man said.

I flinched at the bite in his tone. I hadn't done anything wrong. Wait, now the stranger glared at Ben.

"Hey, there. What can I help you with?" I said.

"He bothering you?"

I plastered on a smile, deciding to stick to honey instead of the vinegar I wanted to spew all over Ben. "He was, but it's all sorted now. Everything's fine. Do you have an appointment?"

"Yep. I'm here to meet with the younger Olsen 'bout a new guitar."

"Looking at her," I said, shooting for the upbeat personality most people expected me to wear.

The guy's brows drew together tight, and he shook his head. "Huh. Didn't expect a woman. Got the sense from your... grandfather?" I nodded, and he continued, "That I'd be meeting someone older—and nowhere near as pretty." He smiled.

"I'm Jenna." I stuck out my hand, and the man clasped it in his larger one. His palm was rough, almost abrasive. Not that mine were the soft white wonders they'd been while I was at

Northern University. No, my hands now were used to cut, shape, and smooth wood, work I found soothing.

He turned my hand and studied the redness on my wrist from Ben's harsh treatment.

"You do this to the gal here?" he asked in a low rumble that sounded like trouble.

Shocker of shocks, I *liked* this man's hand touching mine. Like, a lot. Strange, especially after my rejection of Ben. Ben's gaze bored into the side of my head, and my cheeks flushed at both men's continued scrutiny.

"I asked you a question," he said to Ben. His voice was deep, near as rough as his palm. I liked that, too. Mainly because he sounded nothing like Ben.

"I don't owe you nothing," Ben said, sullen but also wary like he, too, was trying to place this man.

"My body guard's outside," he said, tilting his head back a little. "Should I get him?"

"You *are* the country music star, Camden Grace." Ben smiled like a bright penny. "What are you doing here?"

That's where I'd seen him—practically everywhere since I'd returned to the city. Camden Grace was Austin's hometown darling. Born on a ranch just west of Lake Travis, Camden Grace had crooned his way to the top of the country charts by his mid-twenties. His first album had to be…oh…five years ago. Since then, he'd strummed out a dozen multi-platinum singles and two more full-length albums, and, in the last couple of weeks, some bad press.

"Need a new guitar," Camden rumbled. "J. Olsen's are

the best."

My fingers tingled as my hand slipped from Camden's. I clenched my fist, trying to ignore my attraction. To Camden Grace. Pile up the pepperoni and dive right in; I was always attracted to the *worst* of the male species.

"I love your music, sir." Ben's voice took on the excitement of a small, yappy puppy.

"Can't say I like your treatment of Miss Olsen here much," Cam grunted. "Why don't you skedaddle before you get yourself in a heap of trouble?"

Ben's scowl returned. Uh oh. I knew that look. Ben didn't take well to being ordered around. He'd always been the Bantam rooster in our circle, needing to preen and peck away at others to keep himself at the top of the hen house. I'd have to watch out for Ben's retaliation, which would be swift...and cause me more emotional distress. My hand gripped the bat tighter.

"I didn't see you on the schedule," I said in a rush, trying to diffuse the situation before Ben could escalate it and cost us business. "But I'm glad to walk you through your options, Mr. Grace."

He leaned his hip against the counter and crossed his arms over his broad chest. Standing there, he dwarfed Ben. But it wasn't just the size difference. There was a watchfulness in Camden's eyes, an awareness of danger that Ben, with his soft, privileged life, would never have.

"Cam's fine."

"Right." I turned back to Ben. "I'll need to ask you to leave so I can work with my client."

Ben's scowl deepened, his hands clenching into fists.

Cam dipped his head to acknowledge a large man now peering through the glass. Sunglasses covered his eyes, but his crossed arms meant no-nonsense. His brown hair was buzzed short, and his arms showed off well-defined biceps.

The man opened the door and strode in like he owned the place. "You all right?" he asked Cam. He sounded like a bear—even deeper and growlier than Cam and without that melodic quality.

"This man doesn't want to leave the premises even though the lady's asked so nicely."

I dropped my gaze and bit the inside of my lip to keep from smiling. Polite might be as far as I'd take my request. Nice shouldn't signify—in part because Ben never deserved kindness. Not from me, anyway.

Ben's expression darkened as he looked between us. "I'm going. I'll be back."

"I hope not," I said. "In fact, I'd prefer not to see you again."

Ben leaned back into my personal space and said, "We have unfinished business."

I turned back to Cam, ignoring Ben. "So, what are you looking for, Mr...um, Cam?"

My shoulders unbunched when Ben strode from the shop, the door slamming loud enough to make me jump. Cam's bodyguard wandered forward, placing himself near the glass door, probably so Ben knew he was being watched.

"Not your favorite person?" he asked.

Man, that rough voice sent shivers up and down my spine. Tingles upon tingles danced across my skin. I looked away to cover my reaction.

"Let's focus on your guitar."

"It's not my business," Cam said. He ran his index finger over the redness around my wrist. "And I get you don't want me to pursue him being here further, but he hurt you."

My gaze slammed back to his, eyebrows arched in shock.

"Fear rolled off you when I stepped in here. You don't like him."

I shrugged, unwilling to comment on my nonexistent relationship to a stranger—more, a rich and famous customer. "I don't."

"You need anything else, Cam?" the bodyguard asked.

Cam raised his eyebrows at me. When I didn't answer, he said, "I think we're okay now, Chuck. Just…keep an eye out, will ya?"

"I'll hang out here."

"I'll get you a chair," I said as I turned toward the back. I still gripped my bat. I set it down in the corner, trying to be unobtrusive.

"No need, ma'am."

My steps stuttered at the address—I was twenty-four! I couldn't be a ma'am yet. Whatever. More significant issues to focus on, Jenna. Like staying calm. Icing my throbbing wrist.

"You sure?" I asked.

Chuck nodded. He turned toward the door and crossed his arms. While he looked relaxed, his eyes continued to rove the parking lot. With his big body, short hair, and all-seeing eyes, I'd bet he was former military.

I ran my hands down my thighs and closed my eyes, taking a moment to realign my world—and my place in it.

"Want to come on back, Mr. Grace?"

"Told you, it's Cam. And sure. My leg's not interested in standing today."

"Oh! I'm so sorry! I saw you limping…"

"Shrapnel. From a bomb in the sandbox." At my look of askance, he said, "Iraq."

Golly gee green jelly beans. He played guitar *and* he was a wounded war vet? I'd missed plenty of details about Camden Grace—probably because I'd never been that into country music even when I lived here during high school.

"You were in the army?"

He raised a brow. "Army Ranger at your service, ma'am." His scowl darkened. "Medically retired, though, thanks to my bum leg." For the first time, he appeared uncertain. Lost, even. "Been a long time now."

I motioned him to the back and he moved slower this time, concentrating on each step from his right leg.

"Bad, then? The shrapnel?" I said, gesturing to his leg.

"Took out a chunk of muscle. Never going to win any beauty contests."

I held out a chair and he settled in, wincing. I wasn't so sure— he was beautiful. But he was also a customer, and Ben's physical attack created a severe case of freaking out…which, come to think of it, I hadn't done any of since we started talking. Huh.

I pulled another piece of flannel from my back pocket and twisted it. I needed to take my pills.

I blinked, then flushed. "I'm sorry. I didn't hear you."

"That's the second time you've gotten that look in your eye. What did that flannel ever do to you?"

I laughed, but it was a flat, hollow sound.

"You going to tell me if I need to beat up that kid who was in here before? What I saw—he harassed you."

This time, I smiled with actual warmth. "No, but thank you. Ben and I have a history."

"Got that. What I don't get is why you didn't kick him in the balls like you wanted to."

"It's not his balls I want to drop kick to Saturn," I said, mostly to myself. "That leaves too much of him here."

"Ah. There's a bit of humor. Sass suits you."

"Right." I cleared my throat and settled into my desk, pulling out a paper and pad. "So. A new guitar?"

Cam scratched his cheek, the whiskers making a raspy sound. "Yeah. I busted the last one."

"Well, if you bring it in, we can repair it."

The ruddy stain of embarrassment crept up his neck and crested his cheeks. "Not this one. I—ah—smashed it."

I jerked back, my mouth falling slack. Pop-pop's guitars were expensive, even for a wealthy country singer. Dropping ten grand—or more—to bust a guitar, especially one as beautiful as my grandfather's, was a shame.

"On purpose?"

"Things got a little carried away on the bus, and I took out my temper on the guitar."

He pronounced it the Texan way: *gi*-tar. I liked that, too. Oddly. I wasn't much for an accent of any kind, preferring the men I dated to be as vanilla as possible. Not that I'd dated much—at all—since I'd lived in Seattle. Being a star witness in a trial was hard on anonymity. Being the woman who slept with the drug dealer... I hadn't known Charles dealt drugs at the time, but that didn't make me look any better in the media.

My hand shook and I blinked multiple times, trying to keep my mind here in the present.

No good.

Pre-pills was not the time to think about love, romance, and the lack of sex in my life.

I dug around in my purse and pulled out my pill case. I dumped the two capsules in my hand before dropping them onto my tongue. Then I opened my yogurt smoothie and drank most of it down along with the pills.

Cam watched me, questions building in his eyes. I ignored them as I placed my pill box back in my bag and then shut it in my desk drawer.

"That bothers you. Me busting the instrument."

"Yes," I said.

He rubbed his hand over his lip and swung his left leg forward and back, like a pendulum. I kept my gaze fixed there, unable to meet his eyes.

"I'm not violent. Usually."

I picked up my pencil and tapped it on my pad in front of me. "This new instrument. Got any idea what you're interested in?"

"First I need to address your concerns." He waited until I looked him in the eye. "I found out my father died."

"I'm sorry," I whispered.

"I handled the news poorly. He and I…" Cam sighed, dropped his gaze and rubbed the back of his neck. "As you said, my father and I had a history. Not all good. If it makes you feel any better, I regret my reaction. I regret busting my guitar, and I regret having to call your grandfather to tell him what I did."

"Okay."

"Buried my father two weeks ago. Held my mother through the funeral."

What to say? No words came.

Cam sighed. "All right. Down to business. Something flashy. It's going to be my new stage guitar." A smile tugged at the corner of his lips. "I've been asked to perform at Fort Bliss. For the Fourth of July concert they're putting together."

I'd read an article about Camden Grace headlining the Soldier Celebration tour. All the proceeds from the event went to war veterans and their families. I approved of that cause. But one of the reporters sniped earlier this week that the performance was supposed to help rebuild Cam's deteriorating reputation. "That's in just a few weeks."

His eyebrow shot up and there was the entitled jerk the world loved to hate. "That a problem?"

I sat up straighter, met his eyes. "Yes," I said. "I'm booked."

He leaned in a little closer as he smiled, flashing those damn adorable dimples as his eyes lit up. Confidence. Best aphrodisiac ever.

Of course, he knew he was hella sexy. The man graced magazine covers, billboards.

"Your grandfather spoke highly of your skill, your work ethic. Said if anyone could make me a guitar that sings sweeter than Faith Hill, it was you."

"It's not a question of if I can make you a custom guitar," I began.

"Actually, it is."

He leaned in a little closer. I smelled caramel as his warm breath slid over my skin.

"Unfortunately, creating a quality instrument is a process," I managed to say without growling. I'd just dealt with Ben. No way I was letting another man push me around. "My *name* is attached to your instrument. I only allow the highest quality to leave this building."

Cam settled back on his stool and eyed my hands. "I understand a need for perfection." His gaze rose to mine and the heat in his eyes slammed back through me. "Me, I'm all about it. In fact, that drives my team crazy." He settled his elbows on his thighs and leaned forward again, using that sexy-as-sin face to his advantage. "This is about what your pop-pop said you could do for me. And the fact I'm looking for a perfect-for-me instrument that I plan to boast about at my concert and for the rest of my career. So, question is, can you help me out so I can help you out?"

CHAPTER TWO | Cam

Her eyebrow shot up and fire leaped into her eyes. Eyes that had been wary when I walked in now screamed confidence, competition, irritation, and...yeah, hot, steamy sex.

This woman was too cute. I mean, she was beautiful with all that thick, silky blond hair and big blue eyes, but she faded from professional and even a bit sassy to unsure, which she covered up with the right amount of composure.

Hell if I wasn't *still* a sucker for a gal in need of a thick arm and a strong back. I had both of those and, as my dad liked to point out, I offered them to ladies in distress.

I frowned. Hadn't worked out well with Kim. I laced my fingers and dropped my hands between my knees so Jenna wouldn't see them shake. Did a number on me *and* my family. And fool that I was, I missed all the signs.

Like most of the world, I knew Jenna's name because she'd been the central witness in one of the most-watched litigations of our times. Talk about notoriety.

The girl who didn't die. That was the headline I'd hated then and still found disgusting now.

At least my reputation was well-deserved. Sort of. I destroyed a twelve-thousand dollar instrument two weeks ago, so, yeah, I deserved the digs at my character. But Jenna…from the reports that came out in the trial, she'd been a pawn. In military terms, higher-ups called her hospitalization "collateral damage."

I hated that term near as much as I hated anything that might take the fire, the confidence from this young lady's pretty eyes. Protective instincts locked into full engagement. This time, my need to keep this gal safe had nothing to do with her stunning looks. *Almost* nothing.

Dammit. She was too much for me to take in. If I didn't need this new instrument so bad, I'd limp on out of here. As Chuck said, I reaped what I sewed. Smashing up everything on my bus that night proved damn stupid.

Better than turning to booze again.

Or drugs.

Hadn't tried those yet, though I'd been tempted a few times. Mighty tempted after Kim. Good. Jenna was talking and I could leave my own damn, messed-up head.

"You're right, your backing will help my career." She sighed, and I could practically see her counting hours in the day. "I'll look up the design for your last guitar and start recreating that."

"Don't want another one of those. I want something *you* design and create." I waved my hand to the main area of the shop where twenty or so instruments hung from hooks or sat in stands.

She narrowed her eyes, probably thinking I was hitting on her. Maybe I was. "Okay. What do you want?"

"You make anything flashy?"

Her lips flipped up like she couldn't believe I asked the question. "Sure. I just shipped guitars to Hayden Crewe and Asher Smith."

I whistled.

"Those guys don't play to your kind of fan, though. Their stage guitars needed to be extreme. Hmm, Dane Klein uses one of my designs. He's a member of Lummi Nation—an alt-country band that's closer to your genre."

"Holy cow," I said with a smile. "You only named some of the best musicians on the planet."

Jenna grinned. "There are a few others here in various stages of completion. Jake Etsam asked me to make him a bass. And I have a few other orders, but I'm not at liberty to give out those names or specs."

This gal didn't just wake up with that kind of client list. I might not know much about making a guitar, but I knew the process was meticulous and time-consuming. I also knew she hadn't been back in Austin that long. Less than three years. "Show me some of yours?"

She rose and strode from the room. Her eyes dripped wariness, jerking from my eyes to my hands to anything not related to me, but her gait was smooth as warm oil over hot steel. Damn, she could swing those hips. Best part, the grace was innate, subconscious. Sexy as...

"So, here's one I finished earlier this week. The second one is for Clay Rippey. He's also a member of Lummi Nation—"

"Band based in Seattle. Plays with Dane Klein, who you mentioned a minute ago."

She blinked in surprise. "I have a few others if you don't like these."

I took the first one she held out, her light blue eyes darkening further to a stormy near gray as I took the instrument. The color of Lake Travis on an overcast day.

Fantastic. I was waxing poetically about this woman. Hadn't been so interested in anyone since…well, since Kim.

Time to puzzle over my reaction later. For now, I focused on the instrument she handed me. The wood was smooth, the neck formed from a darker tone than the body or headstock, which were still richer than the typical maple. Mahogany or something like that. The guitar itself was more substantial than my current one—scratch that, the one I used to have. Not heavy or clunky but *solid*. I wrapped my fingers around the neck and strummed. A rich F-chord filled the space.

"The resonance here is amazing," I murmured. I strummed again, head tilted toward the sound chamber. I nodded my head as I played A, then C.

"Nice. I like this one's sound. And the heft. What's it made of?" I traded her the guitar I held for the other instrument. It had a wider body and was made of the more traditional woods. She seemed to brace herself for the exchange.

My chest tightened as I watched her hands shake.

Did she fear me? Because I'd told her I busted my guitar?

Our fingertips brushed. Heat flashed up my arm and coiled tight in my belly. I raised my eyes to hers and swallowed.

Her cheeks flushed and she licked her lips.

Well, now. Much better than fear. *This* kind of reaction I

could work with.

"The first one is alder. With a walnut stain."

"And Clay's?"

"Basswood with a maple overlay. The sides and back are Madagascar rosewood and the fingerboard inlays are sea glass I found on Alki Beach. That's in Seattle."

I studied the small, milky green inlays. A lovely, custom touch that would mean something to the owner. The effort she'd gone to, even if this was a custom guitar, surprised me. "You seem young to be a guitar maker."

Absolute wrong words to try to ease the tension building between us. Her back snapped straighter than my former drill sergeant's and her eyes cooled.

"I enjoy the process. It's soothing and rewarding. I can't say that about many other jobs."

"Not many women choose to make guitars. There's another family place out in North Carolina, I think. She used to be some kind of fancy rocket scientist or something until she got bit by the bug."

Jenna turned away to settle the first guitar into its stand with inordinate care. "I'm not a rocket scientist."

"But one helluva guitar maker." I strummed this instrument. "That sounds mighty fine. You really only been doing this a couple of years?"

"Full time for almost three. But I apprenticed with Pop-pop from the time I was twelve."

I never planned to tell Jenna her grandfather spoke about her at length one of the times I was in the shop—back before she started. Her grandfather liked me for some reason, and I didn't mind listening to him prattle on, so long as I could sit and watch him work.

I had a feeling Jenna wouldn't like that, and I wanted her to be comfortable around me. Better, I wanted her to *want* to spend time with me.

I was thirty-one. Too old for this visceral, shaking-in-my-boots reaction to a woman.

Jenna offered me an electric model this time, and I avoided touching her fingers because even that minimal contact lit me up like a sparkler on Fourth of July. The guitar's body was sleek, a streamlined take on the traditional body shape. I smiled at the Swarovski crystals inlaid in an intricate snowflake pattern.

I strummed again, perturbed by the thoughts racing through my head. Yeah, I wanted Jenna. At least the chance to get to know her better. Kiss those berry-red lips and stroke my thumbs down her supple neck.

"Do you have a buyer for this one?" I asked.

Jenna nodded, her cheeks pink.

"Anyone I'd know?"

Her cheeks brightened but she nodded again. "You'll see her play it at South by Southwest."

"But you won't tell me who?"

She met my eyes. I liked looking at her. "Client privilege."

"Didn't seem to matter with the other names you dropped," I said, raising my eyebrow.

Jenna's smile softened, her eyes brightening. "Kai, Clay, and Dane are good friends. Asher, Hayden, and the rest are willing to let me build my reputation on theirs."

I nodded as I picked out a song, trying to curb my runaway thoughts. Glancing up I caught Jenna's wide-eyed stare. Lifting my head fully, I stared at the transformation in her face. She started when I stopped playing, her hand rising to brush a long strand of blond hair back from her cheeks, her eyes shuttering and her mouth snapping shut.

"That's a beautiful tune."

I smiled, pride puffing out my chest. "Wrote it during my second tour in the sandbox."

She settled on the other side of a paper-strewn desk. "Iraq."

I nodded, pleased she'd remembered.

Jenna leaned forward, watching my fingers work the frets. "How many tours did you do?"

"Too many." I forced my hands to loosen on the guitar. No need to break her pretty instrument because I had head issues. Even all these years later. I reached into my pocket and pulled out a Werther's. I popped the candy into my mouth, letting the cool, hard caramel slick over my tongue and envelop my mouth, soothing the growing dread in my stomach that always came when I spoke of those years.

Candy in, I plucked out another tune, losing myself in the melody. Music helped, just like my psychologist predicted. Some days, music was the only defense, the only reason I was still sane. Well, music and sugar—either Werther's or of the female variety. Both were sweet and satisfying. At least briefly.

"Thank you for your service," she said, head still bowed.

Lip service. I hated that shit. Not the sentiment. I appreciated that I was a vet of a war people might hate but that they treated us soldiers with dignity. After all, I'd chosen to enlist at nineteen, hoping that choice would finally make my father proud of me. Within a few years, after the mess with Kim, combat was the only thing in my life that made sense. Until it broke me, mentally and physically, and all I had left was Werther's and music. I bit into the candy, but it didn't ease the tension building in my chest.

I handed the instrument to her and shifted in the seat. My calf ached from sitting. Hell, it always ached—not that I'd tell anyone. Never had. Didn't plan to start now. Probably always would. And I was a lucky devil—most of me was still, well, me. Couldn't say that about many of my former brothers-in-arms.

I didn't miss the adrenaline or fear like some of my buddies. The camaraderie, sure. Going from bunking with my men to being alone in a dark room at night left way too much time for reflection. And nightmares.

I stood abruptly, needing to do something with the nervous energy building in my legs.

"I like this one." I pointed to the second one I'd played. The acoustic alder wood. Clay's.

"All right." She tapped a pencil against the paper. "And you know our pricing policy?"

"Yep."

"You're not concerned about the fees?"

"You mean the fact I just held ten-grand worth of instrument in my lap?"

She met my gaze. "That one's closer to fifteen."

"But I said I'd give a nice discount because he's such a good repeat customer." Mr. Olsen strode in the back door and shot me a stern look. "And this guitar's for his performance for soldiers. Which he's promised not to bash against a metal floor or anything else metal. Ever."

Next to Mr. Olsen was a man about twenty, twenty-five years younger. Mr. Olsen was tall but with the start of stooped shoulders and a thick, shocking mane of white hair longer than mine. Age spots lined his thin-skinned hands and the sagging skin on his neck, but his eyes were bright and sharp. The younger man could only be his son—and Jenna's father, I'd bet.

Mr. Olsen junior stepped into the shop and walked around me to hug his daughter. After he gave her a quick peck on the cheek, he pulled back and looked me over. Yeah, I got I wasn't good enough for his precious baby girl. Didn't mean I didn't want those lovely lips pressed to mine.

"You coming to dinner this weekend?" the younger Mr. Olsen asked as he stepped back from Jenna.

She nodded and smiled. "Sure, Dad. I'd love to spend some time with you and Mom."

"Good, good. She'll like that. How about you text us the best day?"

"I will." Jenna hugged him one more time while the elder Olsen peered at the guitars next to me, nodding his head as pride lit his rheumy eyes.

Jenna's father walked back out the door with a last wave to his daughter and Mr. Olsen greeted his granddaughter with a kiss on her cheek. Close-knit family.

"Morning, dove. Glad to see you taking care of Cam here.

I didn't get a chance to tell you about his appointment since he didn't call me until last night."

I enjoyed Mr. Olsen's company because he didn't ask a lot of questions, didn't judge me harshly—even when I deserved to be derided. As I did in this case. I'd intentionally set out to destroy one of his hand-made guitars. Rage and pain were no excuse, and I didn't plan to make any. Nor was the fact I'd run out of Werther's—not just in my pockets but on the bus.

I'd rather the world believe I was an angry son-of-a-gun than an ex-soldier full of self-doubt in need of sugar confections to get me through emotionally-charged moments like these past two weeks since I learned my father died.

Jenna's eyes brightened at the sight of her grandfather, and her whole face softened, including those moody eyes. Like the sun coming out after days of cold, gray skies, I felt an answering tug to my lips.

Damn, she had a way about her.

"Hey, Pop-pop. Missed you for coffee this morning. Had to ring the sugar bell alone. Nowhere near as fun."

He hung up his coat before coming over to shake my hand. His grip was firm, his fingers rougher and more callused than mine.

"My granddaughter taking care of you, son?"

"She's been showing me the instruments she made. I want one like this." I pointed to the satin-smooth finished dark wood guitar I'd played second.

Mr. Olsen beamed. "A man of good taste. That's a mighty fine one. Jen here will make you one hell of an instrument. Clarity as close to the angels as we can get."

Jenna's cheeks pinked, but she smiled again. "We do good work, Pop-pop. No reason to go over the top."

"You're making better quality instruments than me." Mr. Olsen raised his hands to show his fingers starting to claw and gnarl with arthritis and age. "She's got an eye for detail you won't find anywhere else, Camden, son."

Mr. Olsen was the only man outside my family to call me Camden. My dad used to, years ago, as he slipped his belt through the loops of his Wranglers. I hated the word—and its association—for years. I popped another candy into my mouth. Thinking about my father's reaction is what got me into this mess. I needed to let all that shit go.

"Did she show you the detail in it?" Mr. Olsen asked, pointing to the guitar I wanted. "It's going to a rocker friend of hers in Seattle. He wanted something of home in it, so she found and polished up that sea glass. Took her hours to get each one the same size and smoothness. And look at the back." Jenna flipped it over. Slight color deviations showed a subtle wave pattern.

"He needs it in less than six weeks," Jenna said, annoyance threading her voice.

I handed her back the guitar before I shoved my hands in my pockets and rolled back on my heels, ignoring the pain shooting down into my calf.

"No, darlin', that's when the concert is. I need the guitar before so I have time to get to know the instrument. Feel comfortable with it and all that." I swallowed my second piece of candy and smiled, infusing it with all the boyish charm I'd long since lost. But, for some reason, the gals still assumed I had an ounce of decency left in me.

I didn't.

After what Kim did—after I took her deception out on my father, my family—how could I?

Jenna leaned forward enough for her light scent to drift into my nose. I sighed, my tensed shoulders relaxing. The light above shone through the delicate shell of her ear, highlighting the curve of her cheekbone, the plump, red bottom lip.

She was beautiful. Sexy without effort. No wonder the punk kid wanted her—and he did want her—which worried me.

I shifted, trying to ease the ache building in my groin. *I* wanted Jenna. Bad, if I were honest with myself.

Wrong though it might be, if I could talk Jenna into a roll in the sheets between meetings for my new instrument, I would. Not because I didn't respect the hell out of Mr. Olsen. I did. Not because I didn't know he'd never let me back in his shop or purchase another of his amazing guitars when I broke his granddaughter's heart. Got that, too.

Jenna stood up and met my gaze with those wide, wary eyes. My eyes dropped to her berry-tinted lips. For the first time in years, I yearned for a woman. Might even be compelled to write a song about her.

This zing of anticipation coiled through me, keeping my mind out of the recurring loop: those bad months in the sandbox, off Kim and my father. If Jenna could distill my focus this well just by being in the same room, then what could she do to quiet my mind when I touched her? I might sleep more than a few hours before the nightmares came.

If I could talk her into spending time with me. Hell, I'd take anything she'd give me—even if that were just sitting in the shop while she built my guitar. This moment of quiet was that unusual. More, it was precious.

Time to cut and run.

"Why don't y'all talk it over? Worst case scenario, I can always play my old guitar." No way Mr. Olsen would let me play that when his name could flash in the bright lights at this gig. *You're a manipulator, Camden*, my father's voice boomed in my head. *A manipulator who doesn't care who he hurts so long as his vision is met. That's not just bad behavior, it'll turn you into a cheat. And I didn't raise a cheat, boy.*

"Oh, we can get you what you need, son."

Jenna straightened, clearly not liking her grandfather stepping in for her. "I'll make sure you get a guitar you're happy with. But I'm going to hold you to keeping it in pristine condition."

I smiled a little. Smart one, this gal. Maybe she wasn't all sugar.

"That's a practice guitar. Nothing too fancy. In fact, I helped your Pop make it. I like to use my hands." I winked at her, intentionally leaving off the fact I'd been an absolute mess when I first showed up here nearly five years ago. Mr. Olsen took pity on me, telling me stories of his time in Korea, how much he missed Jenna's grandmother. The changes in his thought process that took years of distance—and therapy via working with wood—to come to peace with.

The guitar Jenna mentioned had a beautiful sound because Mr. Olsen ensured it did, but he'd made me craft the exterior to help me get past the worst of my demons. I came into the shop every day for five months. The final effort wasn't fit for public consumption, but that guitar was an extension of me—and my struggle to get back to some semblance of normalcy.

"He's right, dove. Cam and I built that instrument together. We made a deal he'd never perform with it. It's not...how do I say this?"

"It's ugly as sin but sounds more beautiful than any angel's voice."

Mr. Olsen chuckled and shook his head. "Summed it up well, there, son."

I smirked, my eyes shifting back to Jenna. "Appreciate it, sir."

"So, we'll make you a pretty one fit for the stage," Mr. Olsen said with a smile.

Still not quite sure why the older man seemed to like me, I smiled back, glad for the approval. One of the hardest realities with being an NCO Ranger team leader at the ripe old age of twenty-one was I was the buck and most decisions for my guys— especially mistakes—stopped with me. But I was no one's team leader these days, and I was a hella long way from a fresh-faced kid now. The mileage of these past years roughened me up and tired me out.

"Since you live in Austin, we can touch base pretty easily. And now that Jenna has a sense of your style, she and I need to go through our wood supply and develop a timetable for your project. I'll have Jenna get with you later today to go over all the details."

Jenna had recovered from my timetable bombshell enough to shut her mouth, but her lips were white with strain. I didn't like that look on her face. Not one bit. Was it from the meds? The man grabbing onto her wrist earlier? My demands? Damn, I didn't want to add to this woman's problems.

Not if I could get her to help me instead. Symbiosis. Mutually beneficial. With lots of orgasms. Once again, that need to hug her tight in my lap and keep her safe from the rest of the world rose in me.

Definitely time to cut out before I lost my ever-loving mind.

"Sure thing, Mr. Olsen. Can you show me some of your instruments on my way out? I'm gonna be talking to George next week and wanted to tell him what you got cooking."

The older man smiled, a beaming kind of good humor and pride, and motioned me forward. I listened with half an ear though my mind enjoyed the clean lines and quality construction. Took going overseas and ending up in a VA hospital in Washington, D.C. to find out that this place I needed, the people, too, were in my backyard.

The world was a crazy, ass-backward place.

As we neared the door, I glanced over my shoulder to make sure Jenna had stayed in the back.

"I need to tell you Jenna had a visitor when I showed up."

Mr. Olsen smiled. "Don't get many drop-ins these days. We're by appointment, but every once in a while, we have some kids from the university wanting to jam. That's why I set up the security cameras."

"He wasn't here to check out the merchandise. His body language was threatening." Lame finish but I didn't know how else to explain my concerns to this man, especially about leaving his beautiful granddaughter alone in the place. I shoved my hand in my pocket and closed it around the smooth plastic wrapper of another candy.

Not yet. Three in twenty minutes showed a lack of control.

The older man's eyes narrowed as his lips pulled down. "You catch his name?"

"Ben. No last name."

Mr. Olsen's mouth tightened in disapproval as he shook his head. "I'd hoped he had the sense God gave a flea and realize he wasn't wanted around here. Never could stand that boy."

"You know him, then?" I asked, curiosity rising.

Mr. Olsen raised his bushy, graying eyebrow. "He was best friends with Jenna's boyfriend back in high school."

"But she's gotta be—"

"Twenty-four, almost twenty-five. So, this was more than six years gone. That boy's always been selfish and needy," Mr. Olsen mumbled, turning away.

I stopped him with a hand on his shoulder, thinking about the raised, red marks on Jenna's wrist. "You think he'll hurt her?" I asked.

The older man's shoulders sagged forward further. "He already has."

CHAPTER THREE | Jenna

My hands clenched around nothing and I missed that small piece of red flannel in my hand. Taking pills in front of Cam lacked professionalism, but their needed calm became vital as I slid further into the past.

Ben's visit upset me more than I wanted to admit. More than it should.

Pop-pop settled his hand on my shoulder, squeezing before his usual three pats. That continuity was one of the best traits in my grandfather. My expectations always met with reality. I breathed out a sigh, letting some of the tension drain from my shoulders.

"I've asked you not to set up appointments when I'm here alone. What if Cam was looking to steal from us? Or…" I racked my brain trying to think up something worse.

"You know I had those surveillance cameras installed a couple years back," Pop-pop said as he settled himself into his chair.

He winced and my anger dissipated in a cloud of concern. Before I could open my mouth to ask about his doctor's appointment, he continued.

"We've got cameras in the parking lot, the front room, back here, and in the workshop. Nearly a hundred of 'em. Figured if I was going to do it, might as well do it up right." His sharp gaze held mine. "Which is why I want to talk about the visitor you had before Cam showed up."

For the second time this morning, my mouth worked before my vocal cords. "H-how did you know?"

He pulled out his cell phone. "They created an app for every-thing."

I snorted at that truth. J. Olsen—the company or the man—never stood on history simply for its sake. While the traditional ways of crafting a guitar brought my grandfather to prominence, upgrading his process—and patenting it—made him wealthy.

"Want to tell me why Ben was here before nine this morning?"

"He stopped by to say hello," I said, proud my voice remained level.

"Jenna." My grandfather's voice filled with censure. "It's not like that young man to do much of anything that doesn't directly benefit his ego."

I smiled, but it was bittersweet. Pop-pop had never liked any of my boyfriends. If I'd gone with my grandfather's gut instinct and never said yes to that first date with Robbie, I'd be carrying a lot less emotional baggage around.

Up in Seattle, with Abbi, I had a bad experience once with drug-laced chocolates—put me in a coma and nearly cost me my life. That experience had humbled me to the point where I needed my family, wanted their advice before I stepped out on my own again, but that didn't mean I planned to follow every bit of it. That would be like putting socks on a cat. I'd spend all my time trying to shake off the warmth only to realize it was keeping me from frostbite.

"Nothing important."

"Did he threaten you?" Pop-pop asked.

"No. Mainly, he wanted to laugh at how pathetic my existence was." I winced, realizing too late that I was talking to my business partner as well as my grandfather.

"Because, at the ripe old age of twenty-four, you're the co-owner of a multi-million-dollar business?"

I squeezed my grandfather's age-spotted hand. "Because I wasn't his—or Robbie's, or some other successful athlete's—arm candy. Me, being part of something successful on my own, never occurred to him. His brain can't comprehend such miracles as independence."

Pop-pop leaned forward and braced his elbows on his thighs. "You don't need a man, Jenna-dove. You got your two hands." He rubbed his thumbs across the back of my hands, his rough skin catching on my own. "A great mind." He smiled. "And more creativity in your pinky finger than most people have in their whole bodies."

I threw my arms around his neck. "Thank you for believing in me," I whispered, head against his shoulder, unable to get my vocal cords to do more.

"That's the easiest part of all. I'm proud of you."

For him, maybe. But to my father, I'd always be a disappointment. In part because of my gender, in part because of my fall-apart my senior year in high school when the pressure for perfection all became too much.

After a quick squeeze to my sides, Pop-pop pulled back. "Now. We have a guitar to make." He grinned. "Rather, *you* have a guitar to make for that country music legend."

"You think he will be?" I asked, something in my throat catching at the thought of Cam surrounded by adoring fans. "I mean, his voice is distinctive. His speaking voice. I didn't hear him sing." I sealed my lips shut. Time to stop talking before the cat and her litter of kittens was out of the bag.

The twinkle in my grandfather's eye proved not only was the whole passel out, but Pop-pop approved of my crush. While part of me thrilled at the idea, to finally have his approval with someone I wanted to get to know better, the other part—still traumatized by my last foray into the world of romance—trembled and wanted to hide.

I hadn't had a serious boyfriend since Robbie. That relationship burned in a pileup of hurt and flames more intense than any country song. And the last man I chose to hook up with was an accessory in my would-be death.

I made the face my mom called "sour lemon". My history with men looked worse than Al Capone's rap sheet. Thankfully, not as long.

"Well, Cam's got the looks, the talent, and he writes songs that aren't stupid or cheesy or forced on him by an idiot executive I see so often nowadays. He's already scored multiple platinum singles and has a couple Grammy nods. That boy's someone to reckon with, and he wants *you* to work with him."

My heart fluttered but in a good way. "So fast! I took four months on Clay's."

"While you worked on *six* other projects. But you're almost finished with those now." He tapped my nose. "Deadlines are good for you. Makes you plan out your time and focus your energy." Pop-pop stood, slapping his knees. "You got that and then some, Jenna-dove. Come on. Let's go pick out the wood you'll need."

I trailed behind him, my body beginning to ache with fatigue from the weight I carried around in my head. I was just me, a girl who was too scared, maybe too scarred, to return to university and finish my degree. That's part of how I ended up here. And that's why building my reputation meant building a lot of guitars. The *best* guitars. Instruments worthy of Pop-pop's workshop.

Not an ideal solution, but then, three years ago I almost died. Shocked by the experience, thrilled to still hug my mother, my siblings, Pop-pop, and my friends, the euphoria of taking a deep breath didn't leave me for months. Neither did the obsessive fear that ingesting food or drink from anyone's kitchen but my mother's—and sometimes even then—would lead to my demise. Leaving the house took more courage than I'd anticipated. Eating out again caused me to break out in a cold sweat *and* hives.

My grandfather saw a young woman fighting for a future.

Me? When I looked in the mirror, I saw the same blue eyes and golden hair he did. But with a shit-ton of determination to be better than any of them expected because of all the failures I'd accrued before I hit twenty-one.

———— ★ ————

I cradled the phone between my ear and my shoulder, mainly because my hands shook too hard for me to hold the device in place.

"Hello?" Cam's deep voice caused a pleasant ripple through

my belly. Not caring about my dates the last few years made the situation both easier and harder—I didn't know how to deal with my flutters or the heat sweeping through my torso.

"Hi. Cam?" Breathy Marilyn Monroe and I had never met before this moment.

"Speaking. Is this Jenna?"

Much as I wanted to clear my throat, that seemed worse than going with the breathy version of my voice. "It is." Wrong. I cleared my throat. "I've picked out some samples for you to approve. After you have the wood chosen, we can go over the schedule for the build out."

"I'm tied up until five-thirty, maybe a little longer. Want to meet up then?"

Pop-pop liked to take off at four for his weekly bingo game. The thought of spending another hour or more in Cam's company, sans supervision both thrilled and terrified me.

I drew in a deep breath through my nose.

This was a sale. Another instrument I'd create, get credit for. That thrill proved stronger than the fear.

"It may take a couple of hours," I said. "Maybe it'd be best—"

"I don't have anywhere else I need to be this evening, and I got the sense you wanted to jump on this project fast."

"True. I'll need every minute of the next few weeks to get this right. In fact, that's one of the details I'd like to go over with you." I pressed my lips together to stop more words from pouring out of my mouth. Cam waited, as if knowing I wasn't finished. "So, Pop-pop's packed up by four. Why don't you call me to let me know you're out front? I can unlock the door and disarm the system."

"Glad to hear you're taking precautions. See you then."

My grandfather looked over and smiled, dipping his head in approval. What had I just agreed to?

I wandered back to the studio, inhaling the sharp tang of fresh cut wood, sawdust and the wood protectant Pop-pop developed and patented back in the sixties. While the guitars were a source of joy and creativity, the three patents my grandfather held were the main source of the business's income.

For the first time in years, my heart rate picked up at the mere thought of a man. My body ignited at the memory of our one touch. I settled back onto my stool, forcing Camden Grace's gravelly voice, those thick biceps and luscious brown eyes from my mind. Which meant I must stop dwelling on the fact I wanted to spend more time with Cam. I pulled my hands from the table and balled them into fists.

I had work to do. Work that required focus.

Desiring Cam was one thing. Acting on it another.

I would *not* act on my newfound crush. Because Cam might well turn out to be another Robbie. Or, worse, another Ben or Charles.

Then, he'd be one of the long line of men who screwed me over.

Been there, done that. Not looking for a repeat.

Ever.

CHAPTER FOUR | Cam

I checked the door first. Locked, as promised. I sighed in relief.

Maybe I was overreacting to the ex-frat boy this morning, but I didn't think so. He was trouble with a capital T.

I pulled out my phone and scrolled through my contacts until I got to Jenna's tiny, smiling picture. Her arm slung over Kai Luchia's shoulder and another attractive woman. Jenna used to be close with Kai, the lead singer of Lummi Nation—at least according to the details I'd read about her today. Yeah, I spent way too long on Google searching for more information about a young woman I had no business stepping out with.

Once again, as it had when I saw the original pictures earlier, jealousy gnawed at the back of my throat. Not something I wanted to inspect too closely. The idea of anyone brushing their lips over Jenna's lush, red mouth had me ready to punch a wall— or better yet, the asshole doing the kissing—square in the throat.

"Hello? Cam?"

"Hey," I said, pulling myself out of my daydream. "I'm out front."

"Be there in a sec."

I clicked off when Jenna appeared through the glass-fronted window. This morning I'd scoped the shop as I left, noting its cameras as well as the double-paned glass door and windows.

With the cost of the instruments in the space, Jenna and her grandfather should have more security measures in place.

Not my problem. Except I'd made Jenna my problem. As soon as I stepped in the door this morning and my mind slowed to a reasonable rate, uncluttered and focused for the first time in ages, I'd known I was going to come back for another hit of her mind-clearing medicine.

And another.

Until I sucked Jenna dry and had to move on, heartbroken I'd destroyed her just as I had the trail of women in my past. My very own Trail of Tears.

But, no…I wouldn't do that again. I wouldn't. I'd made a point the last couple of years to stay uninvolved, unencumbered, as I tried to sort through all the bad in my life. Then, my father up and died and didn't give me the satisfaction of clearing out the guilt.

After letting me in, Jenna pulled the door shut and locked the bolts again. I didn't miss her gaze drifting up and down the street. Worried about the man here earlier, then. The faint stirrings of guilt I felt at telling her grandfather dissipated.

"Let's head back into the workshop. There's something I want to show you before we talk about the detailing."

I gestured for her to lead the way and I enjoyed the view. My brain didn't know where to settle: her hips swinging; those long, luscious legs; or even the bright bounce of her thick ponytail that played peek-a-boo with her sleek neck. She had a freckle on the back of her left ear.

Just one. At least the only one I'd noticed, which made me wonder if there were more under her clothes. I wanted to nibble that spot, wrap my tongue around the tiny, dark blot and suck until she moaned.

"After hearing about your quick turnaround, I thought maybe we could find a good fit with one of the instruments I'd started making to build up inventory. It's no one's commission—just a personal project I wanted to take on."

"You mean you've done more than the commissions? I thought those kept you really busy?"

"They do. But when I work, I don't have to think… I like to stay busy."

Well, now. She might want to fall back on the workaholic aspect—that sounded awful familiar—but her unintentional slip of work keeping her mind off the war in her head. Yeah, that I got all too well. Not unlike how I came about with my practice guitar.

She glanced back at me, and I shoved my hands in my pockets so I didn't try to soothe the worry from those thick-lashed eyes. Brown, not black like most women's. After watching Kim's makeup routine enough times, I'd learned the black came from a tube. Same as Kim's golden curls. I'd bet money none of Jenna came from bottles.

I frowned, thinking of the pills she'd taken this morning. Maybe more of her did than I wanted to acknowledge.

Jenna pulled the skeleton of a guitar's body toward her. The bell was wide like the one she'd shown me earlier but sleeker. She passed it to me and I turned it to the left before flipping it over.

"Why did you do this?" I asked, pointing at the wider sound chamber.

"I wanted to see if I could get the same resonance in a sleeker body."

"Did it work?"

She nibbled at her lower lip. "Mostly. The sound's a little different. But I thought, with the music you sing, your distinctive voice…maybe it'll be an asset."

"You've listened to my music?" I mean, sure, I had millions of fans and lots of hits, thanks to years where I buried myself in work after Kim's death, but Jenna listening was different somehow.

Jenna dropped her eyes, busying herself with another piece of flannel. Her cheeks flushed red. "I downloaded a few songs today." She met my gaze and her face flushed again. "Erm, actually, I downloaded three of your albums."

This woman grew up in a world of talent—the highest echelons of it—so for her to like my music buoyed my ego. Better than I'd received from my father, who'd hated every one of my career choices.

"Ranching's been in this family for more than two hundred years. That's a sight longer'n most people hold onto much of anything. Only one who didn't follow that path was my brother, and he died at twenty-seven, doing just what you want to do."

"What?" I asked.

"I tried to hand you that legacy, but you want to throw it away to drop out of aeroplanes? Just like Jensen did."

"Jensen?" I paused, recalling the name. "I thought that was your first name."

Dad glared harder. "Where'd you see that?"

"On my birth certificate. The Army asked for it."

Dad crossed his thick arms across his chest and squinted into the fading summer sun. "Just when your mama's finally done worrying about you splatting in some place we can't pronounce, you've gone and decided to take up something foolish like music?" My father, his thick brown mustache bristling with frustration, shook his head and turned away. "First career choice and you coulda died. This go-round is about vanity. I don't have anything else to say."

And he hadn't, not about Jensen—the man's name on my birth certificate or my brother's disappearance—since Kim's death. When I enlisted at nineteen, I thought he, like my mother, worried about my safety. But after that "conversation" four years ago, I'd realized I was simply a disappointment. One my father couldn't abide, not even for my mother. Which was why I'd recorded everything I could after Kim's death and before my separation from the Army. In those many long months of desk-work—no more active combat for this grieving Ranger—I honed my songwriting and recorded songs for my thousands of fans, thanks to my Army buddy's YouTube skills.

Which meant my next career, in part, fell into my lap. One that paid way better than Army wages and gave me a way to hire and protect many of my brothers-in-arms.

"Do you want to play it?" Jenna asked, bringing me out of my reflection.

"How? There aren't any frets."

Jenna picked up a finished neck and clamped it to the body of the guitar. "This isn't the fretboard for this guitar, and the clips will distort the sound a little," she said. Her hands moved with speed and grace to attach a set of strings. "Okay. See what you think."

I took the partial instrument from her, turning it over to look at the wood she'd used. It still needed a finished overlay and all the pretty dressing, but the instrument was well-crafted with tight joints. In fact, unless I looked closely, I couldn't see any seams.

My frown deepened as I settled the instrument against my thigh. I'd never considered the pressure of telling a beautiful woman I hated her design before. Sweat beaded on my forehead and my hand shook almost as much as Jenna's had this morning when she handed me some of the guitars she'd made.

I strummed a D-chord, my favorite, with tentative fingers. The sound, as Jenna said, was shallower than the instruments I'd played this morning, but still imbued with a richness that mass-produced instruments couldn't replicate.

I tried a C chord, then B. Glancing up, I began the melody to my favorite song, watching Jenna's face as I picked out the tune. Her eyes flitted from my fingers on the frets down to the body and sound chamber before her brows tugged low. She picked up a small notebook and wrote a few words before setting it down and re-focusing on my finger work.

"Sing."

I startled. "What?"

"While you play. Sing. That way you get an idea of how your instrument—" she patted the front of her throat "—works with this instrument."

"You just want a free concert, sugar."

She laid her pen and notebook down and reached for the

guitar, but I jerked it backward.

"Which I'm more than happy to oblige."

She frowned, adding a scathing look as I continued to pluck out the melody. I waited until she picked up her pen and notepad again.

I bent forward, closer to the instrument. For some reason, singing here in this saw-dust-covered space to Jenna blasted me with nerves I hadn't felt in years. I'd played packed-out stadiums in some of the biggest cities in the world, so no reason this intimate setting should bother me. This moment wasn't different from singing to the guys in our bunkhouse. Except Jenna was a beautiful woman and not a scared nineteen-year-old about to embark on his first—or last—mission into hell.

The words tore from my throat. Words of loss and sorrow and frustrated exhaustion brought on by too many missions and too many lives lost.

I stopped strumming as my voice faded.

"Golly gee wonky whump," Jenna whispered. Her eyes were wide and her mouth popped open. "Your voice."

She hopped off her stool and walked out of the workroom, fanning her face as she mumbled to herself.

I liked the idea of Jenna getting lathered up with my voice. Yep, I liked that idea.

Until I remembered I used to sing to Kim, too. That's how I wooed her.

And that action—bringing that woman into my family—was the reason my father and I never mended our relationship. And now he was dead and I couldn't.

CHAPTER FIVE | Jenna

I'd jumped off my chair, spouting nonsense to gain space. Now I glanced back to find Cam's eyes shuttered, as if he too felt the need to end our time alone. Not that I blamed him. For a man I didn't know, we connected somehow—through physical awareness but also some deeper emotion that seemed impossible for someone I'd met less than twelve hours before.

I didn't do this connection thing anymore. I kept people at arm's length—or further. Bat length more like it. My fingers curled into a fist because I missed the reassuring weight of the metal bat I'd taken to carrying around after some guys threatened my friend Abbi Dorsey.

My breathing escalated.

"You all right, there?" Cam asked.

I nodded, trying to ignore the ringing in my ears.

I was *not* all right.

My bat sat next to my desk. I needed it. Stupid to put so much faith in a metal cylinder, but then, nothing about my brain's reaction to these past few years was logical. Normal.

I would never be normal.

"I like this one, and it could work for my concert, but I still want the one you showed me earlier."

"Two guitars?" I managed to stutter.

He winked all slow and devastating to my crumbling composure. "I'm betting you'll give me a good repeat-customer discount."

My lips seemed to swell and my throat dried out faster than the Mojave Desert.

"I guess we'll have to. So, what did you like specifically?"

Cam's eyes scanned my face and his nostrils flared.

I folded my arms over my chest, ignoring the hammering beat there. "About the instrument."

"The resonance was interesting. Seemed to match well with my voice. Like you said. I'd like a different fretboard. Something a bit wider."

I nodded, flipping back to the page in my notebook and writing it down. "Anything else?"

"If I'm getting two, then I'd like this one to be flashy. More like those instruments you made for Asher Smith and Hayden Crewe."

I couldn't help but smile a little at that. Cam definitely understood the need for showmanship. "I used nickel on Asher's pickguard. We came up with a cool design for it. Pewter inlays in the shape of cats on Hayden's, along with a deep coffee stain."

"Coffee stain?" Cam asked, confusion settling into his eyes.

I shrugged. "For his wife. I didn't need to know the details."

"Right." Cam drew out the word.

"So—wider fretboard, metal pickguard. Some interesting design for the frets." I met his gaze. "Any ideas what you'd like?"

"Airplanes."

I blinked up at him, surprised. His face paled and his lips thinned. Clearly not something he'd intended to say.

"Okay." I made note. "Type?"

"Jet," he rasped. "I'll get you the model my…a relative flew. Died in an accident involving one when I was knee-high to a grasshopper."

I tapped the pen to the paper. "You'll have to look at these every day," I said. I often cautioned my buyers about the strange initial ideas they came up with, trying to steer them away from fads or designs they'd later regret.

"I get it. But this guy…one of the reasons I want them is because…" Cam glanced away. His Adam's apple bobbed. "His name's on my birth certificate. I think he's my father."

"You think?" the words popped out before I could control my runaway mouth.

He cleared his throat, looking almost as uncomfortable as I felt. "I'll just head to the washroom then let you get out of here."

"Why don't we set up another appointment for tomorrow and we can finish discussing the details then? It can be by phone."

"Yeah, sure." He stood and winced, bending down to rub his calf muscle. "Tomorrow afternoon. Phone conference. That'll work. I…ah…I'm going to be tied up."

He didn't lie well, but I let that slide. I watched him walk away, wondering if I should have pushed further. The pain in his eyes, the flat line of his lips made me want to comfort him. A man I didn't really know.

And a client.

———— ★ ————

As promised, Cam called the next afternoon. He seemed more hesitant but I didn't push, assuming he was embarrassed by what he'd told me the night before.

I made some more notes based on his preferences.

"If possible, would you be able to stop by Friday? I'd like to show you the design I'm building in the woods you've said you're interested in. Once we have those finalized, I can start on the finish-out."

"Sure," he said without any enthusiasm. "What time works?"

"I'm here all day, but after lunch would be best. That will give me time to finish the initial pickguard design and draw up your fret inlays."

"I'm in the studio until five. After that okay?"

So much for dinner and my evening run. "I'll make it work," I said.

"See you then." Cam hung up.

Pop-pop looked up from his bench when I wandered into the workshop. "You all right there, Jenna-dove?"

I wasn't sure, so I smiled and nodded, giving my Pop-pop the response he deserved. In fact, I was still shaken from my run-in with Ben. My wrist still ached and now Cam didn't want to spend time with me.

———— ★ ————

Friday morning dragged. I struggled to get the concepts I wanted down on paper—the first step to creating an intricate design.

After lunch, I pulled out the hammered silver I'd decided to use for Cam's pickguard and set about cutting it down to size, ignoring my grandfather's searching looks and my heavy heart.

Much later, after Pop-pop packed up his desk and left for the evening, a sound in the front caused me to frown. I picked up my bat as I stepped forward, expecting to see Cam there. Instead, I stared at foam and bits of bottle glass sliding down the spider-webbed glass of the front door.

"Come on out, Jen. It's time to party."

The shadow loomed—taller, broader, the biggest asshole I ever had the misfortune to meet.

Ben.

I swallowed hard and eased behind the counter, pressing the panic button Pop-pop had installed along with all those cameras.

What the hell was *wrong* with this guy? Why, after all these years, was Ben bothering me like this again?

I heard Cam's uneven tread behind me, felt the heat from his body just before his hand dropped onto my shoulder. I started, turning with the bat raised to strike.

"Whoa there, slugger."

I lowered the bat, my heart pounding so loud I could barely hear Cam's response. "How'd you get in here?" I asked.

"You didn't lock the back door," Cam said.

My eyes widened and I bolted around Cam, who caught me by the waist. "It's locked now. Please tell me the front door is locked."

I nodded. "I never unlocked it this morning. We weren't expecting any clients today except you."

"Good."

I turned, catching Ben's narrowed eyes. I shrank back, cowering into Cam, who cursed softly.

"My security detail is out there. I don't want them messed up in this."

Ben drew his arm back and threw another bottle against the

door, then another and another. I shuddered, hating the sound of glass as it tinkled onto the pavement outside.

Cam brought me closer to him, and I pressed my cheek to Cam's shoulder, a sharp whimper clawing up my throat as I stared at the boy who'd made my life pure hell for years.

Ben planned to hurt me—the promise gleamed in his eyes. I gripped my bat. It kept me safe.

His cell phone pressed to his ear, Cam guarded me. "You boys on this? There's another one in the car? Hell, yes, I'm glad you called the police. This here's personal, and the young buck is more than a little angry. All right. Well, don't get involved unless you have to."

Another beer bottle slammed against the fissured glass of the front door. I tensed, preparing to move forward—to do what, I had no clue, but watching this horror show proved more than I could handle.

"Stay back," Cam barked, dropping his arm to wrap it around me. His cell phone pressed into my hip.

I stopped moving, the authority in his tone not to be ignored. Sirens shrieked into the parking lot.

"You think the cops are going stop me?" Ben snarled. "You owe me, Jenna. You destroyed my life and now I'm going to destroy yours."

He slammed his fist against the glass. He flattened his palms there when the police pressed a gun to his back, his possessive, angry eyes never leaving mine. Once he was cuffed and hauled back, I dropped to the ground, my knees giving out as blackness tinged the edge of my vision.

CHAPTER SIX | Cam

Jenna's breath heaved in harsh gasps, and then she grunted. I refused to offer her comfort until the scumbag and his scumbag friend were in the police cruiser.

Another officer made a motion for me to unlock the door. I nodded but turned on my good heel and made my way back to the counter, my heart rate picking back up when I didn't see Jenna.

She'd slid to the floor, her knees pulled to her chest, her arms wrapped tight around her knees. Might explain the grunt I heard. Her fingers were white where she gripped the bat.

My calf flared with pain as I knelt beside her, causing me to grit my teeth and hold my breath. I blew out an unsteady breath and touched the crown of her head with trembling fingers. "Jenna?"

"He's wrong, he's wrong, he's wrong."

The words jumbled together, a litany or maybe a prayer.

"Jenna. Will you look at me? Please."

Slowly she raised her eyes, the bright golden strands of her hair catching in the overhead lights. Lord, she was lovely. Even wide-eyed with shock and paler than milk custard. My heart slammed against my ribs as I took her in.

I dug into my pocket and pulled out a Werther's. I unwrapped it with hands that shook. Adrenaline dump more than likely.

Before she could protest, I popped the candy between her too-pale lips.

I found another and shoved it in my own mouth.

"Makes everything better."

"That's what Lupin said," Jenna said, chewing her candy slowly.

My blank look caused her to elaborate. "In the Harry Potter books. Harry's teacher gives him chocolate when Harry's overcome by bad memories."

I glanced down at the wrapper, clamped in my fist. "Seems like the character knew a thing or three about psychology. Let's get you up."

She sucked in a breath, then another. Her hands trembled, but she placed them on the floor and started to rise. Pride slammed into my chest and some other emotion clogged my throat as she rose, shaky, but unaided.

"I'm okay," she whispered. "You okay?"

"Yeah. I'm going to open the door now. To let the officers and my guards in." I waited until the panic slid from her eyes and she nodded.

"Quite a domestic out there," the officer said. His sewn-on tag read Briggs.

"Shook her up," I said, raising my chin toward Jenna at the other end of the store, one of her hands flattened against the wall behind her, the other arm clutched around the bat.

My two bodyguards flanked the officer, looking both intimidating and scared as hell. After assuring themselves of my safety, they turned around to watch the other officer shoving the boy who'd assaulted the shop into the back of a squad car. Another officer spoke to the boy—Robbie, I heard the officer call him. Jenna'd mentioned that name. Her ex-boyfriend. Robbie gesticulated toward Ben, then Jenna, his face heavy with a scowl.

Jenna stepped away from the wall and walked forward, her hips swaying in a natural rhythm that got my blood pumping for a different reason.

"You have a problem here, miss?"

"My name's Jenna Olsen." She held out her free hand, the tremors almost invisible, the bat clutched to her chest. "Yes, we did. We have surveillance cameras. I'm sure most of this was caught on one of those."

The officer nodded and made note. "We're going to need a statement so you can press charges."

Jenna's eyes darkened and her mouth pulled down. I put my hand on her shoulder and squeezed gently. "We'll both do so. That man needs to be stopped before he hurts someone." *More*, I thought. Ben hurt Jenna a few days ago with his hands, then again tonight with his ugly words. If she'd been there, within reach, he would have given her much more than a bruised wrist. Of that I had no doubt.

Anger surged as I considered that boy manhandling Jenna— or any woman for that matter.

"Did you know the perpetrator?" The officer's pencil was poised over his notebook.

Jenna nodded. "He's my...he *was* my...friend." Her voice sounded strangled. Interesting.

I laid my hand on the back of her neck and squeezed. The muscles there eased.

"We hadn't seen or spoken in about six years." Her shoulder trembled.

"Ben was in here the other morning, belittling her then." My rage rose, boiling too close to the surface. I swallowed, trying to force the anger back into a tight box where the emotion couldn't hurt anyone.

After seeing the madness unleashed during my tours of duty, I'd managed to be extra cautious about losing my temper. The little piece of excrement Ben crossed the line to out-of-control.

"He said…well, he wanted to scare me. He did scare me," Jenna rasped.

"Why would he want to do that?"

Jenna's brows pulled in tight. Her eyes darted toward me but then she dropped her gaze to her feet and shook her head. Her hair parted in its ponytail, splitting along the back of her neck and showing a flash of delicate pink skin.

"He's been let go of his ball team," Jenna murmured. "He didn't use to take rejection well. Maybe that caused his desire to destroy my property."

"Could be I pissed him off the other day." I rubbed my hand on the back of my neck, wishing I'd played that scene better. "He grabbed Jenna, tried to force her closer, and I suggested he step back and out. Seemed like Ben brought some reinforcements to lay down the law with Jenna, here."

"That how you see it?" Officer Briggs asked Jenna.

She shrugged.

"Is this the first time he's come in?" Officer Briggs asked.

She cleared her throat. "Like I said, I haven't seen Ben in years."

"So. What's your story? Why are you here?" the officer asked, turning toward me.

"Camden is my client. We were finalizing the details I need to make his new instrument."

I'd never heard Jenna so serious. She'd been unsure, a little sassy at times, but this was her in an emotional place she didn't belong. Like she was going over her every action to verify her responses.

Briggs raised his eyebrows. "At seven-thirty at night? Kinda late for that, huh?"

Irritation laced with the adrenaline still pumping through my system—I'd wanted to rip that little runt Ben apart, then claim Jenna as my own. Like a primitive ancestor with no actual thought for her feelings. That made me no better than Ben on some level. Not a realization that sat straight in my gut.

"Not really, considering she's doing a rush job for me. And I had appointments all day with my manager about my upcoming show. I didn't arrive until after six—my first free minutes to visit."

"Right. Okay. Er, you plan to give a statement, Mr. Grace?"

I wasn't surprised the officer knew who I was. Hell, most of the world knew me. My presence here during the break-in increased the likelihood of media attention, and it probably wouldn't be the most positive for Jenna.

Mr. Olsen ran into the building, elbowing the second officer out of the way in his haste to get to Jenna.

"You hurt, Jenna-dove?"

She shook her head. "I had my bat."

The older man snorted. "Bet Ben carried a pistol."

"Licensed," the officer said. "And still holstered."

Jenna's face turned whiter, if that was possible. Her hand settled on the top of her baseball bat, clutching it like it was a lifeline.

"I'm fine." Her eyes met mine over the top of her grandfather's head and she mouthed the words *thank you*.

Yep. Still had a thing for damsels in distress. I was getting too old for these moments. Too jaded, too, because they kept happening. Did I search for them or did these gals find me?

Didn't matter because my name linked to Jenna wouldn't do either of us any good. I should distance myself from this guitar-making siren pronto.

Her grandfather shuffled nearer to me, his face florid from too much exertion or fear. I didn't know, but the redness worried me.

"I thank my lucky stars you were here. Jenna's had it rough these last few years." He rubbed his hand over his face, fingers shaking. "If anyone deserves something good, it's that young lady." He looked up into my eyes. "The guitar's on me. Any other one you want—ever—you let me know."

This time, my face flushed. "Oh, no. No way! I can't accept—"

"Jenna's the youngest of my only son's children. I love them all, including my daughter-in-law who'll rush in here any minute, I'm sure. That said, Jenna's always been special, lively and fun. *My* special girl. You probably saved her life tonight." He laid his hand on my shoulder and squeezed the way my father used to. Back when he was proud of me. "A guitar…hell, five thousand guitars, don't mean near so much to me as my granddaughter, Camden."

I pressed my lips together, tight, trying to ease the sting in my eyes and the lump in my throat. I dipped my head in understanding. "I want two. But I'll pay for the second—"

"Then, you'll have them both. No charge."

A tall, lean lady with hair as blond as Jenna's, though now threaded with silver, barreled in the door. "Jenna!" she cried, her voice cracking.

"Here, Mom." Jenna placed her hand on the counter and teetered for a moment. Her other hand still held the bat. Her mother sped over to her, wool suit coat flapping around her hips.

"Oh, baby. I was so scared."

Jenna's mother enveloped her in a hug, her cheek pressed tight to her daughter's. She kept murmuring words as she petted Jenna's head, touched her shoulder, her back.

"Why can't that piece of scum leave you alone?" Mrs. Olsen asked, her voice unsteady. "He hurt you in high school, and he's hurting you now."

"Hurt her in high school, how?" Officer Briggs asked.

Jenna turned white and I inched closer, needing to hear the answer to the policeman's question.

But another officer stepped over and requested the bat. Jenna handed it to him with obvious reluctance.

"Will I get that back?" she asked.

"Did you use it at all?" he asked.

"No."

"Then you'll get it back."

"When?" Jenna's voice shook.

I'd been right. That bat was her security measure. Damn, I didn't like her needing a weapon of any kind.

The officer shrugged. He turned to me and motioned me to

then follow him to the back room to answer more questions. My leg ached, and I clenched my teeth against the pain and frustration in missing Jenna's answer. What had Ben done to her before?

Much like Jenna the other morning, I needed one of my pain pills and soon. I positioned my chair and stretched out my legs, wincing. I crossed my arms over my chest and kept an eye on Jenna through the doorway as I answered the officer's questions.

The officer closed his notebook. "Thank you for your time, Mr. Grace."

I leaned forward and placed my palm on the back of the chair he sat in.

"Can you do me a favor?"

The officer looked up, waiting.

"That bat's awful important to Jenna. Seeing as how tonight went down, I understand why. Bet you do, too." I paused, waiting for him to nod in understanding. "So, I'd appreciate you giving that back to her. She'll sleep better knowing that boy's being held on the charges and her bat's next to her bed."

The officer studied me for a long minute. Probably trying to decide if I was involved with Jenna as more than a client. I kept my easy smile in place.

"I have a sixteen-year-old daughter. She carries pepper spray and a Taser. Can't ever be too safe."

I patted the crisp blue uniform at his shoulder. "Glad we agree."

"I'm a big fan, Mr. Grace. Wish we hadn't met like this, though." His eyes skittered toward the door, narrowing at the corners. Judging Jenna—incorrectly, I'd wager.

Yep, I'd be smart to leave the lady alone. My years of bad

behavior, my needs, and my idiosyncrasies, hell even my fame rubbed onto her.

Jenna already struggled with a past and some unresolved issues.

I unfolded my arm and reached into my pocket, digging out another Werther's. I popped it into my mouth. The warm caramel flavor helped, slowed my spinning mind. But not as much as Jenna. For whatever reason, she eased the vicious aches and roils of my brain.

Jenna raised her head and met my eyes across the room. One beat turned to three, five, twenty and we stared at each other.

And with each breath, we both relaxed. With each breath, our focus narrowed down to the most important person in the room: each other.

Hell.

I wanted this woman. Couldn't explain why or how she affected me so, especially when no other woman ever had.

"You ready to go, Mr. Grace?"

"She's making me a guitar," I murmured.

The officer responded with a noncommittal sound.

I tore my gaze from Jenna and the rip in connection cut into my soul. The last of the caramel melted over my tongue and I wanted to whimper at the unfairness of the night—at Jenna's plight. "She's professional. Best in the business. That's why I'm here. I'd appreciate you letting your boys know."

The officer's eyes widened and darted toward Jenna only to return to my face. I wasn't claiming her—wasn't sure I ever would now that I'd seen what a mess she was dealing with. My publicist would have a fit if I tried. But that didn't mean I couldn't offer

Jenna some professional cover—a bit of protection such as it was.

"Now, I'm off to get my PR machine rolling. My publicist is not going to like her late night."

"You got that right."

This from Chuck, who'd entered the room when the officer brought me back here. He'd stood, arms crossed, the scowl permanently stamped on his face. Chuck smiled. "Well, now. This ought to get mighty interesting."

"You would think that," I muttered.

"Well, you just threatened to call Brenda after hours—she gets real pissy when you do that, no matter the reason."

"I can't help this attack."

Chuck bumped me with his shoulder—he wasn't much bigger than I was. We'd always had a similar build, but I'd been his team leader, thanks to good test scores in Ranger School and the bad luck of me wanting a promotion.

Chuck nudged me forward. "Better get to that call. And get out of here before any of the reporters show up."

Jenna's face was buried in her mama's shoulder as we passed. Her grandfather stood close, watchful, tense. In case they needed to catch her, I'd bet. I didn't want to interrupt, but neither did I want to leave without saying goodbye.

Chuck nudged me forward again, making the choice for me.

CHAPTER SEVEN | Jenna

I dropped my keys on the granite of my newly-purchased down-town loft. A perk of being the co-owner of J. Olsen's Guitar Company included the financial security my position brought. More than that, though, I enjoyed the time with my Pop-pop. He made me laugh, something I didn't do enough of these days. My attitude improved while at school up in Seattle, but the near-death experience changed me again.

Not just inside my head, where the doctors loved to map and poke, but my connections with family and friends. Some days I still didn't understand how much.

Today I did. My body ached with fatigue, not just from answering the myriad phone calls from friends and reporters who'd read about Ben's attack last night. I should be at the shop, steaming and molding the wood Cam chose for his new guitar. And I needed to finish three other projects.

Instead, I cut out after lunch, unable to take the pounding in my head or the worry in Pop-pop's eyes.

I leaned my bat—thank goodness the officer gave that back to me this morning—against the island and strolled over to the large windows, looking out at the bustling entertainment district. College students and hipsters meandered through the streets, searching for a bite of good food and an earful of live music. Both were in full supply here.

Here I was: in the heart of Austin's trendy downtown, a mere stone's throw from some of the world's best live music. One day I'd get out there and go to a concert.

I snorted.

No way I'd ever be brave enough to force my feet into another concert venue. Even before meeting and connecting with the guys in Lummi Nation, I'd been traumatized by a concertgoer—namely Ben Wilkins, the boy terror who wouldn't stay in my past.

Nope. Not going there again.

I liked that I could walk or bike to the shop located on Sixth Street—the same location of J. Olsen's Guitar Company since my great-granddaddy started it back in the 1930s, well before live music lent Austin its vibrancy, and back when country and western music twanged supreme.

We'd built more guitars for rockers and even folk singers during the last ten years than country music singers—not that country wasn't a big draw in Austin. It was. But so was folk, alternative, indie, jazz, and just about any other genre of music I could name.

One large benefit of living within a mile of my job: walking to and from work meant I skipped out on a much longer commute. Austin's traffic was notoriously bad. Back when Dell and a few other tech companies built their presence in the area, the local politicians and city planners didn't set up the city's infrastructure for the coming population explosion. And, in Texas, people liked the liberty of driving their own vehicle.

But putting millions of commuters on narrow roads led to

immediate gridlock, something I didn't handle well. I lacked the patience to drive, mainly I couldn't be still. Stillness allowed my brain to fly in too many directions. Tasks, even simple busy work, solved some of that crazed mind. Some. Not all. Most nights I ran for an hour, sometimes two on my gym's treadmill, pushing myself until standing proved difficult and exhaustion slammed through me.

Then, finally, my mind calmed and I slept. Sometimes I even managed several hours.

My twelve-minute walks to and from work were the grand total of today's workout, mainly because I found dealing with people, even someone who'd do no more than offer me a towel as they looked at my membership card, to be too tiring.

No one I knew now would believe I'd been an outgoing cheer-leader in high school. My hospitalizations, especially the second one in Seattle, must have changed my brain chemistry. That's why the doctors liked to map my brain.

I settled on my couch, enjoying this space. It was simple, clean, safe. Most importantly, quiet. While I'd loved living with my roommate at Northern, I preferred the hushed solitude of my thousand-square-foot palace more. Here, I could breathe.

Here, I could, maybe, finally learn to be Jenna Olsen again. Whoever the hell that turned out to be.

I settled deeper into the larger of the two sofas and shut my eyes, too exhausted after last night's sleeplessness and today's constant requests to worry about finding myself wherever I was locked up.

———— ★ ————

The sound of my phone ringing shocked me back to consciousness. Without much thought, I snatched it out of my pocket.

"What? Where?"

A deep, rough chuckle greeted my ear. "Don't tell me I woke you."

"Kay. I won't." I yawned. "What time is it?"

"A little after six. I called to apologize for running out last night. I had to get with my PR team and start the spin machine. I hope you haven't been bothered."

I snorted.

Cam chuckled. "Too much to hope for, huh?"

"I left at two-thirty with a phone system that couldn't accept more calls and nearly three hundred unread emails. I'm sure it's worse now."

There was a pause. I wondered if Cam was shifting his weight onto and then away from his bad calf. He didn't seem to notice he did that. "I'd tell you I was sorry for the trouble I caused, but I'm not sorry I was there last night, Jenna. Because that hunk of human excrement wanted to hurt you."

"Hunk of human excrement?" I asked, amused.

"Seemed nicer than what I wanted to call him, you being a lady and all. My mama doesn't allow cussing around ladies."

"I've learned a few bad words in my day," I said. "And not all of them from my brothers or father."

"Nothing wrong with that. But we're off task. Talked with your grandfather earlier when I stopped by."

"When was that?"

"'Bout four, I guess."

"Sorry I missed you. We still need to meet to finalize those details."

In an honest moment, I admitted I wasn't ready to deal with Cam—and my growing feelings for him tonight.

"Can we meet tomorrow? I'm not at work, and I can't seem to wake up all the way." No way I was going to tell him that I had never been so desperate to have him like me.

"We could, but I have an idea I want to go over with you. Came to me this morning when I was in the shower."

Great. Now, on top of everything else, I was going to have the image of Cam, naked, in the shower covered in soap, branded in my overwrought brain.

Damn brain created one hell of an image, and I needed to fact check its veracity.

"I'll throw in dinner to sweeten the deal," he said.

My heart flipped at the idea of going on a date with Cam. He was so sexy. And a bigger star than Kai and the rest of his band, meaning we'd get mobbed by fans. That was rule *numero uno* of no-go in Jenna-Land: no crowds equaled minimal freak-outs.

"I'm not up for an evening out."

"Didn't think you would be after last night. I'll bring food to you. You like 'cue?"

"Am I from Texas?" I retorted.

Cam chuckled. "Want pulled pork or brisket?"

"Um…both? With a loaded baked potato."

"More of a Pappa's girl, huh? Sacrilege to my true-blood Stubb's. I'll throw in some ribs."

"Whatever," I said on a yawn. "If you bring ribs, be prepared to see me covered in sauce."

Cam groaned. "Really? Not an image I needed."

"Not one I meant to send," I said with a smile because yes, it was. To get even for his oh-so-not-innocent shower comment. "I have some Beerworks Peacemaker my brother left here when we were watching the game."

"You like college football?"

"Cam," I said on a sigh. "We've established I'm from Texas. I have two older brothers. Yes, I like football, both professional and college. As if there's another sport I'd watch."

"All good points. I have an older brother, too. A whole eleven minutes older. See, we have tons in common, Jenna. Now, text me your address and I'll be there in…"

"At least an hour," I said, rolling my eyes. "Sugar plums are made faster than you'll pick up an order at Stubb's."

"Oh, ye of little faith. I'm taking that as a bet."

"What? Whoa! I don't bet. I never said anything about a bet."

"Too late."

My heart rate kicked up to that of a galloping horse. "No, siree with a cherry on top. Nope."

"You afraid? C'mon, I'll make it easy on you. If I can get there faster than an hour, I get to take you out on a date. Day of my choosing but in the next week."

"This is stupid…"

"And if you win, you get to take *me* out on a date."

"Win-lose ratio's off there, buddy."

But he'd already hung up. Somehow that didn't surprise me. Camden Grace got what he wanted—when he wanted it. All those fans, hits, and money created that alpha personality. Or maybe he was always the top dog and could now enforce his desires.

"What did you get me into, Pop-pop?" I tossed my phone back onto my coffee table and rubbed my palms over my face.

For now, Cam seemed interested in spending time with me. And I might...yeah, for better—probably worse—want to see him, too.

CHAPTER EIGHT | Cam

I hadn't told Jenna I'd called ahead and placed an order for all the things we discussed. Definitely helped to have her grandfather's blessing—and his willingness to share Jenna's favorite foods. I finally understood why he hadn't told me Jenna worked with him. Over the past couple of years, I'd heard all about the pretty little gal who was the apple of her pop's eye, but the wily bugger never once mentioned she was his protégé—or such a well-respected artisan in her own right.

He knew that would have intrigued me even more. And Jenna needed to recover, to build her portfolio and self-worth. To learn to trust again.

I chuckled, shaking my head at Mr. Olsen's brilliance.

If Jenna refused to see me, or if I'd read the signs wrong last night during our epic, intense stare and she wasn't interested, then I'd be eating quality barbecue for the next couple of nights. Nah, I'd drop some off with Katie Rose. I liked being in the same city as my baby sister again. At least for a few weeks...until my gig schedule kicked back into gear.

That's why getting this guitar finished by July 4th rocketed to the top of my priority list. My calendar was blocked off with performances in and around Austin for a few weeks as I prepped for a winter tour that would set me up for the South by Southwest Musical Festival in March.

A smile tugged the corner of my mouth, and I was pleased to know I surprised Jenna *and* planned to spend multiple hours in her company over the next week.

Something about this woman called to me—on a deeper level than even Kim had.

No need to get in over my head and realize I was drowning once I couldn't get back out of the ocean. Nope, this time I'd play it smart. Starting with a simple meal together. I'd keep the physical stuff that I'd fantasized about to a minimum to see if the sweet bite of need held on through another conversation.

I knocked on Jenna's door forty-nine minutes later, hands laden with canvas sacks filled with food. She opened the door and her eyes widened.

So did mine but for different reasons. Her just-out-of-the-shower hotness lit a fire deep in my belly. Her skin still held the faint flush of hot water, bringing out the blue from the gray in her eyes, and her wet hair—still bright gold—slicked back from her face, dampening the cotton of her Lummi Nation T-shirt. For some reason, seeing her in another musician's shirt caused jealousy to slam back through me.

"Wow. You must be hungry," Jenna said.

"Or I really wanted to spend more time with you." I smiled and leaned forward a little instead, liking the whiff of fresh that wafted up from Jenna's damp hair. It was soft and sweet, but not cloying. Maybe some kind of fruit—pear? Yeah, pear. I liked it.

She smiled at that, eyes dancing. "Since you brought payment, I'll let you over the threshold."

"Thanks. And you better be hungry. I got some of everything."

She held the door open, closing and locking it after I made it into her large loft. The exposed bricks were a mix of local yellow and a mellow red. The ten-foot ceilings were studded with thick, dark wood beams echoed in the floors. The large Oriental rug in creams and blue brought together the light tan leather couches. A distressed round oak table and four matching chairs in the same warm cream as the rug sat nearer the open kitchen with its maple cabinets and rich blue granite countertops.

The space was airy with a hip, urban vibe—totally different from my folks' dated farmhouse or the terrible tent conditions we'd lived in during most of my second tour.

More like my new-and-improved cabin I'd built toward the back of the family ranch.

"Nerves take away my hunger." She looked down at her bare feet.

"Got a secret for you, sugar. I don't care much for being the center of attention either."

Her head shot up. "Teasing brings out some serious sass. A defense mechanism learned thanks to those two older brothers."

I raised a brow. "I don't tease about important issues. Though I do like your sass."

She studied me as she had the day I blurted out my parentage—or at least my thoughts that the man who raised me wasn't my biological father. I wondered again why I was here. Part of me wanted to turn tail and run, but the other part, the part that calmed when I saw her, the part where my brain clicked into quiet mode when I smelled her scent, wanted to get closer.

As close as she'd let me for as long as she'd let me.

I placed the two bags of food on the counter. Thinking that Jenna was some kind of saving grace would probably bite us both in the ass.

"Quite the spread you got here," I said.

"That's my line. But for the food." She waved her hand to encompass the containers I pulled from the bags. "Thank you for all this. If you hadn't called, I probably would've skipped dinner."

"Never a good idea to miss your squares."

"I was pretty out of it. Not sure I would've noticed."

She pulled down a couple of plates and topped them with the silverware she'd already gathered. Setting those on the counter near the food, she turned to the fridge and pulled out a couple of bottles, raising her eyebrows in question.

"Got me a gig at Shiner's this weekend."

Jenna smiled. "The bar here off Sixth Street? Congratulations."

"Will you come and listen?" I asked. My palms sweat and my throat dried out faster than a puddle in the sun.

"Um." She bowed her head. "I don't really do live shows."

"You should swing by," I said. "You know, for research on my instrument and instrument." Not why I wanted her there—I just did. Because I liked her. "And I'd feel better knowing someone there was watching over my sister."

"When is it?" Jenna's tone was hesitant but I counted myself lucky she was considering the option.

"Sunday."

She sucked in a breath and balled up the plastic bags the food had come in, shoving them to the back of the counter.

"Can I think about it?"

"Yep. Hit me," I said as I opened the first container. We groaned simultaneously as the spicy-sweet tang of sauce hit our noses.

"Can't get stuff like this in Seattle," Jenna said, as she used a fork to pile meat onto her plate. "At least not one I could find."

"Definitely a Texas specialty."

"I quit eating meat when I lived in Seattle. They just couldn't cook it right."

"You did your freshman and sophomore years there?"

Jenna nodded, handing me a plate. I started dishing food on to it.

"I'm still working on my degree here, but it's slower going now that I have a full-time job and demanding clients."

"You should tell those boys where to shove their extra requests," I said with a smile.

"I would, but there's only one guy who does it, and my Pop-pop likes him."

I leaned my hip against the counter and laid my hand on her hip. "Is that the only reason I'm here, Jenna? Because your grandfather approves of me?"

Pink suffused her neck but she kept her gaze firm on mine. "No. I like you, too. And anyway, you're my client. I have to please you."

Please me. There were lots of ways she could do that and none of them forced her to use her hands. Though that could add to the mutual pleasure if she did.

I picked up my piled plate and carried it to the table, hoping the short space between us would help me regain some control over my raging thoughts.

"I liked your design. All of 'em, really."

"You did?" she asked, satisfaction lacing her tone.

"You're mighty talented with those hands."

She looked down, her cheeks even brighter. Yep, I liked teasing this woman. Teased myself, but in these moments, my mind wasn't on how I should've done better during my last tour, how I should've fixed the mess I'd made of Kim's life, or worse still, my brother's continued radio silence.

I scowled but shoved the thought deep in my head and focused instead on the pretty, sweet-smelling lady in front of me.

"With the way you bolted, I assumed we were out the commission completely." Her voice stayed quiet, her eyes glued to her plate.

I glared at the silverware next to my plate as guilt racked me. I hadn't handled myself well last night. My past mistakes had nothing to do with Jenna, and she didn't deserve my bad manners because of them.

"My guards hustled me out of your place quick-step. I called my people. Brenda, my PR rep, wasn't too pleased with her late hours last night."

"You were spooked." She took a bite and chewed. She dragged her fork through the barbecue sauce pooling on her plate. "From me? My drama with Ben-the-giant-asshole?"

I shoved a bite of pulled pork in my mouth, buying some time before answering. Jenna hopped up and came back from the kitchen with the salt shaker. This time I noticed the bounce of her breasts under her tee. No bra. Noticing wasn't going to help my growing interest. Hell, I'd been attracted to her from the first moment, but now, after how she handled herself last night—she elevated past interest into full-blown need.

Right. Might as well be honest. I was too old and too tired for anything less than interest in me, the man. Not Camden Grace, the performer.

"Both. Mostly from memories. They sneak up on me sometimes."

Her eyes lifted to mine, the bite of potato halfway to her mouth. "I hate when they do that. Memories, emotions, whatever. You saw me that first morning. I take meds for anxiety. My psychiatrist added another for mood stabilization when I came back to Austin. I was a mess after…" She set her fork back on her plate, her lips thinning as she dropped her gaze. "I struggled with the fallout. From surviving."

"Why's that?" I asked, also setting my silverware aside.

Somehow this conversation turned heavy, the air thick with emotional pitfalls.

"Because I really should have died. I had a lot—I mean *a lot*—of GHB in my system. And I'm the one who made Abbi eat one of the drug-laced chocolates. She was hurt worse than me, really, so it's just not right that I made it."

"She's fine now, though. Happy, even. I saw her and Clay at one of the festivals a couple of months ago."

"You know them?" she asked, a delighted smile spreading across her face. I liked that level of happiness.

"Yep. Performing is a small world when you get into it. Clay's talented. Abbi's fun."

"You're right on both counts."

Her mouth settled back in a grim line, and I clenched my fist around my silverware. I wanted that smile back on her face. She deserved it.

"I don't handle those events well. Festivals, concerts." She shrugged, but her shoulders and mouth remained taut. "Too much noise, people. I don't do crowds well."

She met my gaze.

"That's why I'm not excited about your invitation to your gig on Sunday. I'm thrilled you invited me, but I'm not sure I can handle…" She looked back down. "I'm not sure I can handle you. What I'd need to be *for* you."

Jenna's bravery came from speaking her mind, admitting her weaknesses.

"No shame in that. Took me four months state-side not to want to drop to the ground at the first sound of yelling. My body was programmed to think it was a bomb or IED."

Jenna smirked, picked up her fork. "Aren't we a pair?"

I also picked up my fork and pointed it at her. "You're almost as much of a mess as I am."

"Different kind of traumatic stress," she said with a shrug. "There's no real comparison. An Army Ranger. That's impressive."

I shrugged. I didn't enlist, or even push myself to make the Ranger cut, because I wanted to impress others. I did it for Kim— college didn't work out for me, and I wanted to give her the financial stability a rancher or college drop-out rarely achieved.

"What were those memories that spooked you? Of the war?"

Jenna asked.

"Sometimes, but that was a long time ago and I've gotten better at holding them back." I shook my head. "The ones I can't control are of my wife."

Jenna's fork clattered to her plate. "You're *married*?"

The look of horror on her face was priceless, though the whiteness in her fingertips as she gripped the edge of the table worried me.

"I've been lusting after a married man," she whispered.

Her words caused warmth to spread through my chest. She hadn't Googled me or even pumped her grandfather for information. The elder Olsen collected most of the highlights from my sordid past, thanks to the hours I'd spent in his shop over the past few years.

"This is low, even for me," she said, her eyes filling with tears.

Aw, nuh uh. Jenna planned to beat herself up.

"No, I *was* married." My words tripped out, over each other because she had to understand. I sighed as I rubbed the back of my neck. "Years ago. I'm not anymore."

"Then you're divorced?" The way she asked the question reminded me of someone trying to spin a Rubik's cube the first time. None of the syllables or words fit together.

I twirled my fork, my mind revving up to that unhealthy speed for the first time since Jenna opened the door. I exhaled in a slow even stream from my nose, as I'd been taught during sharpshooter training. During those years, focus kept me alive. Now, focus kept the worst of the memories at bay.

Did I want to do this? No real choice, and Jenna had shared

a painful bit of her past with me. The least I could do was return the favor. Not that I'd share the whole, sordid story. Only my family—and Kim's—were privy to how disastrous our relationship became.

"She killed herself."

If anything, Jenna's face scrunched even further into horror. "Oh, I'm sorry. I wish you were divorced. I mean, I don't, if you still loved her, but that's better than—I'm *so* sorry."

"So am I. But not for the reasons you think. Kim and I… We had a rough relationship. Her death was just the culmination of some bad years."

There. That sounded like I'd closed that door—dealt with Kim's betrayals and the much deeper, more bitter fallout with my family.

Jenna stared at me, her food once again forgotten. I didn't like the shadows blooming in those eyes. "Will you…can you tell me what you mean? Cuz right now, my imagination's working hard to build a picture."

My neck tensed. I hated talking about Kim. Mainly because I hated how much her death affected me *still*. "About?"

She picked up her fork and fiddled with a chunk of potato, dragging it through a small puddle of sour cream. "What was rough?"

The way she asked the question, the forced nonchalance told me more than the words themselves would. Jenna's grandfather said as much but I expected he meant emotionally—as in teen angst over a bad relationship flaming itself out. Ben seemed the type to dominate a woman.

Damn, now *I* needed more answers. Answers Jenna wanted to

keep hidden, bottled up and repressed. We really were a pair.

"Kim was a free spirit. Too free." I dug my fingernail into the edge of my beer label, peeling the damp paper down with ease. "She wanted me, but that didn't mean she wanted to give up her other boyfriend." I raised my gaze, gauged Jenna's reaction. "Or her other one."

This time Jenna's face registered shock instead of horror. "She married you, but she still slept around?"

"Yeah." I lifted the bottle to my mouth, letting the long pull of cold liquid wash the filthy taste from my mouth. This was the part I didn't like to rehash, but Jenna needed the reassurance I wasn't an abuser, and now that I'd started talking…well, I wanted to keep on doing so.

"Kim's home life was hard. Her father was commandeering, not affectionate at all. She looked elsewhere. Lots of elsewheres. Especially after I shipped out. I was gone way more than I was home, so Kim moved onto the ranch." And, more than likely, into my brother's bed.

I refused to tell Jenna just how sordid the details were. She didn't need to know, and I really didn't want to tell her.

"No wonder you have nightmares."

I shrugged. "I didn't know. Not for a few years anyway."

"You don't have to tell me any more," Jenna whispered. Her eyes remained wide and wary. Not much different from how I felt.

My lips curled up in a sardonic smile. "I don't like talking about this so might as well do it once and be done. My sister called, gushing about Kim being pregnant though I'd been in Iraq for almost six months. Once my sister figured out that math…

Kim was just two months along then. She lived at my parents' house. They weren't too happy harboring a cheat. My dad booted her soon as Katie Rose—my sister—spilled the beans."

Starting the disintegration of *that* relationship. Not that my father and I were best buds before. But he spent the rest of his life wrestling with his part in Kim's demise and blaming me for the guilt that ate at him. Worst part was, he pushed away my mama, my baby sister, and my brother, too.

We all broke because I brought Kim in our lives. Guilt dug its vicious talons deep into my chest, gripping and wringing my heart. We still hadn't heard a peep from Carter since my dad's death two weeks ago, much to my mother's sadness. Katie Rose said Mom cried herself to sleep again last night.

Jenna made a sound of distress before she picked up her beer. Her sip was less liberal than mine.

"No one knows what happened, exactly, but Kim died less than a month later. An overdose." I touched my fingertips to my elbow, giving Jenna the silent cue for the level of drugs Kim was into. "My dad and I rubbed each other wrong from the big fight we'd had at Kim's funeral, and he up and died before we got around to talking it through."

Jenna's hand covered mine where it rested on my opposite arm. How her hand, the tools of her trade, were so soft and white, baffled me. Her palm warmed the back of my hand and we settled there for a long minute.

"Your guitar—the one you broke—you said something about your father's death?" she asked.

"Yep. But wasn't just that guitar." I met her gaze. "I busted the whole trailer—every instrument. That's how I dealt with the emotional overload."

After a long, tense pause, she raised her gaze and met mine again. "I had a psychotic episode. That's what the psychiatrist called it."

"Like a breakdown?"

She nodded. "I was hospitalized after the anxiety got to be too much. I'd always been fine—never had anything like that happen before."

I narrowed my eyes. "What triggered it?"

For whatever reason, I wanted to know more about Jenna—all her secrets, her quirks. Her heartache so I could hug it from her. My turn to drop my gaze and steady my breathing.

"The total cliché. Robbie screwed my best friend—not much of one if she fell into bed with my boyfriend."

This time I picked up her hand and squeezed her fingers in sympathy. "Right. Not much of one. What happened?"

"Well, I found out later Fiona and Ben plotted the whole thing. They'd dated a while, but Fiona wanted Robbie. Ben wanted me. They set it up. And…it worked out just like they planned." Goosebumps rose on her skin and she looked away.

Not a proud memory. Something I could understand, especially at that age. Hell, I was barely a year older when I married Kim—and caused my own family to disintegrate.

"Sort of. Fiona got pregnant."

I raised my beer. "Not that different from most high school dramas, really. Too many hormones and not enough sense."

Jenna shook her head as a tiny smirk uncurled on her lips.

"There's more to it, but I'd rather leave it there for now."

I leaned back in my chair and crossed my arms over my chest. "You mean unfinished business between you and Robbie? Or you and Ben?"

Jenna raised her beer and tapped the neck against mine.

"On my end? Neither."

"You knew more than you told Officer Briggs."

Jenna shrugged. "Seems like Ben needs to use me for something stupid and tied to his ego."

"Must have a big one, that young'un."

She giggled and I smiled in return, liking the sparkle in her eyes. Then she sighed and her eyes turned serious.

She leaned forward, placing her elbows on the table and dropped her chin between her fists. "Exes mean baggage."

"Truckloads full of it. And about an even weight of regret."

I picked up my last rib and tore off a bite of meat, chewing. I pointed at her plate. "Eat up."

She looked down, her mouth firming closed. "All this sharing killed my appetite."

"Find it again so I don't have to worry about you wasting away to nothing, sweetheart."

She picked up her fork and popped the now-cold potato in her mouth. We ate in silence for a few moments, each of us working over and through the other's history.

"I don't regret breaking up with Robbie." She wrapped the napkin around her thumb and began picking at it. "Not anymore. I did for a long time because I worried I wouldn't be popular or go to any of the good parties. Stupid things like that, but they meant the world to me at the time. So much so, I made myself sick with them. And I let myself believe I'd betrayed his trust somehow."

"Sounds to me like that young man needs to learn more about how to treat a lady and less about how to manipulate one."

I pushed my plate back and wiped my fingers on a napkin before it joined the rib bones. "I need to tell you something, sugar."

"That you like pet names that start with 's'?"

"No, smartass." I paused, waiting for her to give me her full attention. Didn't wait long. Whatever was between us, it was mutual. And strong. "I like you."

She raised an eyebrow as she picked up her beer. Most of it was still in the bottle. Not much of a drinker—good to know.

"Even after my sordid history?"

"Yep."

"But…" Her eyebrows scrunched together. "Why?"

"Don't really know exactly. But I do. Not just your talent, your sass. Bottom line: I like you, Jenna."

She set her bottle down. "I like you, too. A lot." She leaned forward so I could see the swirls of gray in those blue eyes. "Liking you as much as I do freaks me out."

"Me, too, darlin'. Me, too."

CHAPTER NINE | Jenna

"But fear won't stop me from wanting to see you again."

His voice remained strong and sure. His career gave him confidence—not just in his talents but in women wanting him.

I picked up my napkin and twisted it over and over, unsure how else to get rid of the nervous energy building, building, building inside me. Cam laid his hand over mine, his mouth turning down when he felt them shaking. After another long pause, I met his gaze.

"Do you think that's smart?"

"Us?" He leaned back in his chair, crossing his arms over his chest. "No. After seeing Ben in action last night, I didn't plan to see you again."

I went completely still, unable even to take a full breath. "So you did think about cutting all ties?"

He scratched the side of his head. "You're your kind of messed up. I'm both messed up *and* famous, which causes more psychological distress."

I winced but didn't dispute his comments. "There really isn't time. I'm going to be working a lot. On your guitar."

"But since I plan to purchase the one you started, it'll get done faster, right?"

I stood, picking up my plate and walking it to the kitchen.

The distance did me good. "Look, Cam, my head's been scrambled for years by name-calling and…other drama. Then it was scrambled again by drugs. I might seem wholly functional, but I'm not."

"Not much different from popping a bag full of candies, but you want to make some point."

I smiled at his levity before I glanced down, shuffling my feet against the pretty hardwood. "I'm focused on keeping Pop-pop's reputation strong and making sure I don't mess myself up further. Dating a celebrity…"

"Because of the crowds and fans, or because of the traveling?"

I threw my hands up in the air. "All of it. I don't do crowds. I can't travel with you. I'm not built that way. Not since…" I swallowed. "Look, as you pointed out, you planned to walk away."

I didn't like to be reminded of how I'd felt—caged, unable to fight or flee. I needed space. *Now.*

From Cam. From…all of it. I'd already given him so much of me tonight. Broken off chunks—the parts of me that remained raw. Cam wielded the power to hurt me, something I hadn't ceded to anyone in *years.*

I searched his eyes. Cam seemed like a caring man. Pop-pop liked him.

"My lifestyle, the performing, doesn't allow you to have control of your environment."

"True."

Cam scooted closer. He wore those motorcycle boots that drove my ovaries into overdrive.

"But you like *me*," Cam said, his voice softer, almost crooning.

"You're attracted to *me*. Physically."

Oh, now he was going to use his voice to seduce. I opened the dishwasher and began loading it, keeping one eye on Cam. "I am." And because my mouth refused to listen to my brain, I added, "Very."

He shifted, his face pulling into a grimace. But he ignored the irritation—probably in his calf—and walked up behind me, laying his hands on my waist. Slowly, he turned me around. Once my eyes met his, he dipped his head. My gaze dropped to his lips and I tilted my chin up, surprising myself by meeting him halfway, my fingers tangling in the hair at his nape.

The first brush of our lips shot tingles through my cheeks, across my neck and breasts and down my spine. He pulled me in tighter, placing his lips firmly over mine. A small, soft whimper slipped from my throat as his tongue licked across my lower lip, seeking entrance.

I opened for him, and we both moaned at the taste of desire overlaying the tangy-sweetness from the barbecue sauce. I cupped the back of his head while he tilted my chin to the left so his tongue delved deeper into my mouth, slicking across my cheek before sliding against my tongue in a sinuous dance.

Moments later, once I was drugged with desire and need, he eased back. Cam's chest rose and fell in synchronicity with the rapid pulse in his neck. My eyes fluttered closed as he leaned forward to press soft kisses to my eyelids.

"What's between us is more than I've felt for anyone in years. Maybe ever. Hard to say because this here is fresh and lovely."

My lashes fluttered, and I met his warm brown eyes.

"I want to give us a whirl. Please think about it."

"My last relationship was just sex," I said.

He ran his thumb down my cheek. "Done that a time or two myself."

Probably more. Sex was easy when you were famous, easier still when you were as good-looking as Cam was.

"My friends had all paired off and I was lonely." I shook my head—to negate my reasons or to forget the relationship, I wasn't sure. I'd been confused about why I started sleeping with Charles in the first place, and now, after that kiss, after feeling Cam's reaction to me, hearing his story, my confusion mounted. I stiffened my spine, ready to do the impossible—to push him away. "I don't have good taste in men, Cam."

I turned back to the sink, my hands gripped tight at the counter's edge. "Please go."

"All right," he said, all easy grace and sexy, deep voice. "We'll talk it through tomorrow."

"I don't think—"

"Your grandfather promised me a guitar—actually, he promised me a good half-dozen—and I plan to follow up to make you follow through." After a moment's hesitation, he leaned forward, his chest snuggled to my back. My knees wobbled and my breath caught. I turned my head enough to see his eyes darken, a sure sign he'd noticed my reaction. He pressed a soft, sinful kiss to my cheek.

"We both have lots of reasons this is a bad idea. But you know what I thought last night when I was lying there in my bed? That when I look at you, I know it's all going to be okay. I need that in my life, Jenna."

"Cam." My voice shattered. Maybe I did a little, too. Oh, I wanted this man.

He arched more tightly to my back, making sure his hips met with my bottom. I bit my tongue at the heat of him there.

He pressed another kiss to the edge of my jaw. I released a sound more like a sob than a moan.

Go! Just go before I beg you to stay and damn the consequences.

"See you 'round, Jenna."

With that, he walked out of my kitchen. I waited until the door shut before I opened my eyes again.

My breath stuttered, but I managed to keep the frustration and exhaustion at bay. After scraping and scrubbing the other plate, I turned back to my counters, soapy sponge in hand. All the food Cam bought lay there, open and taunting me.

I kicked him out after he listened to my sad story, told me his own. After he bought me dinner and kissed me. For a few moments, I'd been normal, happy even. Until I busted up that illusion because I hadn't told him my transgressions—the reason Ben showed up at my place of business. And I didn't want to, ever. I didn't want to see the desire and interest fade from his eyes and turn to scorn.

CHAPTER TEN | Cam

In combat, there were times—not many—when the best strategy was retreat. Tonight's decision was about regrouping and planning a new strategy. I'd pushed Jenna into admitting she liked me and she wanted me.

And damn, I wanted her. Wanted that blond hair falling across my hands as I cupped her softer-than-satin cheeks. Wanted her ruby-red lips pressed to mine. Wanted her sassiness and her wariness.

I wanted, and I detested this feeling.

I leaned back against the wall in her building, letting the creamy caramel I'd popped into my mouth ease the tight ache in my chest. Took two more pieces of candy, but I peeled myself off the wall and sauntered toward the elevator.

Once Jenna discovered my next counterattack, she might be angry. Hell, I hoped she'd yell at me. That was better than the defeated, scared and scarred woman standing before me tonight. I didn't like her as she was when I left. Almost couldn't leave because of it.

I moved to my truck, nodding to Chuck. "Any news?" I asked.

"The guy lawyered up and got himself released on bond."

I firmed my jaw. Not good news. I needed Jenna protected, whether she wanted that or not—whether she thought it was good for her mentally or not.

I got it. Those first few months after Kim's death proved near impossible. My head was so screwed up, not understanding it—and the rest of me—was safe. I hated Kim for dying, hated her for cheating and using me the way she had. Embarrassment warred with anger, a toxic stew that boiled over at inopportune times. Like when my father pointed out I'd been too young to marry, too young to know my mind or expect Kim to know hers.

But I had married her then because I wanted to make her happy, wanted to save her from the emotional desert that was her life. And I'd loved her. Stupid though my emotions proved to be, I'd loved her like I'd bet Jenna loved Robbie—in that all-consuming, blind-to-flaws manner that first loves seemed to garner.

Which was why I slammed back at my father, telling him he shouldn't have kicked Kim out of our house, that she was *my* wife, my responsibility that I'd left in his care while I fought in the war he believed in. And he killed her.

Not our first set of angry words and definitely not our last. But, that night, I also learned my brother Carter didn't plan to come back to Austin. That's when I knew—deep in my bones—something terrible happened. Something my brother and father refused to speak about. Something involving Kim.

Fragile, destructible Kim. Just like Jenna claimed to be.

But Jenna, unlike most other people, understood the difficulties of simply being in a room with people. With managing expectations and shoving down those fears.

Jenna was as real as any woman I'd ever met. Genuine in her curiosity and her compassion. Focused and skilled as a craftsperson. Dedicated and ambitious in her business and designs.

A chimera of feminism, professionalism, and delicacy.

A woman I wanted to touch, to learn and taste. To love for days…maybe weeks and years.

But more than all that, Jenna, thanks to her independent streak, wasn't someone I was willing to let slide through my fingers simply because she was afraid of what she felt for me. She looked after herself. She'd proven it in college and now, living on her own and creating such beautiful instruments.

Nope. I had the money, the power and the fame to ensure she was safe, and I planned to do just that. Not just with me but against Ben and any other men like him. Which was why I dialed Mr. Olsen's home number.

"Hello?"

"Hey, Mr. Olsen. It's Cam. I was at Jenna's having dinner—"

"That's my granddaughter, young man."

"I'm aware. We had dinner. I told her I liked her. She booted me out."

Mr. Olsen grunted.

"But that's not the point of this call. That…Ben? He's out on bail."

"I heard."

I smiled. "Figured you'd be in the know. Here's the deal. I want to make sure Jenna's safe. She's making it hard."

"She's been hurt by her previous boyfriends. Of course she's making your courting difficult. Makes sense to see if you'll stick."

I chuckled. Damn, I liked the old fella. "Don't worry, I like her feistiness. But here's the deal. Ben's got a record."

Mr. Olsen sucked in a breath. "How do you know that?"

"I have a team of people that I pay quite well to know all the details of a situation. They can find out all kinds of things. It's sealed, by the way, meaning Ben was a minor."

"What should I do?" Mr. Olsen asked.

"Right now? How about a bodyguard or two? We can help Jenna shape her public image. As a businesswoman and a survivor, not a victim of an ill-formed plot to kill Abbi Dorsey."

Silence built between us, but I waited. I might be a manipulative ass, but I never pushed.

I popped the last of the caramels into my mouth, humming with pleasure at the taste but also at the memory of how Jenna felt in my arms, how soft her lips were, how good her body felt pressed to mine.

"Okay. Tell me what you need from me, son."

I grinned broader than the Cheshire cat as I put my truck in gear.

———————— ★ ————————

I smiled, making sure both my dimples flashed, when Jenna walked into the back room of the shop two days later. She shook her head, a smile tugging at her pretty lips.

"You're going to tell me something about tenacity, aren't you?" she said.

"For the dogs," I said, waving my hand.

"He brought you donuts, dove."

Jenna dropped her purse into her drawer and placed both hands on top, leaning forward just a little. I liked the position. Made her mouth closer to mine.

"You don't play fair."

"Also for the dogs, sugar. Now, come on over here and eat this fresh, delicious donut. It's one of those fancy ones from the shop down the street. I wasn't sure which was your favorite so I picked up some choices."

I lifted the box so she could read the name in shiny gold letters: "Gourdough's Public House."

"Do you have The Freebird in there?" she asked, her voice quavering with unrelenting need.

Mr. Olsen chuckled. He'd told me Jenna came home from Seattle with an irrational fear of eating foods she hadn't prepared. Mr. Olsen bribed Jenna with a donut comprised of cheesecake filling, slathered in cream cheese frosting and piled with strawberries and blackberries before being drizzled in graham cracker crumbs.

I held out the donut, set in the middle of a napkin. Jenna dove at it. She bit into the luscious cake with a moan of pleasure.

My breath caught in my throat when Jenna tipped her head back, a look of sheer bliss forming on her face as she chewed.

"I'll be in the workshop," Mr. Olsen said, still shaking his head. He moseyed through the door, shutting it behind him. George Jones's voice wafted through the speakers, Mr. Olsen singing along.

Jenna licked her lips and sank her teeth into the confection again, this time keeping her eyes locked with mine. I shifted on the stool, unable to find relief from my growing arousal as Jenna continued to make sexy noises as she nibbled at the donut.

She wiped her hands, sighing in pleasure before patting her belly.

"I have to tell you, Jenna. That might have been the most sensual experience of my life." I stood and moved toward her. "I've never been so turned on by eating before, but right now, I got fire raging straight to my—"

"Don't say it! My grandfather is just through there." She waved at the closed door.

I cupped the back of her neck, tugging her toward me. "Then don't you tease me like that. I haven't seen you in days, and I've dreamt of those lips. Seeing them wrapped around that donut nearly did me in."

"Why haven't you been around?" she asked.

"Writing songs, helping my mother work through the paper-work that comes with being a widow." My accountant and lawyer handled all that paperwork, but I had spent time with my mother and sister and cursed my brother for his continued disappearance when my mother needed them most.

Jenna's lips curved up in a smile as her eyes softened. "That's sweet. To help her out."

"She's a great lady, and I have the resources to take some of the burden off her." Not to mention I was the reason for the burden—that my father keeled over at sixty-five in the first place.

Jenna shoved her thumb into her mouth, no doubt to lick off the last of her treat. I groaned as I leaned in, my lips a hair's breadth from hers. Her thumb fell from her mouth as her lips parted, her soft exhale hitting my face and ratcheting up my desire.

Before I could react, she said, "Let me show you what I've got." She washed her hands and then brought out the guitar.

She settled it carefully on a large glass table tucked next to the back door.

"I want to set the back in walnut. You were in Iraq, you talked about airplanes, so I wanted to use that in the design."

She showed me a color image of what looked like a rolling sand dune—my personal hell of the sandbox—but not. Softer. Subtler, more like…well, more like clouds in the sky. What I'd see when I flew in a plane.

"I like this," I said, touching the paper, surprised by how cold it felt. The design made me remember the hot sun, but not in a bad way—more like an encompassing warmth. "I'm surprised by how much."

"I know you don't have great memories of Iraq. I don't want to change that. But it's part of you. You carry it here." She placed her hand over my heart, and for some reason that made my throat swell.

She got me. She got that I couldn't—wouldn't—let that part of me go, but it had shaped me just as she was shaping the wood, molding it into something better.

Something beautiful.

I coughed, trying to cover the emotion building in my chest, causing my heart to pound. I leaned forward, intentionally knocking her hand from my chest.

She stepped back a little, frowning. Yeah, I got it—I'd run hot, now cold.

I hadn't expected her to see me so clearly.

The ache built again.

She riffled through her papers and brought out a design.

Again, it was fluid, nothing too rigid or even straightforward. But it reminded me…it was my ranch with the stream and tall grasses. Even the large rock cropping on the far side of the watering hole.

"This is amazing," I murmured.

"I'll etch it into the silver. Not too deep. Just enough for you to know it's there."

"Won't be noticeable from the stage?" I asked.

Jenna shook her head. "Not unless people are up close."

"I love that. All right. This is all great. A couple of things: I'd like the neck out of walnut, not alder."

"Are you sure? The alder would be—"

"I'd prefer the stock to match the body. Okay?"

She nodded, that small scowl still pinching her brows.

"We all done?" I asked.

"Yes, once you sign off on these pages for my file."

I took the pen she offered and scrawled my name. Then, because I could, because I wanted to turn the knot in my chest into something better, I lifted her up onto the table next to the guitar. Her eyes widened as I leaned over her.

"What—"

"I have to kiss you now, sugar," I rasped, trying to hold back the emotions. "I can't wait any longer."

But I did wait—not giving her much space, holding my breath as she held hers, eyes searching, delving into mine. She dipped her head to acquiesce even as she closed the tiny distance separating us.

I took her mouth in a demanding kiss that caused her to

whimper in need. She gripped my wrists, tugging me closer as I plundered her sweet mouth, my tongue bursting with the flavors of her donut, my teeth nibbling, licking and sucking so that she was just as hot for me as I was for her.

I pulled back in slow degrees. Not because I wanted to. Hell, I wanted to take her right here, right now. But her grandfather was in the next room.

With one last lick and nibble, I settled back on a wooden stool. Heat blistered my veins and raged with the pounding in both my head and lower belly. I had zero control around this woman.

That realization, more than any other, slicked my back with cold perspiration.

"Goddammit, woman, I haven't been this hot and bothered since—"

"Kim?" she asked.

I absorbed the blow, but now my heart raced for an entirely different reason. I snagged the bag of donuts I'd set on her desk earlier, clutching the paper in my hands so tightly, I expected all of it to combust.

"No, I never felt like this for Kim," I managed to say in an even voice. "But bringing her up now, after I shared that with you in confidence, proved as hurtful as you hoped."

I stood and stalked out the back door before she had time to respond.

Yanking open the door to my truck, I pressed the ignition button and sped out of the parking lot, not caring about spewing gravel.

A block up the road, I pulled over into a gas station and tried to regulate my breathing. Much as Jenna eased the whirring in my head, she caused it to escalate with her words just now.

She'd lashed at me out of fear. Hurtful but understandable. Maybe not forgivable. I opened the donut bag and sank my teeth into the chocolatey-est one I'd bought.

I moan tore from my throat. *Good* didn't come close to describing the dance of pleasure my taste buds were doing.

Thunder rumbled and the leaden skies opened, dousing my truck and the surrounding pavement in a thick wall of rain. Lightning kicked through the sky, barely visible through the sheets of water.

I savored each bite of the donut, going so far as to lick my fingers to ensure I snagged each delicious crumb. I leaned back against the seat of my truck, enjoying the sound of pounding rain, and shut my eyes, trying to hold on to the pleasure still singing from my mouth.

The knock on the window broke my moment of peace, and Jenna's pale face and huddled form ruined it further.

I flung open my door, causing her to stumble back. "What the hell are you doing out there?"

Her teeth chattered and she clutched her arms to her wet shirt. The rain was hotter than sin, but she seemed chilled. "I'm s-s-sorry."

"Get your butt in the cab and warm up."

She started to walk around to the passenger door, but I snagged her wrist and towed her back. Before she could protest, I placed my hands under her armpits and hauled her into the driver's seat. A long honk signaled some part of Jenna on the wheel, but I was too busy getting the door closed to notice.

"You have got to stop running on pure emotion, sugar," I said, settling back against the leather seat and maneuvering her body so she draped over me.

"I really d-d-don't run on j-just emotion. Except with you. I-I like that n-nickname. Though I'm n-not always s-sweet." She shuddered again even as she burrowed closer.

I wrapped my arms around her wet, cold shoulders, rubbing my palms up and down her icy arms. "Don't I know it."

The horn honked again, so I used my left hand to press the toggle switch to move my seat back. Jenna settled more firmly in my lap and sighed as her cheek pressed against my throat.

We sat there until her shivers ceased.

"You're right. I said that to hurt you."

I used my right hand to tip her chin up. "I don't think you want to hurt me." I waited for her to nod in agreement. "You want to push me away. Like you did the other night."

"Yes."

This time, she tried to lower her lashes to hide from me, but she forgot I had a younger sister *and* I'd been married. I'd learned a few tricks of my own. Silence once again permeated the space, undercut by the occasional door slam or car honk outside my truck cab.

"I just managed my way through a deep hurt, and I…" She paused.

I stared at the crown of her head, willing her to look up. She didn't.

"I don't want to hurt you," I said.

"No, you want me to give you *all* of me. But you'll move on. You're famous," she muttered. "And…and you don't stay in one place for more than a few days."

Her eyes were stormy with fear but desire lurked behind that. Desire I could work with to overcome the fear. Why I kept pushing her, I couldn't say. Just that, on a visceral level, I craved this woman—her scent, her taste, but most of all, how she made me feel. The calm she brought to my overwrought head.

"When I'm touring, I'm not here much. You're right. But the only big event on my agenda right now is on the Fourth." Sort of, but I had weeks until then—weeks to convince her to stick around. To be with me. "I need to write another album, then record it. I plan to do both of those here in Austin so I can be nearer to my mother and sister. They need me right now."

"But then you'll leave again," she said, her shoulder rolling forward in defeat. She knew musicians—hell, she was close friends with many of them. She wouldn't let me hide behind my half-truth, not that she should.

"And I…I don't want to be alone." She whispered the last like one would a terrible confession. Maybe to Jenna loneliness was.

I placed my hands on both sides of her waist and rubbed my thumbs along her rib cage. Her top was damp but no longer dripping. The skin beneath was warm. I wanted to touch her—feel its silkiness again.

"*Eventually*, I'll need to tour."

That made it sound farther off than it was. Not smart…not playing the long game here. I was trying to win the immediate skirmish. Because I needed to kiss her mouth. *Now*.

"That's where a large portion of my income comes from," I admitted.

She dropped her head back into the crook of my shoulder. "I've seen how hard that grind is on relationships. I've seen how it nearly broke some of my friends—and they're so in love it's gross."

I rubbed my hand up and down her back in what I hoped was a soothing rhythm. In her hunched position, I could feel each of her vertebrae, reinforcing Jenna's physical fragility.

Of all the women to be attracted to, I chose the one who needed me as much—more?—than I needed her. Fate was a cruel wench.

"How about this?" I kept my voice coaxing, kind. "How about we get to know each other better over these next few weeks while you finish up my instrument. From there, we can see if we want to jump in deeper or not. Planning right now seems a bit counterintuitive what with us not knowing if we'll even be able to stand each other in a month or two. But for now...I can help you. Keep you safe from Ben while we see where—if—we want to go somewhere."

She raised her head again, her eyes darting from one of mine to the other. "You'd wait for me? I mean, we could hang out and talk, and this isn't just about sex?"

The last words rushed together. I smiled. Part of her charm was her directness—her willingness to face a situation head-on even though the topic was stressful.

"I can't say I don't want you." I pulled her down tighter into my lap and she bit her lip when she felt the bulge behind my zipper. "But I am a thirty-one-year-old man, and I have been known to exercise restraint a time or two."

"I get Cam restrained?"

"You get Cam the man."

She giggled even as she wrinkled her nose. "I am not calling you that."

"Never expected you to. But I'm serious. I don't want to be a performer with you. I want... You put my mind at ease, Jenna. I can't explain to you how important that is. How rare."

She cupped my cheeks, and her eyes were clear blue when she said, "I know."

She did. Jenna understood those demons buried deep, so far down they'd never get ripped out nor would they ever go completely mute.

"I'm afraid I'm going to fall in love with you," she said on a sigh. "Because of how safe you make me feel."

"I am potent."

At her look, I chuckled, but cuddled her closer.

"Attachment is always a possibility, and I told you, you're better for me than my Werther's." I waited another moment, my hand delving into her long, silky hair, smoothing down the strands. "Do you accept my proposition?"

"Since it isn't indecent—" she raised her eyebrow "—*yet*, I will accept." She paused. "I'd like the bodyguard, the protection your name brings."

In that moment, with her words, I got a full sense of how hard Jenna worked these past few days—hell, maybe years—to put on a bright enough façade for the world. She didn't feel safe.

Not even in her own shop. Even with all that, she came to work each day and created something magical.

As my fingers tried to curl into fists, I forced them back open. I inhaled slowly and exhaled slower still. I'd deal with my reaction later. Right now, I'd gotten what I wanted—Jenna, here in my arms.

"But I also want the opportunity to change it to indecent and all about sex if I so choose," Jenna continued, unaware of the depth of my response to her words. "Based on our mutual need for each other."

I clasped her hips, anchoring her to my lap. "Well, that there's a deal I'm happy to make." I leaned in and kissed the tip of her nose. "Now, I better get you back to the shop. People have been snapping our photo for the last few minutes."

"What?" she gaped at me. "No!" She turned to look out the steaming window, and sure enough, there was a small crowd with their phones raised.

"I did not sign up for this," Jenna moaned as she climbed into the seat next to me. "Why didn't you tell me?"

"Two reasons. First, I love how you fit in my lap." I slipped my seatbelt into its lock and waited for her to do the same before I shifted the truck into gear.

"And?" she prompted, pushing a few strands of golden hair from her bright pink cheeks.

"I'm not sure I want to tell you." I pulled the truck out into the street, turning back toward her shop.

"But you will anyway. I'm going to demand honesty, Cam."

"I'll give it long as you do the same."

She nodded, her eyes solemn. "Deal."

Well, now was as good a time to spring this as any. I clutched the wheel, hoping my talk with her grandfather proved enough. "Because I liked those people thinking we're together. I like my fans knowing I'm dating you. I like the idea that the little shit Ben and even the media knows you're mine."

Jenna folded her arms over her chest as she leaned back into the sumptuous leather. I'd paid a wheelbarrow-full of money for this truck. The ride was smooth and the leather was near as soft as the skin on Jenna's neck. I liked nuzzling into Jenna's neck more.

"Does that mean you're mine?" she asked, her voice carefully neutral.

I pulled around to the spot I'd been in earlier and killed the engine.

"Absolutely." I raised my eyebrows and gave her the look I used on my men. "I don't share."

When she opened her mouth—probably to argue with me, stubborn woman—I leaned in and kissed her lips. This kiss was soft, more of a light glide. She lifted her hand to the back of my neck and tugged me in closer, those beautiful red lips rubbing over mine. I pulled back slowly.

"I'll see you tomorrow," I said, smoothing my thumb across her cheek.

"What's tomorrow?" she asked, her eyes still clouded with desire.

"The day you quit pretending you're too busy, and we finally go out on a date."

She fumbled to open her door, and a blast of hot, humid air

sliced through my T-shirt.

"It's too hot."

"Not for what I got planned."

"I don't do crowds." She stepped out of the truck.

"I'll be with you. Everything will be fine." I leaned over and pulled on the door handle to escape before she came up with another reason to fight me. "See you tomorrow, sugar."

I slammed the door shut, smirking at the disgruntled look on her face.

Yep, dating Jenna was going to be fun.

CHAPTER ELEVEN | Jenna

Coming back into the office, I found a piece of paper on my desk. I wasn't sure when he left it there, but I was noticing that Cam was stealthy. His penmanship showed thought and control. And it was neater than mine. Each stroke was as bold as he was, the lines clean and strong. I liked the shape of the black ink on the page.

Who was I kidding? I liked Camden Grace—his voice, his eyes, his touch, his kiss, his desire to care for me, keep me safe, and even his handwriting. Too much.

Looking forward to seeing you tomorrow.

Cam

My fingertips drifted over the page once more, lips curving up at his confidence. Finally, I turned away to fire up my computer and catch up on the morning business.

When I stepped into the workshop, I found Pop-pop bent over his table, nose so close to the wood the two were almost touching.

"Good chat with Cam?" Pop-pop didn't bother to look up.

"Maybe." I sighed. "I don't know."

"Why's that?"

"He's older."

This time my grandfather lifted his head, his eyes bright under the bushy, white brows. "Not by that much."

"You're right. But…he's been married, Pop-pop. I can't take care of a plant. I've just learned to manage myself."

"You're quite good at that, dove. Look at all your success here."

"How can I handle being involved with a man who has millions of adoring fans?"

Pop-pop slid off his stool and wrapped his arm around my shoulder. "You're thinking of Robbie."

I nodded. "I know they're different people. I know I'm older. Supposedly wiser."

"More cautious."

I dipped my head in acknowledgment.

"Let me ask you something." Pop-pop wiped his hand on a rag. "Even when you were in Seattle, were you happy?"

I chewed on my lip. After a long moment of reflection, I shook my head. "I had moments of happiness. I have the best group of ladies there. They watch my back."

"But you're here. In Austin. Not in Seattle with your—" he pursed his lips "—home girls."

I rolled my eyes, a smile tugging at the corners of my mouth. "I don't need a man to complete me, Pop-pop. You said so yourself just a few days ago."

Pop-pop's eyes remained sharp and fixed on my face. "But you didn't like watching them all pair off either."

The wise and sneaky man. He got right at the heart of the issue.

He tapped my nose with a begrimed forefinger. "You crave love, Jenna-dove. You soak it up and dish it back a hundred times over. I don't think you need a husband to fulfill you—hell, you and I have both made sure of that—but you do need someone to talk to, someone who gets you."

He turned back to his table, hunching over his work.

I opened my mouth to argue. I watched him for a moment, replayed my conversations with Cam over in my head.

And I'd be smart to listen to Pop-pop's words, especially when it came to relationships. Pop-pop and Grammy were married for fifty-four years before cancer took her from him. And while Pop-pop still enjoyed his work, his eyes no longer held the same light or gleamed with the same relish for life.

Which meant being in a relationship could hurt more than it soothed.

I closed my mouth and headed to my side of the long, thick-hewn table, caught up in the tumult roiling through my head.

I pulled the body design Cam approved closer to me. After studying the pieces, I went over to match walnut wood for a neck. After a distracted search, I finally found a piece I liked from our supply. I ran back to my desk to get the spec sheet and then spent the next few hours cutting, molding, and sanding the wood. I stopped sanding, grimacing when my hands cramped, and picked up a pen to write down the material I wanted to try for the frets. I hoped they'd pick up the distinct vibration I wanted the guitar to emanate.

If not, the standard steel would work. Wouldn't be as flashy or as interesting, but sometimes tried and true were the best choice.

"You almost finished for the night?"

I jumped at Pop-pop's voice, my heart beating with erratic speed. "You scared me!"

"Because you've been in a kind of trance for hours. I asked

you at six if you were ready to shut down and you didn't even answer."

I massaged my aching right hand. "What time is it?"

"After eight, and way past this old man's dinner time."

No wonder my hands hurt. I'd been at it for almost nine hours. "Sorry! Let's lock up so you can get home to your meal and shows."

He raised his brows. "I'd be happy to take my best girl out to dinner if you'd like to talk it through some more?"

I bee-lined to my desk and pulled out my purse, guilt eating at me. My poor grandfather didn't need to babysit me. Part of the reason I agreed to work with him was so I could look out for and after him. I had to do better. He deserved better.

"Do you want to? Or are you just being sweet? I'm thinking you want to get home to catch the last of the Rangers game and kick back in your lounger."

Pop-pop smiled as I slid past him, keys in hand to lock up the back door.

"I took care of the front already. I'd be fine with a beer and the game."

I leaned in and kissed his cheek. He smelled of wood and his aftershave. Something no other man in my life could harness. After a brief hesitation, I hugged him because I needed to. He patted my back, holding me for a moment longer.

"Then get on home and enjoy that beer. Put those feet up and yell at your TV."

"After I drop you home."

I glanced out into the dark night, the knots of Friday night revelers spilling out onto Sixth Street. My hands began to shake at the thought of being surrounded by those large, fleshy bodies. Like I was that day when I fell in front of reporters. Or that night when Ben… I swallowed hard and turned toward Pop-pop's Prius.

"Thanks."

————— ★ —————

Cam called me about nine o'clock that night.

"What time are you up and about tomorrow?"

I chewed my lip. "Well, I'm usually up around six-thirty, but I'd like to get in my work-out before we do whatever it is you won't tell me we're going to do."

"Cagey way to ask, and I'm still not telling. How about this? Be ready at ten. That work?"

"I guess."

"Relax," he said, his voice soothing. "You'll have fun. Low-key. No crowds."

"My mind spins in about fifty different directions, trying to come up with scenarios." I huffed out a breath. "I don't do surprises well, Cam. Two of them nearly got me killed. And I'm opposed to blood and physical pain. I squeal like a girl—my brothers say so."

He hummed into the phone, and I assumed he was mulling something over. "Fair enough. I don't want you stressed and worrying all night, sugar. How about this? We're coming out to my property. There's the river you put in the etching. Lots of fields. A few cows."

"Killer cows?"

He chuckled like he found the question funny. Um, this was

Texas, the land of longhorns—cows with *long* horns. Not taking chances.

"Not our girls. And this whole property is surrounded by a big fence. I promise there'll be no media to take your picture or ask you questions like's been happening since you and I first hit the papers. Just a day to relax."

My grip on my phone eased, as did my shoulders. "Okay. That sounds…honestly, that sounds *muy bueno*. Like a taquito."

He hummed in his throat again. Probably because my mouth ran away before my brain could catch up. "You know what's better than a taquito? The thought of you in a swimsuit. Please tell me you own a bikini."

The laugh caught me by surprise, but I enjoyed the release of the last of the tension in my shoulders. "I do. It's retro."

"Hell if I care what style so long as I get to see lots of your pretty skin."

"Our agreement, Cam."

"I plan to look. Maybe touch. Just a bit."

His voice dropped on the last word and my chest went fluttery, my belly filling with a delicious heat. Whoa, Nelly and the cart behind the horse. This man was potent—even through a device.

"You know, if you'd told me about this before, I could have bought a sexier bikini."

"Don't want you any different than you are, sugar," Cam said, his response fast enough I believed his sincerity. The warmth in my belly spread upward, toward my pounding heart. "Just want you comfortable and relaxed. And wet. With me."

With these words, heat in my belly slid down into my thighs.

"I'm going to get off the phone now."

"Don't do that." I could almost see his pouting lips. "This was just getting fun."

I smiled, even as desire pulsed through me. "Nope. I said no sex, and I meant it. Not even phone sex. Especially not phone sex."

The distinct sound of plastic being unwrapped filled the speaker. "Don't want an imitation of the real deal. Cuz, I have to tell you, I've been imagining how good it'll be with you. Sliding into your tight, hot—"

Baby Jesus in a peach tree, the man was potent. Like moonshine on a hot summer night. "Good night, Cam. See you tomorrow at ten."

"Sweet dreams, sugar."

I clicked off my phone and flopped back on my bed, a groan building in my chest.

He did that on purpose—made me all wanton and needy. I smiled, and within a second, I laughed. The chuckles continued until I finally sat up and padded to the bathroom to brush my teeth and wash my face.

I plugged in my earbuds and flipped to my music library. I pulled up Cam's music and hit play, closing my eyes and sliding into sleep with Cam's voice crooning in my ear.

Almost as good as the real thing.

Almost.

CHAPTER TWELVE | Cam

First rule of engagement: expect the situation to go FUBAR at any moment. I pocketed my keys and pulled my ball cap low over my brow, trying to slink past a couple of journalists milling out front of Jenna's building. Getting us out of here without being seen might prove more difficult than I'd hoped.

Once in the lobby, I dialed up my head of security. "Got us a situation," I said without preamble, letting Chuck know what's what, and how I wanted to handle the reporters.

"I have Brian in sedan two, and I'll take care of your problem out front. Have fun today."

"You just want me in a better mood."

"Sure as shit," Chuck grunted. A fine man from middle-of-nowhere Texas making the best out of his sad lot. Getting him on my payroll helped us both out. Me, more, though, I was sure of it.

Chuck was smart, ambitious, and too savvy not to do well. Right now, he made a pile of cash as my head of security, but I told him he didn't have to stick around.

So far, four years into our new setup, he stuck as close as he had back in the sandbox. His eventual departure would devastate me. That's what came from hiring a brother-in-arms. Brian, good man though he was, he and I never fought together. Not the same level of loyalty.

"I haven't been that bad," I scoffed.

"Only time I saw you worse was right after Joey died."

I closed my eyes, as pain lashed up my throat. Joey should be here now. "Thanks for the reminder of my fuckup."

"Come on, chief. That wasn't on you. You had your orders and the intel was supposed to be spot-on."

We shared a sardonic laugh. After our first trip out across the wire, we'd all learned to be skeptical of any intel. Lots of good men died because of it.

"That's not where I was going with my point."

"You got one?" I grumbled.

"Yep. Two, actually. Your dad dying took you down."

He didn't know the half of it. Mostly because emotions weren't really part of our relationship. Poker, beer, angry, sullen and even contemplative silences epitomized the ten-plus years we'd hung out together. Chuck was one of my best friends but he only saw me lose it once—on the bus when I went ballistic and destroyed everything in reach.

"Even Kim's death didn't take out your knees like losing your dad. Think that says who you had unfinished business with. And, two, I like the guitar gal."

More words than Chuck normally strung together in a day. Obviously, he'd wanted to say something for a while.

"Her name's Jenna."

"I totally see the attraction."

"You better not act on it," I growled. At one of my best friends. A man I knew placed loyalty above all else—we'd lived through too much not to trust each other. This is what came, in part, from losing faith in my twin.

I should call him. Better than getting on a plane to punch him for his…I'd call it a relationship, but he hadn't stuck around long enough after Kim disappeared to show any kind of caring. Which meant the brother with whom I'd shared my every secret, the young man I'd loved more than anyone, was as dead to me as my wife and my father. That's what really set me off: knowing I'd never get the full story as to why my brother betrayed me on such a visceral level.

"I hear ya, chief. I never would. But I will make sure both you and she are safe and not bothered."

Chuck's voice brought me back to the present. I stared at the attractive red brick wall near the bank of elevators. I was here in Jenna's building, planning a day with the lady who sparked my imagination and desire but also calmed these raging thoughts. I'd deal with my brother later…or not at all.

———— ★ ————

I knocked on Jenna's door, trying to shut down the nerves fluttering in my belly.

She opened it, and I took a long moment to drink her in. Her straight blond hair was pulled up and off her face in a high, thick ponytail that cascaded over her left shoulder. A shoulder covered in a thin strap.

Her dress. I swallowed. The bold color, a pinkish-purple, offset the tiny rows of ruffles at her chest and hem. The soft material swished over her breasts and danced across her flat stomach before flaring at her hips. Never in my life had a dress seduced me with such ease.

"Hey, sugar," I said once my gaze finally flashed back up to her amused one. "That's a nice getup."

"I'm going to take that as a compliment." She held open the door and I stepped inside, snagging my arm around her waist and dipping her back. I pressed a heated kiss to her jawline. And with that touch, with the feel of her in my arms, my mind slowed. I sighed against her warm skin, my muscles easing.

Much as this sensation should scare me, the calm it brought was addicting.

"You okay?" she asked, worry in her voice. Her hands, though, clutched at my shoulder. Nails digging into my flesh through the soft T-shirt I wore, just for her.

"I am now. Like my shirt?" I stood her up and stepped back, puffing out my chest with pride.

A guitar outlined in white with wings fluttered across my stomach. Music floated from the top edge and the notes spelled out Cam and Jenna.

"Etsy?" she asked, her fingertips lightly tracing our names, making me shiver.

"Didn't think of that one. Got it from one of those make-your-own-shirt sites. My sister loves funky tees. I've learned a few things."

Jenna's eyes smiled up into mine. "It's cute."

"Not quite the reaction I'd hoped for."

Jenna laughed, delighted, no doubt, by my petulance. She leaned into my chest and pressed her soft lips to mine.

"I like the shirt. Very much."

I pulled back even as my hand came up to palm her neck.

"Better."

Her lips curved into the start of a smile as I sealed my lips over hers. This kiss proved hotter than our last. My heart and my mind sped up, but the images getting my blood pumping were sexy in nature—something to jump behind and ask for another helping of. My body thought so, too. I moaned as I retreated.

"Didn't know your nickname would be so perfect for you."

Her lashes fluttered as her eyes opened. "Are you saying I'm sweet?"

"Just right here." I took her lips again in another long, slow kiss. Temptation and weak men and all that business. But I managed to curb my growing hunger and set her back. "Grab what you need. We'll be gone most of the day."

She walked to her kitchen bar and slid sunglasses onto the top of her head while she grabbed a beige leather tote. I noted the saddle stitching with respect. Jenna had an eye, not just for the pretty but the well-constructed.

"Do I need a towel?" she asked.

"Gotcha covered. Same goes with sunscreen."

Jenna headed toward the door, snagging my hand on the way. A smile tugged my lips at her cute move. For whatever reason, I loved this woman's spurts of sassy.

My phone dinged and I tugged it from my shorts pocket. I nodded, pleased to see Chuck handled the situation below, meaning Jenna need never know about the paparazzi in her lobby.

"Oh! Wait!" She scurried back into her apartment and grabbed a cute little beige cap. She plopped her sunglasses on her

nose and tugged the hat onto her head, adjusting her ponytail.
Most of her face fell into shadow or behind those large sunglasses.
Just her ruby-red lips and rounded chin were visible.

"Think it's enough to get us past the photographers down-
stairs?" she asked.

I pulled out a caramel while she locked the door. "How'd you
know about them?"

"I live in a building with security. It's the lobby guard's duty to
let me know when anything out of the ordinary pops up."

I bent down, careful of her little cap brim to brush my lips
over hers again. "You're full of spunk, sugar. But this time, I
handled the out-of-the-ordinary."

I slid my palm back against hers, a little shiver of awareness
building across my shoulders. She squeezed my hand and trotted
behind me onto the elevator and then out to my truck. Not a
single lens or photo click. I needed to give Chuck a raise.

After bucking the thousands of other drivers' desire to get to
their destination, I sighed in relief as we pulled onto the long
gravel drive. Jenna lifted her head, brows drawing close as she
eyed the passing oaks and pines with confusion.

"I didn't realize you lived in the Hill Country."

"The edge of it, sure. This is my family's ranch. Been in our
family for almost two hundred years." I glanced around, my heart
aching as I saw what my money bought—that my father's years
of sweat and toil couldn't. He'd been proud of the changes, but
also frustrated my choices led to me being able to do what he
couldn't. That man's pride had been larger than this spread, and it
was no wonder we butted heads so often—even before I made the

mistake of bringing Kim into our lives.

"It's beautiful," Jenna sighed.

I agreed. It was, now. But five years ago, after I de-commissioned, the place was ramshackle with broken fences and rotten roofs on the bunkhouse. The main house looked like something out of Amityville Horror and the cattle roamed free-range—not by choice but lack of quality cowhands. Without Carter here to help run the cattle and maintain the perimeter, the place fell further into disrepair.

After my father's death a month ago, I'd taken over the operation. Well, my business manager had. While I'd made slow progress over the past few years on the fencing and barns on my few free days, now, every outbuilding, well, tank, and home on the property was on schedule to be modernized. The equipment shone in the late afternoon sun as we rounded one of the barns and headed deeper back onto the eight-thousand acres.

"You don't live in the main house?" Jenna asked.

I shook my head. "That's my parents' place. My mother's still there. With Katie Rose. My sister. She moved back home this year after a bad experience up north after she graduated from UT." I glanced at her from the corner of my eye, trying to gauge her reaction. "You'll meet them soon, I'd bet. If they aren't waiting at my place, I'll be shocked."

Surprise widened Jenna's eyes. "Meet your family? Now?"

I took her hand in mine. "Not to worry, sugar. They've been asking about you, and they're real excited."

"I don't…"

"If my brother were around, I'd worry he'd try to steal you, just for the hell of it."

"I'm not a pair of jeans," Jenna grumbled. "I can make up my own mind."

I brought her knuckle to my lips, unwilling to tell her how much I'd needed even that faint reassurance. Not that I planned to tell Jenna about my brother's actions. But...still...the idea of them together angered me. More, it ripped at my chest. Something I refused to examine.

"Feisty and independent suit you."

She turned to look at me as I parked in front of my two-story bungalow. Built out of native stone, the soft yellow felt homey. The deep wrap-around porch was painted a clean white. The windows were also a cheery white, bookended by glossy green shutters. I smiled in satisfaction, as I did each time I saw my home.

The front door opened and Katie Rose's wild auburn ringlets bounced around her head as she trotted forward, nearly tumbling down the steps in eagerness to get to Jenna.

I glared at my sister, giving her my best be-nice-or-else scowl.

"I'm Kate. Cam's sister. Please do *not* call me Katie Rose. He's the only one who does, mainly because he knows I hate it."

Jenna's eyes widened during the speech, but she took Katie Rose's hand and smiled wide. "He calls me sugar. I think he's trying to keep us both young and me sweet."

Katie Rose laughed, throwing her arms over Jenna's shoulder and pulling her through the front door. "You're probably right. Sounds like a Cam type of manipulation."

Jenna's voice still carried out the door as she said, "What else does he try to manipulate? I need lessons."

CHAPTER THIRTEEN | Jenna

"I'm so glad to meet you," Kate, *not* Katie Rose, said as she led me deeper into the house. "Cam's talked my ear off about you. He's usually so confident with the ladies, but you've got him tied up in knots. He's been worried about that guy who threw stuff at your store. Real worried."

At her words, my stomach wrapped and warped itself. "Really?"

"Oh, yeah. He's been planning all kinds of stuff with his people to make sure you're okay. I haven't seen him this preoccupied in a long time."

Something in her tone brought up my conversation with Cam when he brought me dinner. A wave of cool air slid over my skin just then, and I shivered.

"I don't plan to hurt him."

She turned around to stand right in front of me. "Good to hear, cuz he's been hurt before. Real bad."

"By Kim," I murmured.

Katie Rose's eyes ran over me. "He's told you heaps about himself for knowing you such a short time."

I nodded, determined not to give away any other information to the vivacious redhead.

"You want some tea? Mama made it so it's sure to be good.

Cam can cook but his sweet tea is atrocious."

"Sure. Um, so you still live at home?"

Kate's shoulders stiffened but she kept her voice light as she pulled the tea from the fridge and poured me a glass.

"I do. I had a bit of a bad situation. And Daddy never managed this place… Well, it's been stressful a few years since my brothers lit out—and even after Cam came home. Daddy was always out, leaving Mama lonesome. This was before, when Cam was touring pretty much all the time." She fastened on a bright sunny smile that didn't do anything to push away the shadows in her eyes. "Moving back home was mutually beneficial—I helped out Mama and Daddy by doing the books, ordering the feed, getting the cattle squared away—that kind of thing. Cam didn't have to feel so guilty about his travel."

"I moved back home after I OD'ed. Granted I didn't mean to, but that doesn't change the fact I struggled for a while after the hospital released me."

As I'd assumed, Kate knew all about my story—at least what happened in Seattle. She nodded, her eyes clear and not as judgmental as I'd anticipated.

"There're times it's the right move. I'm twenty-four, almost twenty-five now, and I have a business degree from UT, an internship with Boeing, and now I'm working on my master's back here at UT. But it's time for me to get out and on my own two feet."

"Are both of your degrees in business?"

"Yep. Operation management, now marketing. I liked finance okay, but decided I'm more of a people-person than a numbers gal."

I nodded and took a sip of my drink. "And are you working?" I asked.

Kate shook her head. "Not outside of the ranch, no. And that's a shame for me because Cam's got his business manager handling most of the issues here. If it weren't for school, I'd be twiddling my thumbs in boredom. I need to be out, sending resumes and hitting up the job sites, but…well, Daddy's death's been hard."

I pulled my card out of my purse and handed it to Cam's sister. "I'm not sure it'll work out, and I'm definitely not sure exactly what the job description entails, but we need a person with the right skill set to move the shop into this century. My grandfather isn't in as much as he used to be, and I'd like company." And the safety of numbers. "Maybe we can help each other."

Kate set her drink on the counter and stared at me as she clutched the card. I fidgeted, worry pouring over me that I'd overstepped the role I was supposed to play as Cam's…whatever he and I were to each other. Maybe he wouldn't want me to offer his sister a job—to further entwine our two families, especially when our relationship was up in the air and in need of labels and parameters.

"If you don't want to come by next week, I'll understand. It's not a formal interview. It's just that I know I could modernize the business side of the shop, make it more accessible and welcoming for our clients and do some actual marketing instead of relying solely on word-of-mouth…"

I stopped talking when Kate threw her arms around me and hugged me hard.

"Oh my gosh! Are you kidding? This is *exactly* the kind of thing I want to do! I love your guitars. I love the music business, but unlike Cam, I don't have any real talent. I mean, I'm passable on the piano, but that's thanks to sixteen years of lessons. Oh!" Kate stepped back and jumped up and down, her eyes shining with excitement. "Do you think I can learn all about guitar making, too? I mean, I know some stuff, but your guitars are so amazing and I—"

"What're you rambling on about, Katie Rose?" Cam asked. He slipped his arm around me, eyeing his sister with concern.

"She's going to come visit the shop next week," I said. "I'm considering—"

"Jenna's been nice enough to offer me a tour and show me what she's working on for you." Kate cut in, her eyes begging me not to tell Cam the real reason for her visit.

I picked up my iced tea and drank, unwilling to lie to Cam but not wanting to upset his sister. Crap. What had I gotten myself in to?

CHAPTER FOURTEEN | Cam

After I finagled my sister to leave, still unsure what she'd cooked up with Jenna, I changed into my board shorts. I led Jenna down to the water. The narrow pool wasn't deep—barely four feet, but with the current churning through, I used it as a natural, tepid equivalent to a hot tub.

I helped Jenna into the water and we both sighed as we leaned back against the rock ledge I'd had built into the side.

"Thanks for bringing me down here," she said after a long silence. "I needed this."

"No problem. Though, I'm sorry to have caused the need for relaxation."

"Not you. The situation—your fame. But." She bit her lip. I wished I could see her eyes behind the tinted lenses of her sunglasses. "I like spending time with you."

"Mmm, I'm glad." I pulled her closer to me, liking the way she let her legs float up as if she trusted me to never let her go.

Strange that I had no problem with that thought. I should.

I eased back. "So, tell me something new. Something interesting about you."

She settled back, her head against the edge of the pool. "What did you want to know?"

"Middle name?"

"Marie." She shrugged. "Not very interesting."

"I'll be the judge of what interests me, Jenna Marie."

She crinkled her nose, and I laughed at the death look she shot me.

"What's yours?"

"Bexar."

She raised an eyebrow. "Your parents named you Bear?"

I shook my head, smirking. Even though we'd both grown up in the area, Jenna didn't have even a hint of a Texas accent. Her mother wasn't a born-and-bred Texan, though, so maybe that accounted for some of the difference.

"No. Bexar. Like the county near San Antonio."

"How'd you end up with that for a middle name?"

"It was my great-great grandmother's surname. She was one of the county's first families."

"Wow. You said you'd been here a long time. Those roots are dug deep."

I pressed my shoulder against the side of the pool, lifting my right leg up with a grimace.

"You need to get out?"

"Nah. That actually makes it stiffer. The water here is supposed to be good for it. Something about the minerals. Why guitars?"

"Because I like them. Always have."

"I liked singing but it wasn't my first career choice. Just one I fell into."

She cocked her head to the side. "How do you fall into being a famous musician?"

"Not dying in a war. Getting wounded just enough to make

me a hero. Losing my wife in such sad circumstances. And Chuck's knowledge of YouTube."

"Chuck?"

"My head of security. He posted videos of me singing for his friends back here. They liked it, so they shared them. Soon, I was the singing warrior. I hated that moniker, refused to use it. I'm me, just like you're you. Nothing too special."

She grimaced. "I'll beg to differ. Being around you is like me trying to do geometry."

"What do you mean?"

"You're more than just you. It's like…I understand we're talking about angles and circles but that's about it."

I shifted again, trying to ease the ache in my calf. "But you build guitars for a living. You have to make the pieces fit together."

She swiped a long tendril of hair back from her cheek. "You're being literal now. And there's a template."

"Do you ever give yourself credit for anything?" The words blasted from my mouth, harsher than I intended, probably because she just wouldn't see herself as I saw her.

"I'm a mess. Like a lava pool kind of hot mess. Get too close, I won't just burn you. More like strip your bones and say 'ah'."

I snorted. "Quite the image you created."

She shrugged. "A special talent to confuse and scare people with just my mouth."

My gaze dropped to her lips. Oh, I could think of some things to do with her mouth. None of which involved scaring me. Those berry-stained lips parted and she inched in. Yes, she'd noticed my attention.

"Look, Jenna, you're making this awful damn hard."

"What am I making hard?"

"Dating you. I don't tend to spend time with the ladies just for kicks."

"I could kick you. You could see if you liked it."

"Thanks, no. I'm not much for violence."

"Says the man who shot a really big gun."

I smirked but managed to control my retort. "From the gal who wields a really big bat."

I tried to hide my next grimace, annoyed by how much my leg hurt today. Getting comfortable proved near impossible.

"His name is Gerald. You're in pain," she said, startling me. "Here. Lean into me and let your legs float."

Her mouth might spout a huge pile of cow patty, but she was observant. And caring. I did as she suggested, my head positioned in the cradle between her neck and chest. She was soft and smelled delicious. Something girly and fine. Not the best time to notice that—if I didn't get the image of her wet flesh out of my mind soon, I was going to embarrass myself.

"Back to us," I said, trying to refocus on something other than how good she felt against my back. "I don't mean to confuse you. And, yes, we're dating. Exclusively. Again, we decided that yesterday."

"What if you change your mind?" Her voice trembled.

"You always need to do worst-case scenario?"

She took such a big breath, her breasts pressed against my back. "You asked why I don't like crowds." She swallowed, her body tensing beneath mine. "I was at a concert. I told you, Ben decided he wanted me, so he cozied in close. We weren't dating, but we were…always together."

I nodded my understanding of what she didn't want to say. I picked up one of her hands and laid it on my stomach, my palm on top of hers, and waited.

"Robbie made noise about us getting back together. He didn't love his new girlfriend like he loved me. It was a mistake. You get the idea. By then, I'd been through the shitstorm. I was struggling to attend classes, sure everyone was laughing at me behind my back. That everyone had chosen Robbie's side."

She fell silent. I linked my fingers through hers, keeping them resting on my stomach.

"We—Ben and I—went to this concert. It was kind of a senior class thing. Most everyone was there. Robbie showed up. Ben lied to him, and Robbie—he called me names, bad names. Everyone heard."

I made to turn, but she laid her other hand on top of my stomach. The muscles there clenched at her touch and I sucked in a breath. Fine. I could let her talk like this though I'd prefer to see her eyes.

"What he said, that's on him, not you."

She huffed out a sardonic sound, not even a laugh.

"I tried to leave, too, but Ben… He slammed me against the wall and told me I'd teased him long enough."

Her breathing escalated as she relived those terrifying moments. "I was scared. So scared. I screamed. At first no one heard me over the music."

"Where was Robbie in all this?" I asked.

"He left. Ben said we'd been hooking up the whole time Robbie and I were together. That I liked Ben more because I was with him now. That I liked it rough and Robbie didn't do it for me. He said he'd prove it."

CHAPTER FIFTEEN | Jenna

This was why I didn't want to talk about my past. The pain, the fear, even the betrayal bit sharply into my chest, nipping at my throat.

"What happened?" Cam asked, his voice softer than it had been. He rested against me, waiting.

"A few people turned around. But no one came to help me. They just watched. Some were curious, others whispered." I shrugged. "Finally, I yelled 'fire!'"

I paused, my throat too dry to continue. Finally, I croaked, "There's a reason you don't do that."

Cam's heart thudded, hard and staccato against his ribs. "Stampede?"

"Ben let go of me and I fell. The police found me on the floor."

"You were trampled?"

His shock was palpable. He did turn around. I stared into his wide eyes.

"Yeah. Broke my arm and sprained both my ankles. I was lucky."

He absorbed my words, his mouth flattening.

"The police were involved. They wanted to charge me."

"Did they?"

"No. The video cameras caught it all, but I was sent to the

psychiatric ward for observation and therapy."

He tightened his arm a little. "I bet this is the incident that's sealed on your boy's record."

"Not my boy. Never, *ever* mine." I sighed. "Well, my mistake, clearly."

We were silent, listening to the soft rush of water.

"You want to finish telling me?"

No, I didn't. But I knew all about curiosity—and where it took my brain. "I told you, I had a hard time with going to class anyway, so, in a sense, I liked the mental health facility my parents found for me to go to. It's in New Hampshire, in an old barn. It was…it was a cocoon. I did my work and graduated before I left the facility."

With a careful hand, he pulled off my sunglasses, forcing me to meet his eyes. "And then?"

I shrugged. "I went to college. Against my parents' wishes. Two years later, I was home after another hospitalization."

Cam narrowed his eyes. "Did you see Robbie or Ben again—after that night?"

I shook my head. "No reason to. Plus, the intake psychiatrist called them triggers. As in, if I saw them, I'd trigger back into the panic."

"Did you?"

I kept my eyes firmly locked on his. "No. I was sad for a while that Robbie thought I'd cheated. Especially with Ben. But, no—I don't want him back."

Cam slid his hand behind my head, cupping the back of my neck. He wrapped his other arm around my waist and turned so

I draped across his chest, my legs tangled with his. Part of me was surprised he was still here, in the water with me.

My story didn't entail the same physical violation many young women faced, but it was sordid and left me feeling unclean for years. A large part of why I didn't date much.

"That's a long answer to your question, but yes, I always do worst-case. After that night at the concert… I was too naïve to think that way. But it's one of the techniques we worked on during my stay at the Peace Barn."

Cam's lips quirked a little at my quip. Not enough to reach his eyes, which remained dark, serious.

"Ben doesn't get to touch you. Ever. I'll make sure of it." Cam's voice was laced with that same commanding tone he'd used when Ben assaulted my shop.

I touched his cheek, trying to show him there was only one man I wanted to touch me. "I don't want him to."

"I'm getting you another bodyguard."

"Whoa. Slow that roll, Music Man. I don't need two beefy dudes scowling at me and the world."

"Yes to the muscles and scowls. Lots of scowling to let the world know I mean to keep you safe." He tightened his hold on me. "And mine." He ran his nose along my jaw and down my neck. "You're mine, Jenna Marie."

My pulse leaped. Cam smiled before he pressed a kiss to it.

"What about what I want?" Putting up this fight seemed important. Cam could—would—steamroll me if I let him.

He eased back a little. Not enough to give me space. "We're together. Exclusive. You ease my mind, sugar. I don't know how to explain it. But the noise stops. I find peace in our time together, and I don't plan to give that up. Plus, you're a looker."

I rolled my eyes. "Not selling this 'mine' business anymore."

He grinned. "You like me, I like you. We get to know each other better. Will the past come out? Absolutely. Do I care what anyone else thinks? Not a'tall."

"You say that now, but the digs, the comments, they can be so mean."

His face turned fierce, his eyes fiery. "We ignore them. None of that—" he waved his hand to encompass the rest of the world "—matters. What you and I think about each other matters. And, I have to tell you, sugar, this right here makes me mighty happy."

The rest of my arguments disintegrated after he spoke. I wanted him. I wanted a relationship—to feel secure in someone else's affection.

"Okay."

"Now, get pissy so we can enjoy the rest of the day."

I sighed. "You already set me up with a security contingent, didn't you?"

"Smarts and beauty." Cam nuzzled my jaw, kissed down my neck.

I didn't argue. One, Cam would do it anyway. He was stubborn like that. And, two, after Ben's most recent attack on my place of business, I didn't want to argue.

"I'm keeping my bat."

"At all times. Plus a Taser or pepper spray. You know how to shoot a pistol?"

I reared back and let him see my fierceness. "I do. But I will not carry a gun. You can have a guy with me who carries a gun, but I won't do it." Much as I didn't want to explain myself, we were building trust and he needed to understand. "There was a girl. She was Micah—my oldest brother's girlfriend."

"Aw, hell."

I nodded because Cam understood my reticence about weapons now. "She carried. She had her permit. She was in a car accident. That didn't kill her. Her weapon—in her purse—went off. Got her in the temple. She would have walked away from the accident with a few bruises."

"Did he love her?"

My heart warmed that Cam didn't try to talk me out of my position—and because he worried about my brother, a man he'd never met. "Yes," I said, my voice soft with the regret as it always was when I thought of Micah and Shannon. "He did."

Cam pressed a kiss to my temple. "All right. I won't ask you again to get a pistol. But we'll practice. Keep your aim sharp."

I wrapped my arms around his neck. This was what a relationship should be. Caring. And compromise *because* of the caring. "I can do that."

"Later. Right now, I need to hold you a bit."

We snuggled together as mosquitoes buzzed and birds chattered. The water rushed by, relaxing us both. Sometime later, when my eyes grew heavy, Cam shifted me before tilting up my chin.

"No other bombshells I need to know about?"

I dropped my eyes as I shook my head.

"Good. Let's head up. We'll have some lunch."

My stomach clenched, and I knew I wouldn't eat much.

———————— ★ ————————

The warm feeling Cam created on our date lingered long enough for him to talk me into attending his show Sunday. Listening to Cam play live—even with a tinny, store-bought guitar—proved again how much I liked him.

"You look at him just like he looks at you," Kate said, coming to stand next to me backstage where I stood, entranced by Cam's ability. As if he sensed my eyes on him, he turned his head and winked.

A soft sigh fluttered from my mouth.

"Damn, girl, you got it bad."

My face flushed hot, and I wondered if I'd made a mistake to invite Cam's sister to come into the shop. She tended to be more, well, difficult to manage than I'd anticipated. As if she read my thoughts, she turned toward me just as Cam finished his song.

"I don't have to come in if you're having second thoughts."

"Oh." My cheeks heated again. "I'm not sure it'll work out, but, you know, it'd be fun to see how we'd fit together in a professional setting."

Crap in a crabtree. Why hadn't I considered that I'd be Kate's boss. Yeah. Awkward.

Cam leaned into the microphone. "As y'all know, I'm playing a show at Fort Bliss on Independence Day."

He waited for the hollering and applause to die down. "One of the reasons is because I spent seven years in the Army. I believe in our independence." Again he waited for the applause to fade. "And in our military men and women. The vets. Those who don't get to come home but leave behind grieving families."

Cam strummed the guitar. The melody was soft, haunting. I brought my hands up to my lips. This song touched me each time I heard it, and that was before I found out Cam wrote it for one of his soldiers.

Kate bumped my shoulder with hers. "He's got talent. Not just for the melody and lyrics but for drawing out the right emotion in the crowd."

I nodded, still wrapped up in Cam's mesmerizing voice and larger-than-life personality.

"I'll see you tomorrow, Jenna. Thanks again for letting me swing by," Kate said as Cam finished his last song. "I'm really excited about talking with you more."

"Sure. See you."

How to explain her presence to Pop-pop? I shrugged the worry off and focused on Cam, smiling as he walked toward me. He wrapped me in his arms, and I reveled in this man's ability to tug me close with such ease.

I placed my hands on his cheeks and leaned in to kiss him. "You are an amazing performer."

He shrugged. "Would have been a better concert with a better instrument."

"I'll be back at it tomorrow," I said.

Cam shook his head. One of the dark locks of his hair stuck to his damp brow. "Didn't mean it to be a swipe. I'm a little off-kilter. Talking about my soldiers does that to me."

I shoved my hand into my pocket and pulled out a hard candy, letting it lie in my flat palm.

"You bought me Werther's?" He took the caramel and unwrapped it. After popping it into his mouth, he leaned down and kissed me again.

"You're better than any candy, Sweet Jenna Marie."

I pressed my lips to his, hard, needing him to understand how much I cared, not only about his kind words but about him.

"Let's get out of here." Cam threw his arm over my shoulder.

"Where are we going?" I asked.

Cam stopped walking and handed his guitar to one of the roadies that he'd introduced me to earlier. Cam's team was larger than my friends in Lummi Nation but smaller than some of the bigger acts I'd made instruments for. Made sense, but I was more shocked by the fact Cam knew everyone's name. Lots of the people who worked for him used to be under his command. Apparently, his desire to help, to protect, rolled over into his desire to employ his former soldiers. Kate told me he made sure they had health insurance and retirement plans—at a significant cost out of his own bottom line.

He dipped his head at a large man in the corner wearing all black. At my gaze, Cam headed in his direction.

"Chuck, this is Jenna. *My* girlfriend." My brows drew together at the emphasis on "my".

Chuck laughed. "I get that, chief. Hey, Jenna. Glad you're with Cam, here."

"Chuck's my head of security," Cam said. "And one of my best friends. He was my second-in-command during my last three tours."

Something dark moved in both their eyes. Not good memories, wherever they went.

"You headed out?" Chuck asked.

Cam nodded.

Chuck motioned us forward and fell in a few paces behind. I glanced back but Chuck wasn't looking at us; his eyes darted around, assessing the people backstage. No doubt trying to find risks before they became threats.

"Where are we going?" I asked.

Cam glanced down at me from the corner of his eye. "You okay if I stay at your place tonight?"

"Um. Sure."

Cam stopped walking a few steps from the back door. "You don't sound sure."

My cheeks reddened as I worried about Chuck overhearing our conversation. Why was this so weird? I liked Cam, wanted to spend more time with him, but something about him having a huge staff caused my chest to tighten and proved, yet again, how different our lives were.

"No, I want you there," I said quickly.

Cam narrowed his eyes as if he didn't believe me. I pushed open the doorway and pulled Cam into the dark night.

The screams were the first indication something was wrong. The second was the slam of still-shrieking bodies. The breath hissed from my lungs with one particularly hard swipe of an elbow or knee.

I started to fall, fear causing my ears to ring and dark spots to fill my vision. Cam yelled, as did Chuck, but the fear from the shifting press of bodies overwhelmed me. I tried to get upright, but I couldn't breathe, and when another blow came to my solar plexus, I whimpered as I collapsed.

Cam lifted me in his arms, holding me tight and high, away from the clawing hands but nearer the screaming mouths. I shuddered, pressing my face into his neck and cinching my arms tight around him. My breath broke into staccato pants.

"Step back," Cam shouted. "Y'all need to give us some space. Jenna's hurt."

I heard other men bellowing. More people pressed against my back, and I clung tighter to Cam and his familiar scent. I focused on the feel of his shoulders under my hands, trying to drown out the high-pitched squeals.

Ambushed by fans. I heard the words, but they didn't compute in my frazzled mind. I forced my eyes tight, trying to hold in the tears, the hysteria that threatened to burst forth. I was there, back there, on the floor of that other club, surrounded by people who were supposed to be my friends, their feet and knees within inches of my face. I pleaded to Ben, who stood over me, to step back so I could stand. To help me up.

He laughed. An ugly, harsh sound. Then he walked away as more bodies swarmed over me.

Before I could process further, Cam jogged forward, his gait unsteady. Chuck yelled from my right, another man answered from the left. Where were we going? I wanted to ask, but I was too afraid, my mouth too dry, to lift my head.

Another round of screams. Cam grunted as a body slammed into his back. Another caught him in his side. Someone yanked my hair. I screamed as I began to tumble out of Cam's arms.

"Jenna? Can you hear me, sugar?"

I opened my eyes, immediately squinting at the twirling, bright red and blue lights.

"What? Where?"

"We're in an ambulance."

"Why?" I started to sit up, but a set of hands pressed me back down. The panic built and a machine beeped a loud warning.

"Jenna. Look at me."

Cam's clipped command did not brook disobedience. My eyes sought his.

"You're safe, and I'm with you. Okay?"

I nodded, but my mind still rebelled, still sought the danger. My gaze bounced from Cam's to the EMT's—the person who held me down.

"We've got to finish cleaning out your cuts, ma'am."

"Wha…what happened?" I asked as I laid back against the hard mattress.

"Ambush," Cam said, eyes dark and mouth set in a flat, angry line. "Took seven members of my crew to get those women off us."

"I fell."

Cam shook his head. "I didn't drop you."

His shirt was ripped. So were the knees of his jeans. "You fell."

"I wasn't letting you go."

The cloud in my head vanished at his words, at the heated look in his eyes. *I wasn't letting you go.*

He meant it. He planned to let those woman, at least I assumed they were women based on the pitch of the voice, hurt

him, but he hadn't dropped me. Would have—probably did—
protect me with his own body.

I reached up and placed my palm on his cheek.

"Thank you."

CHAPTER SIXTEEN | Cam

Rage burned under my concern for Jenna's safety—and my gladness that she'd let me stay with her. All I knew so far was the fans were led around to the back of the building. Chuck spoke, well, more like yelled at the police who were supposed to help with security. He'd get answers.

I bit my lip against the ache in my legs. Both my knees dripped blood and I rolled my shoulder, trying to ease the ache from the nail scratches there and on my neck.

No wonder Jenna hated crowds and feeling hemmed in. I'd fought in multiple battles, stared men in the eye as we grappled with a knife. But the experience tonight, when the mob of mostly young women attacked, scared me spitless when they tried to rip Jenna from my arms to get to me.

I leaned in, my forehead touching hers, reveling in the feel of her hands on me. I didn't deserve that soft look, the gratitude. "I'm finding that I'd do just about anything for you, sugar."

She pressed her lips to mine, and I closed my eyes against the overwhelming sense of rightness of holding, kissing her. I pulled back, needing further reassurance.

"You okay? Anything hurt?"

Her brows scrunched as she considered the question. "My head. Probably from when someone yanked my hair."

The rage slid back over me, burning the edges of my skin. "No one should have touched you. I'm so sorry you were hurt." I touched her temple. "You banged your head as I went down. Don't know what on. Then you fainted."

She lowered her lashes. "That was the fear." She swallowed and refused to meet my gaze.

Shit. She had every right to be afraid. I'd brought her into this mess—my life. "I was afraid, too."

Chuck stepped to the back of the ambulance and patted the door. "Got him."

"Him, who?" I asked, scooching closer to Jenna. The need to protect her grew with each breath. My heart tripped. I couldn't lose her—couldn't let anything bad happen to her.

"Benjamin Wilkins."

Beside me, Jenna tensed. "What, exactly, did he do?"

"Who's Benjamin Wilkins?" I asked, annoyance making my voice sharp.

"Ben. The guy from my guitar shop," Jenna added, a frown building on her face.

"The little shit's been out on bail, which we knew. So now we get to add intent to harm and assaulting an officer. He clobbered one of the cops on the head to let those fans loose back here. Smart about it, too, because he waited until I received the all-clear from the officer before whacking him."

Chuck crossed his arms and by the pained scowl on his face, I knew he took the security breach personally.

"He'll stay in jail this time?" Jenna asked.

Chuck looked at me. I tipped Jenna's chin up, trying to make the moment a bit more private—control mattered to Jenna and I wanted to give her as much of it as possible.

"You want him to?"

Jenna nibbled at the corner of her lip. "Is it wrong to say yes?"

"Hell, no," Chuck said.

"No, sugar. He's tried to hurt you. Twice. I can call my attorney."

"Three times," she said.

"What?" The word slid from my lips as a growl.

"I-I remembered. When the women started grabbing at you and me. I remembered that Ben stood over me when I fell to the floor of that club."

She waited until I dipped my head. I remembered the story she told me. My hands clenched into fists and I breathed through my nose real slow to ease my racing heart.

"He stood there, making sure I couldn't stand and then…then he kicked me." Her eyebrows pulled tight over her nose. "That must have been when I passed out."

"You want him in jail, and I'll get my PR machine involved so they can get your story out there. I don't care if he plays ball for the Yankees."

"He doesn't play for anyone now. I think that's part of why he's acting out."

"He needs to be shut down."

The last words sifted through my gritted teeth. The EMT finished cleaning Jenna up and eyed me with concern. Whatever. Jenna hurting at the hands of Ben brought forth all my protective instincts—and made me want to rip him to shreds.

I cleared my throat from the emotional debris. "Whatever you want."

Jenna searched my eyes. "I want him to go away. Whatever and however that's best. I don't want him to hurt you, either."

"I'm fine." I brushed off the concern but my knees and calf throbbed more with each breath. I glanced back at Chuck, making sure he saw the danger in my eyes. "We'll take care of this. Make sure he stays away."

Chuck dipped his head in understanding and stepped back before pivoting on his heel. He'd take care of Ben. I narrowed my eyes. I would, too, in a statement put out soon by my publicist.

She rested her head on my shoulder, and once again I focused on how right she felt in my arms. "Let's get your leg looked at," she murmured.

"It's fine."

"Cam?"

I looked down into her upturned face.

"Don't play tough guy right now."

I couldn't help the smile that tugged at my lips. "You think I play at it?"

She moved back, scooting her legs over the side of the EMT bed so that I could settle more fully next to her.

"I think you're Army Ranger tough and brave. And right now, you have a serious boo-boo that needs attention." She dipped her blond head toward the EMT who gathered the necessary equipment to clean out my abrasions.

I went along with the motions, needing the time to get my anger back under control.

"You need an X-ray of your knee and lower leg, sir," the EMT said. "One of the bones might be fractured."

"It's not," I said, pressing a kiss to Jenna's forehead—the non-scraped side.

My blood pressure soared again as I thought of those women yanking on her. Thankfully, Jenna fainted before she heard the derogatory words they hurled toward her. I never would have dropped her, but after experiencing the vitriol first-hand, my fears ratcheted up. Those women hated Jenna—I wasn't sure if it was envy or spite or something that piece-of-excrement Ben said, but whatever caused the outpouring of hate, it scared me. Big time. Which was why Jenna must have her own security detail.

And…much as I hated to do so, I needed to re-think my relationship with her. What I could and did bring to her life.

First, I needed to hold her until my mind slowed far enough for me to develop a strategy to keep my female fans *and* Jenna.

Much as I might like the idea of scrapping the fame to live a quiet life, too many of my former soldiers depended on me. I'd made them a promise before I met Jenna. She might be my main interest, but my men, now security and roadies, were my family—the one that brought me through Kim's death and the dark place I fell after my father's decision to throw her out.

My arms tightened around Jenna. I needed time to figure out how to keep her and my men secure.

I closed my eyes as the EMT wrapped my leg.

Brenda was going to demand a raise.

If she could figure out this shitstorm, she deserved one.

CHAPTER SEVENTEEN | Jenna

"I don't wanna get an X-ray," Cam muttered.

I'm sure he didn't, but something else bothered him more than a trip to urgent care.

"I'll go with you. Hold your hand the whole time."

"You can't go in the room with me. You know that." He sounded petulant, but he rubbed the thumb of his left hand against my wrist.

"Do you not want to go because you're worried it's broken?"

"I don't wanna miss time with you, sugar."

"I just said I'd go with you."

"And then you'll be exhausted for work tomorrow. And I want to hold you in my arms again tonight. The rest can wait."

I turned toward him after I stepped out of the ambulance.

"No. Either you go to get your leg checked out now or I go home. Alone."

Instead of anger, Cam threw his head back and laughed.

I frowned, trying to look fierce and serious.

"Oh, I get you're not joking, sugar. I just like how bossy you got. Like I matter."

He tugged me forward, wincing as his leg twisted a little.

"You do," I said, slowing my steps so as not to hurt him more.

"Good. That's why we're together." He turned to face me

once we stood next to the passenger side of the SUV Chuck drove. Cam tucked my hair behind my ear, then leaned in closer and pressed a kiss to my jaw. "I don't like to think about what could've happened here tonight."

He opened the car door and helped me in the back seat.

"Gotta make a call."

I nodded, liking that he took my hand once he'd pressed the buttons. "Brenda, I need... You're already on it? Good. What do you need from me? All right. Jenna said there's a video of him attacking her some years back."

He looked at me, even as my stomach plummeted. I didn't want those images, my struggles out there for the world to see—to pick apart.

"What place were you at with Ben?"

"I don't think that's a good idea," I said.

He touched my cheek, tipping my chin up toward him to better gauge my response. "We need to get in front of this. Tell me the name of the venue so Brenda can start dripping it before some troll does."

"Moody Theater," I muttered, my stomach twinging harder. "But I really don't want..."

"You hear that?" Cam said, putting the phone back to his ear.

He spoke with Brenda the rest of the way to the urgent care facility. Cam, being big-time country star Camden Grace, was seen quickly, and the doctor noted the knees were simply badly scraped and his shin bruised, not broken. After we received pain pills and a lesson in how to alleviate pressure, I was beyond exhausted.

"You're owly-eyed," Cam said. "Let's get you home."

I considered asking Cam to give me space, to let me process the night and the way he'd just steam-rolled me, not even listening to my concerns.

I opened my mouth twice, but truth was, I didn't want to be alone. Each time I closed my eyes, I relived the frantic faces of those teenagers from my past overshadowed by the female fans running toward us tonight. Their shrill screams and their hands. I shivered, hugging my arms tight to my body as I tried to ward off the memories.

Cam shooed me to the bathroom and double-checked my locks, turning off lights and cursing when he ran into something in the living room. I met him in the bedroom, face washed and teeth brushed.

He pressed a kiss to my forehead and I eased my body against his, thankful he was there and hating myself for the weakness of needing him. That had to make me weak, right, to need his presence to silence the screams in my head?

Cam brushed his teeth and came out of the bathroom in just his boxer briefs. I had to close my eyes but already the image of his toned chest, the rippling abdominal muscles and tight hips was tattooed in my brain.

As he hauled me closer, my eyes closed and the silence finally prevailed. I slid into an exhausted slumber.

———— ★ ————

I woke hours later, alone. Turning, I placed my hand on the sheet. Cool.

I sat up, eyes adjusting to the dark. I slipped from the bed and padded into the living room. Cam stood with his back to me, facing the large picture window. His hands pressed against the glass, his head bowed. He'd pulled on his jeans but left them unbuttoned. At his feet lay multiple foil wrappers.

As I approached, the scent of caramel became more distinct.

"I keep seeing the look in your eyes when that woman yanked your hair. Your neck arched back and I worried it would snap. All my fucking fault."

"No," I said. "Ben was involved so it's not your fault. He let those women back there."

"Ben might have let them through, but they were my fans. And when you looked at me, and I couldn't focus on those women. On the threat like I should. I wanted to take the fear from your eyes. But I put you in that situation."

I swallowed hard. I didn't want to do this, dredge up this part of my past. But Cam needed to understand—and maybe, maybe I needed to forgive my seventeen-year-old self.

"There was a rumor. After I left school to go to the Peace Barn."

"All right."

"Girls said I miscarried Ben's baby."

Cam turned toward me, brows low, mouth flat. "Did you?"

I shook my head. "I've never been pregnant. Just stupid enough to have sex with him," I added at Cam's building scowl.

If I'd been smarter, I would have left as soon as Ben showed me Fiona and Robbie together. But I wasn't smart and I let him nail me in the back seat of his father's Land Rover that night. That's all it was—Ben, getting off.

Afterward, I'd curled up in a ball, too numb to cry and too

hurt to focus on anything.

"Why's he acting like this if it was just a rumor?"

I sighed, wrapping my arms around my waist. Cam grunted before he pulled me to him, the rough edges of his bandaged hand pulling at my skin.

"Before I left… Before the scene at the concert… I started bleeding, and I had cramps."

Cam kept his arms around me but his muscles shifted, tensed. "But you weren't pregnant?" His voice lost some of its warm edge.

He was thinking about Kim, thinking I'd made the same choice as Kim—to cheat and then to get rid of the baby. I tipped my face back and tried to step out of his arms. He tightened his hold but his eyes…they held the bleakest shadows.

"No, Cam. No."

"You can't leave the story there." Urgency built with each of his words. He ached inside, just as I did because he thought I was like Kim. "Did you cheat?"

He hurt. Because of me.

When would the cycle end? I'd tried so hard to be better, live better. And yet…once again, I hurt a person I cared about.

"I just told you I didn't."

"But they all think you did. There's gotta be some truth in that."

I stiffened my spine and stepped back.

"There wasn't. Not any. But I can't say I appreciate you believing Ben over me."

He finally dropped his arms. He pulled another candy from his pocket, his hands shaking as he unwrapped the plastic. His eyes never left mine as the wrapper fell from his fingers. He shoved the Werther's in his mouth and sucked.

"Never said I did."

"Then you're letting your pain from the past get in the way of thinking clearly."

"Like you did tonight?" he shot back. "Don't think I didn't read your face—you didn't want Brenda to pull that footage. Why's that, Jenna? What are we going to see?"

"I get that you're hurting—that you think somehow this is Kim all over again—but that was low, Cam. That was mean."

"Cuz I called you on it?"

I lifted my chin, blinking back the tears I refused to let fall. "Because you'd actually believe that about me."

He spun on his heel. "I need some space."

"You need to trust me," I shot back.

"Like you do me? Don't tell me you didn't blame me when those gals came charging at us."

My hands clenched and my heart raced. "So did you."

No. I didn't want him to leave. I wanted to finish this fight.

I wanted him to hold me.

But the door shut with a soft click.

Just as I realized something terrible. I cared about Cam. More than I had for any man in my life.

I slid to the floor, my cheek to my pulled-up knees and stared out at the predawn skyline winking back at me.

———— ★ ————

Pop-pop wasn't in today. He had his annual physical and then lunch with my dad. I loved how close the two of them were, but

I also sighed with relief, thankful not to explain Kate's presence or whatever I was doing with Cam. Nothing good, obviously, since he'd left.

I pulled out my phone, refusing to think about Cam more. My mother left me messages last night, as did Pop-pop and my brothers, all of which I answered so no one would panic or worry about me. I texted them all again, letting them know I was at the shop and planned to stay until six. No point in going home—there was no one to meet me.

I missed Cam.

I sipped the coffee I made, hating it almost as much as my screwed-up life.

I cleared out a bunch of emails before I heard the knock on the door. I took a deep breath and went to face Cam's sister.

"Heya, Jenna." Kate bounced into the store, holding on tight to a bag while her eyes danced around the shop. "This place is amazing." Her voice was as reverent as one expected for a church.

"Glad you like it. Want to look around for a minute?" I turned back to the door, making sure to lock the deadbolt. Ben might be in custody, but I wasn't taking any chances.

"Later, if that's okay," Katie Rose said. "I brought you donuts. They're not from that fancy place Cam said you liked because I didn't want to be late, but I hope they're still good."

"You going to eat one with me?" I asked.

Kate's eyes twinkled. "I could. But I already ate two on the way over." She shrugged. "They smelled fantastic, and I was starving."

I took the sack from her as I laughed. Relief washed through me. I'd be okay. Cam had only been in my life a few days.

Maybe my face gave me away. Kate spun back to me and asked, "What's going on with you and my brother? I mean, really."

"I don't know." I set the donuts on the counter, no longer interested in food. Not even fried sugar bread.

"Did y'all fight?"

I shrugged. I sighed, dejection settling over me in a thick, unwelcome cloak. Familiar and hated, I wanted to step out from under it but couldn't. I'd brought this current situation on myself.

"Okay," Kate said, her voice as shaky as I felt. "No talk of Cam. Um, do you want me to leave?"

"No! I mean, please don't. I get…it's so quiet here."

She rested her hand on top of my clenched one next to the bag of donuts. "And you fall into your head." She said the words with a conviction that cemented the kinship between us.

Politely dismissing Kate would be smart.

Why couldn't I be smart?

Because you're lonely. And scared. Not just of Cam never speaking to you again, but of remaining alone—of never getting past your stupid decisions, no matter how far in the past they are.

"Why don't you come to the workshop? I'll show you what I'm working on."

Kate trailed behind. I talked her through the current stage of the guitar and what I needed to accomplish today. She settled on a nearby stool, her eyes following my every move.

"Why do you use such thin pieces?" she asked after I laid a second piece next to the first, using a roller to ensure no air bubbles remained between the two types of wood and the adhesive.

"Because we don't want the guitar to be too heavy. That would cause shoulder aches for the performer."

She hummed her understanding.

The next time I needed the adhesive, she handed it to me. Once I'd set the wood, she pressed the roller into my hand.

"You're observant," I said.

"Not just about your process here."

I glanced up, catching her worried gaze.

"I won't ask," she said. "But Cam… I saw him this morning. He looks at least as bad as you."

I dropped my eyes back to my work, biting the inside of my cheek. *That's* why tears formed in my eyes. Not because I worried I'd lost him forever.

"But since we're not talking about him, why don't you show me your process to onboard a new client? And then we can talk about ways to grow the business without straining you and your grandfather more time-wise."

"You think that's possible?" I asked.

Kate shrugged. "I won't know anything until I get a better grasp of the business."

I led her from the shop. Focusing on work would help.

And I needed to stay focused. This, my business, was important—the most important piece of my life. Cam, well, Cam would have to decide if he wanted to hear my explanation.

CHAPTER EIGHTEEN | Cam

I set my practice guitar to the side and settled my heels against the thick, white banister separating my porch from the garden below.

"You come to tell me all about your day?" I asked Katie Rose.

She picked up my tumbler and sniffed. With a wrinkled nose, she turned and threw the contents of the glass into the roses. Whiskey wouldn't do the flowers any favors, but the liquor wasn't helping my leg or the deep lashings in my heart.

I couldn't get Jenna's words out of my head.

She was like Kim. Just like the woman I married who broke my family.

I leaned my head back and closed my eyes, swallowing down the bitter regret and the disgust for my inability to learn from my mistakes.

"She's as much of a mess as you. Well, maybe not. She didn't get drunk. Just tried not to cry as she worked on your guitar today."

I absorbed what Katie Rose said—and the tone she said it in. "Don't want to go into it."

"And I don't want to be in the middle. But you're both miserable and want to be with each other."

"Not if it's toxic."

I flinched and yelped when Katie's hand cracked against my arm. Closing my eyes proved just how much Jenna messed with my head. Katie Rose loved to wallop my arm.

"What's that for?"

"So many things." She scowled. "But I think I'm most annoyed that you're thinking of Kim and overlaying that on Jenna."

I shook my head, opening my mouth to tell her.

"Save it, big brother. I don't want to hear you rip into a woman I happen to respect. Have you seen her work? I mean, the meticulousness she puts into every detail? She's a freaking genius. I like Jenna. Even at twelve, I didn't like Kim."

With that she turned on her heel and strode down my porch steps and back up the path toward the big house.

"And for the record, I'm pretty sure this is all your fault. You're the one who talked her into going to the concert and got her attacked. Her arms are black and blue and she kept wincing."

Katie Rose flounced off, once again proving she had to get in the last word. Granted, those words dug in deep, just like she intended.

---- ★ ----

Each time I fell into slumber that night, Jenna's somber eyes pulled me toward her and I woke with a start, resisting her and her history.

She kept working on my guitar. Katie Rose sent a picture of it late the next afternoon. The instrument glowed, the edges seamless. Jenna proved her craftsmanship in each of the pieces she created.

I missed her.

My mother stopped by with a platter of hot fried chicken. My favorite. I bit into one of the legs with half-hearted enthusiasm.

"You need to call your brother, Camden."

"Don't see how that'll help anything. He won't talk to me. He didn't even bother to come home for Dad's funeral."

Mom's lips rolled into her mouth and her eyes got a nasty, distant look in them. She pulled her phone from her purse and pressed a few buttons.

"Hi, Carter. Thank you. Yes, I'm okay. But Camden isn't. I'm going to put him on the phone and I want you to be *honest* with him."

My mama's voice, combined with that look in her eye, made my guts twist hard in my stomach. I took the phone much as one did a live bomb. Getting it to my ear seemed to take forever.

"Carter, so nice of you to talk to me again."

"Cut the shit, Cam. We both know Mama's making me do it. And we both know you're so bristly because of the woman you've been stepping out with. Did you break up with her because you almost got her killed?"

That was the problem with a twin—I hadn't seen him in almost five years, but he knew my habits and moods.

I blew out a breath, trying to stream out the hurt I'd felt since Jenna told me the truth about Ben. "No. I would have though. Planned to. But… She turned out to be just like Kim."

Carter barked out a laugh. "I know not-one-thing about your new gal, but I know she's *nothing* like your wife."

Now his words were like gutshot. "Did you screw her?" I asked.

My mother shut her eyes and gripped the edge of the counter but didn't walk away. Because she knew…she must know. As sure of it as I'd been—that this was the reason Carter refused to come home.

"No." His voice was emphatic. I could feel the glare sizzling through the phone line. "But I am the reason she died." He swallowed hard, a thick rasp of emotion bubbling from his throat. "I should look you in the eye when I tell you this."

"You'd have to be willing to be in the same room as me—and you haven't done that in years."

"Because I feel guilty!" Carter yelled. "I'm the one who threw Kim out."

I leaned back against my kitchen counter. "Naw. That was Dad."

Carter bit out a curse. "*Dad* was the one screwing Kim. I caught him. In the barn. Pants around his ankles."

My eyes slammed shut, trying to block out the image.

"But...then...why did *you* leave?"

"Kim had made advances toward me. I told her no. You were my brother—more importantly, my twin, which she said was why she wanted me. I turned her down in a not very nice way. There was no way I'd betray you like that, bro."

I'd hated thinking he had.

Carter's voice was soft, so full of sadness when he continued speaking. "Cam, the baby Kim carried...that was Dad's kid."

I slid down to the floor. "What?"

"He told me. After I caught them. Dad planned to run off with Kim. I said no way. Kim had to leave. I packed her up and drove her to the airport. I bought her a ticket to Las Vegas. Where her sister's at."

Kim's younger sister, Connie, made a great living as a burlesque dancer in Vegas.

"That's after I beat the shit out of Dad. He had more coming, but Mom came out and found me pummeling him."

I raised my gaze to my mother's. Tears streamed down her face and her arms wrapped tight around her waist as if she were trying to hold the pain in. She knew this story—what Carter said. She knew and she, like my brother, kept it from me.

"By that point, Dad couldn't walk. I wanted to leave him in the barn, but Mom made me carry his sorry, selfish ass inside. Then I collected Kim's crap and drove her to the airport. But she didn't get on the plane."

"She was found dead, what? A week later, in an alley near downtown."

"Yeah, I know. From too much heroin. She must've been using for a while, just none of us knew what to look for."

"Dad too?" I kept my gaze firm on Mom.

She nodded, pressing her hand to her lips, ugly memories flashing through her eyes.

"That's why I moved. I just couldn't look at that sorry excuse for manhood—let alone fatherhood—anymore. Mom wouldn't leave him. And you were already mad at him. Rightly so, I reckoned. No reason to further rock the boat."

"I had no idea I brought such a pestilence into our house."

"You didn't." Mom's voice was thready but gained strength. "I did. I did this to our family."

She twisted her hands together before smoothing them down the front of her shirt, then over her hips. I'd never seen my mother so anxious before.

"Your father was having an affair with that girl before you

married her. That's why he was angry about your marriage."

"You hearing this?" I asked Carter. I pulled the phone from my ear and pressed the speaker button.

"Piece of shit," Carter replied. I wasn't sure if he meant Dad or Kim. Didn't matter, really.

"She told your father that-a-way, she could be closer to him and no one would wonder about their relationship," Mama said. "At least, that's what he told me."

When I married her, Kim was nineteen. My dad was fifty-two.

Mom swiped at her cheek. "He would have to divorce me and shell out so much of the ranch. Or sell it off. I almost did, anyway."

"Why didn't you, Mama?" Carter asked.

"Because I knew how much it meant to Camden. *He* was the victim in all this. No reason to sell his home just because Laurence was a lying, cheating snake."

"What about Kim?" I rasped. "She participated."

Mom nodded. "True, but your father was the adult. She was eighteen when he started stepping out with her—way old enough to know better, even if she wasn't."

"Wish I'd hit him harder," Carter growled. "I hate that he hurt you, Mama."

She raised her chin. "He did. But he was never the love of my life so it's not like he could wound me as deep as, say, Jenna's hurt you, Camden."

I set the phone on the tile next to me and rubbed my hands through my hair and then down my face.

"How are we still a family?" I asked.

"Because neither Kim nor Laurence had the love in them to *be* part of this family. We have each other and we're going to fix this mess. Once and for all. You hear me, Carter?"

"Yes, Mama."

"I expect you to get home soon. I know it's hard with your own spread. But you get home and you hug your brother. Soon."

"Yes, Mama."

"Camden's heard enough but you're going to answer his calls and tell him whatever else he needs to know."

"Yes, Mama."

"I love you, son," Mama said, picking up the phone from next to my hip. She crouched in front of me, and I wasn't sure if she spoke to Carter or me.

"Love you, too, Mama. Thanks for making me come clean."

"Bye, now."

She clicked off before settling on her knees next to me. She grimaced a little before clutching my hands in hers. "I owe you an apology, son."

I shook my head.

"I knew about their affair. Not until after your wedding. I just…I couldn't figure out how to tell you without hurting you."

"What about your hurt?" I asked.

She smiled, but it was a sad one. "That happened before you were born, Camden. I lost my love to a stupid training exercise. Air Force," she said at my look. "I was pregnant at the time." She smiled, and it was soft and genuine. "I was never happier than that day I found out." She raised her eyebrows. "Laurence's older brother. Just seemed smart to marry Laurence and let him raise his brother's boys."

"Boys?" I asked. But, really, I already knew. Had known.

My mother reached forward and cupped my cheek, her smile sad. "You're Jensen's boys."

"The name on the birth certificate. Jensen. I asked Dad... Laurence about it once. He never answered me."

"He wanted to pretend you were his. That made him more okay with the whole situation, though, honestly, Camden, you and Carter are the beneficiaries of this ranch. I didn't understand until later that's part of why Laurence married me."

I tilted my head back away from my mother's hand. I needed a bit of space, needed to process her words. "You were young."

"Twenty-two wasn't young to have kids, not for this part of Texas thirty years ago. My only regret was Jensen and I never married. But that didn't stop me from putting his name on your birth certificate. Laurence never got over that."

"Does Katie Rose know?"

Mom shook her head. "Kate was...an effort to make Laurence and I work. Didn't help at all, not that anything would have. Laurence tried, and he was a good father."

I snorted.

"What he did to you, Camden, is atrocious."

"He hurt you, too."

Mom shrugged. "By then, nothing Laurence did surprised me. He was nothing like Jensen. But I'd appreciate you not saying as much to Katie Rose."

As if I'd hurt Katie Rose with that truth. I loved that little girl and always would—full sister or half-sister, she was my baby sister either way.

Her smile turned rueful. "Laurence loved me—for a while—but I never loved him, and he knew it. That's part of why he took up with other ladies. Kim wasn't the first."

I stood, grimacing at the ache in my leg. I pulled Mom up slowly, letting her find her feet.

"Seems like there's been lots of half-truths in this family."

She kept her eyes steady on me. "And that needs to stop. You weren't at fault for Kim's actions, any more than I'm to blame for Laurence's." She hesitated. "He was a good father when you were little."

I opened my mouth to argue with her, but my mother shook her head.

"I need to accept I made mistakes, Camden. They've hurt you. So much." She pressed her lips together but they still trembled. "I've lost Carter to his place up in Wyoming. Serves me right, too."

"Mama—"

"Now, I don't know what's going on between you and Jenna, but I think you need to understand Kim's choices were her own and had *nothing* to do with you." At my flinch, she cupped my cheeks harder. "That girl needed something no one—not your father—"

"Laurence," I corrected her. Much easier to ignore how he taught me to ride, to rope a steer, to dance and fight dirty. He was my uncle—a cheating man who didn't deserve any of the positive feelings I had, and definitely none of the guilt I'd carried around since his death. No, since Kim's.

"Laurence or you could provide. But don't let that past hurt destroy your future happiness, son. Don't make more mistakes because I was too scared to tell you the truth."

I pulled my mama in and hugged her. She wrapped her arms around my waist and squeezed back, hard. She needed this moment though I wasn't sure yet what these revelations meant. My mind pinged from one thought to another, unable to settle.

"I'm sorry my decisions led you to this point, Camden. I'm so sorry."

I rested my cheek against the crown of her head. "I needed to know."

She stepped back. "Does knowing the truth make it easier? Can you find your way back to Jenna now?"

Good questions for which I didn't have a good answer. I just knew I craved her calming influence. Instead, I popped another Werther's into my mouth.

———— ★ ————

I spent the next few days processing what I'd learned. Finding out Laurence was my uncle, not my father, helped.

Sort of.

Being a cuckold to my own damn uncle sucked. Hard. He'd been my father—the man I turned to for advice about everything from sports to calving, to women. Yeah, the irony of that proved great.

By the end of the week, I hadn't slept more than a few hours in all the nights combined. I spent the time staring at bad day-time TV and scribbling in my notebook only to cross out the shitty lyrics I managed to compile, and despairing at my cut-and-run with Jenna.

Speaking to Carter further soothed my abraded soul.

I set my phone down now, having just completed another call with my brother. Hearing his voice, his concern for me—hell, even better was hearing the pride he felt in my success. I'd needed that, along with the promise he'd come into town soon—around the Fourth of July.

I looked forward to seeing him.

I missed Jenna more.

But…trusting her, after I'd put trust in Kim and the man I'd considered father, proved hard.

Jenna hadn't contacted me. Maybe she was glad to be rid of me.

Not according to Katie Rose. My sister told me each day just how sad Jenna looked—as if my hasty exit blew apart her own fragile grasp on trust.

Speaking of sisters, Katie Rose flopped down into the Adirondack chair next to me with a huge sigh.

"What?" I grumbled. In part I didn't want to see her, but another part of me hated keeping a secret from her. Carter thought we should tell her, but Carter wasn't here for the fallout, which meant his vote counted less.

"Shut that growling off."

I swallowed down the retort.

"You need to go out," she said.

"Don't want to."

Katie Rose turned toward me. "That's obvious. You look worse than you did when you came home from your last deployment." She waved her hand in front of her nose. "Smell worse, too."

"I'm not in the mood."

"Cam, you haven't done more than sulk inside or outside for

almost week. You even turned down Mama's fried chicken. *Twice.*"

Not for the reasons she thought. I loved my mother, sure, but she kept some mighty big secrets from us. And we were all paying the price for them. I closed my eyes, unsure how best to handle this conversation with my sister.

"I'll be social when I'm ready."

"The way you're going, that'll be never. You and Jenna had a misunderstanding." At my sharp look, she held up her hands. "The only way it's going to get better is for you to talk to her or to lap up some fan fawning."

"No."

I hadn't told anyone, not even Chuck, that my chest tightened and my heart pelted out a mad beat at the thought of being surrounded again—part of the reason I couldn't get Jenna out of my head. What if I caused her anxiety to spike? What if Jenna needed *more* meds to get through the day because I all but forced her to come to my show? Then dropped her faster than a hot potato.

She should be angry with me.

I scowled, trying yet again to tamp down on my desire to see Jenna—and my guilt at how I'd left her without waiting for an explanation. I missed touching her skin and the way her hair slid through my fingers.

The need to spend time with her grew each day, and misery ate at my consciousness.

I stood abruptly, oversetting my inked-up notebook.

"Fine. I'll go talk to Jenna."

"You can't."

I turned back to glare at my sister. "What do you mean, I can't? Isn't that what you've been harping on?"

Katie Rose raised a fine, auburn brow. "She left earlier today to deliver a couple of guitars."

I stared at her, my brain dulled. Jenna lived and worked in Austin. She wouldn't leave. "Left?"

"Yeah. She's in Seattle for the weekend."

I stilled. Seattle. Where her friends were. A place she loved. "Was she supposed to go?"

Katie Rose shook her head, biting back a smile. "Nope. Mr. Olsen sent her. Said she needed to get out of her mope. He's none too happy with you these days, either."

She'd go out with her friends and have fun. Maybe hook up with some guy who'd tell her how beautiful she was. Kiss her mouth and love her body.

Oh, hell, no.

I stomped into the house and slammed my door shut.

———— ★ ————

No way I was letting her go to Seattle without proper protection. The guards I'd hired to watch her, Mitch and Jared, weren't enough. Not after last week. Not if she was in another city, too far for me to help should she need me.

At least, that's what I told myself as I showered, shaved, and packed.

Katie Rose, the nuisance, waved as I sped my truck toward the airport, Chuck and three more of my team following in the car behind because Chuck refused to ride with me.

"You've had a bug up your ass for days. I'm not taking on any more of that nastiness. And don't go spouting off on the fact you have daddy issues. You're not the only one, but I treat my friends decent still."

I rolled my shoulders as I remembered Chuck's words. Guess my bad mood rippled out to cover the rest of my companions.

I owed Chuck a bottle of Macallan. I shifted in my seat. If I'd been as bad as Katie Rose said, I owed him a case.

For the duration of the flight, I made a point to improve my attitude. Chuck still scowled whenever he looked at me, but some of his humor softened the tension around his eyes.

We checked into the hotel—the same one Jenna checked into a few hours ago. I booked out an entire floor for privacy, which meant each of the guards had their own room, but I left my suit-case and guitar still packed on the bed as I pulled out my phone.

"She back yet?" I asked Chuck.

"I knew your better humor was an act," he said on a sigh. "No, she's out to dinner with some friends. At least that's what I was told."

"Do you know where?"

"I don't. And I don't think it's a good idea for you to chase after her right now. She'll be back later."

"But what if she isn't alone?"

"You should have thought of that before you left her in the middle of the night, chief."

Chuck's valid statement didn't lessen the ache in my chest.

Jenna was beautiful. While she might not be out searching, another lover might have found her while I wallowed in my past. I never let her explain. I let my unanswered questions and fears with Kim lead me by the nose straight out of Jenna's place. More fool I, especially to find out my dad—no, *Uncle* Laurence's part in the whole sordid mess.

I used my nervous energy to put away my clothes, and then I tried to pick out a new tune. Nothing felt right. TV, even with over one hundred channels, couldn't hold my attention. I grabbed my phone and shoved it and my keycard into my pocket as I headed toward the elevator. Maybe a drink or even a walk outside would cool me down.

I pressed the down button on the bank of elevators and waited, tapping my foot with impatience. With a soft ping, the arrow over the middle car lit, and I stepped toward it, anxious to get out of my room and, more importantly, out of my head.

The doors opened and I stared straight into Jenna's eyes. Hers rounded, her mouth falling open. I grabbed her wrist and pulled her toward me, my eyes never leaving hers.

Until the kick to the shins and another hit on my arm, followed by loud shrieks of "Let her go."

I shifted my gaze to see Abbi Dorsey on Jenna's left and a curvy brunette I thought dated the bassist in Lummi Nation on Jenna's right.

A door down the hall slammed into the wall and feet pattered near silently on the thick carpet.

"Dammit, Cam. We thought there was a problem."

"There is," Jenna said, motioning to my hold on her wrist.

I should let her go, let her get back to her friends. I knew this. Instead, I stepped closer until the scent of Jenna's shampoo filled my nose. Pear. The damn scent smelled like home.

I'd missed this woman.

"I just want to chat with Jenna here," I said.

Abbi narrowed her stunning blue eyes. "From what we've heard, she should never talk to you again."

"Be that as it may, I flew out here because I couldn't stand it a moment longer. Could y'all give us a few minutes? I promise to return her to you—in one piece in…" My gaze slid back to Jenna's.

"Twenty minutes." Her facial muscles were rigid, her eyes guarded.

Well, hell. I dipped my head in acknowledgment. "Twenty minutes."

Chuck motioned to Abbi and the other gal…Nessa, yeah, that was her name. "You want to join us for a drink? Or a movie?"

"Jenna isn't going to be gone with Cam long enough for a show," Nessa said, putting her hands on her hips, which caused her blue dress to tighten across her chest. Chuck made a soft noise, his gaze landing on Nessa's incredible cleavage.

"Nes has a boyfriend," Jenna said to Chuck, yanking her wrist from my hand. She pulled her keycard from her purse and handed it to Abbi, who took in all of us once more.

"Are you going to be okay?" Abbi asked. "You don't have to go with him."

Jenna shrugged, her face turned away from me. "I'll see you in nineteen minutes."

Abbi and Nessa nodded, concern obvious in their expressions. I waved Jenna to go ahead of me while Chuck crossed his arms over his chest and leaned against the elevator bank, no doubt planning to chat with the other gals until another elevator stopped on this floor.

"This one here's me," I said, rubbing my clammy palms on my jeans before pulling out my key card. I managed to get it in the lock without my hand shaking too much.

Now that Jenna walked into the room, now that she turned back to look at me, her eyes shadowed with grief and something akin to anger, my voice refused to work.

"Why did you fly out here, Cam? What could you possibly want?"

I opened my mouth, my heart thundering in my ears. I cleared my throat. Stepping closer I raised my hand to touch her cheek but Jenna flinched back. My chest ached, my knees weakened.

"Found out that the baby Kim carried was my uncle's. The man I thought of as my father."

She blinked, then blinked again. "What?"

I rubbed the back of my neck, unsure why I'd started there. Not what I'd meant to say. "Katie Rose doesn't know. I mean, that my brother and I aren't...that we just share our mother with her."

Jenna shook her head as if I'd overloaded her with information.

"That's not what my leaving was about though. I messed up. I couldn't figure out how to make it right between us because I figured if you were hurt because of me, then I should let you go. But then you told me about the miscarriage."

"There was no miscarriage."

I nodded. "Right. Still, at the time, all I heard was pregnancy and I thought you must be like Kim. But you're not. You're *nothing* like her."

Jenna's eyes narrowed as I spoke. She released a heavy breath. "You didn't even listen to my explanation. That hurt me, Cam."

"The moment I walked out your door, I started bleeding."

"I wanted to talk to you." She stood taller. "I wanted you to hold me. Like you promised you would, especially after I was hurt attending *your* concert."

"I…" How to explain about the adrenaline, the fear for her life? For my panicky reaction to the mere idea of being in or near a crowd again? "I want you to finish telling me about Ben."

She wrapped her arms around her middle. "*Now* that's important to you?"

The derision in her voice caused me to flinch but I managed a nod.

The anger in her eyes, the firm set of her lips crumpled. "You want to know about *him*? Fine."

CHAPTER NINETEEN | Jenna

The fresh slice of Cam's concern—not for me but for *Ben* and what happened all those years ago—kept me from finding pleasure in his shocked look.

Served him right. He'd thought the worst of me and disappeared for days without so much as a "how ya doing" after that mob attack.

"There is literally not one other thing to tell you. I hadn't seen Ben since that night at the concert until he walked into my shop. I assume he thinks I miscarried because that was the rumor going around the school in the weeks before. I don't know for sure because I've had no further interaction with him. It was an ovarian cyst, by the way. My doctor believes it may have ruptured because of stress."

I looked away, hating feeling so dejected, so out-of-control. That's part of why I decided to fly up here. I needed space, not just from Cam and the media, but from Cam's sister, Kate, simply because she reminded me of him—of the safety and closeness I'd managed to lose within days of finding it.

"Why didn't you tell me then?" he rasped.

"Why didn't you stick around if you wanted to know so bad?" I shot back.

He dropped his head into his hands and his shoulders heaved.

His breath slid into his mouth in a thick rasp.

I inched toward the door, needing to get away from all these emotions. As if he felt my withdrawal, Cam leaped to his feet and wrapped me in his arms. I stiffened. Cam's touch, his scent, relaxed me even as I tried to break free.

"Just let me hold you a second, sugar. Like I should have then. I know I need to apologize but just…let's be still."

"No." The word ripped from my throat, guttural, animalistic.

He dropped his arms and stepped back.

"You don't get to pretend everything's fine. Everything is *not* fine. You…" My chin trembled. "You left me." I gasped for air, my chest and throat tight. "I was attacked, and *you left me*."

Cam's eyes widened with each word before moisture filled his eyes again. "I… Oh, Jenna, I fucked up bad."

I headed to the door and opened it. I turned to look back at him and said, "I know."

I shut the door and leaned back against it. Cam's father's—no, uncle's—death and meeting me, my historical similarities to Kim—I got why he had issues. He'd been slammed by an emotional tidal wave. But, the problem was, he tried to drag me out to sea with him, and I refused to go.

I could *not* go under.

I swiped at the moisture on my cheeks as I walked down the hall. Nessa and Abbi still waited there with Chuck. All three looked at me with sympathy and maybe even pity. Abbi wrapped her arm around my shoulder while Nessa grabbed my hand, squeezing my cold fingers.

I smiled a little at them before turning back to face the

elevator doors.

I refused to look back when I heard a door open down the hall. Just as I refused to let Cam any deeper into my life and heart.

The doors slid shut and we rode upstairs to the suite I'd treated myself to during this weekend away.

Abbi and Nessa tried to fuss over me, but I shook my head. "Let's watch the movie," I said.

Abbi nibbled on her lip while Nessa wrung her hands.

"Either we watch a movie or we call it a night, ladies. I can't talk about him. Please."

When I blinked back this round of tears, Abbi and Nes nodded.

Nes, the greedy girl, grabbed the remote and started surfing the movie channels. We settled back in, watching Henry Cavill pretend to be Clark Kent, an average Smallville teen.

Thank goodness for my friends, both of whom rested their heads on my shoulders.

Still, when they left to go home to their men—men who loved them, doubts, failings, quirks and all—the hotel suite turned dark and quiet and sleep evaded me.

After a couple hours of restlessness, I rose and stood at the window and wished for the warmth and intimacy Cam and I started to build before our pasts rammed ugly heads.

———— ★ ————

The knocking on my door came within moments of my phone's text chimes. I buried my face under the pillow and pulled it tight over my ears.

Neither stopped.

With an angry huff, I threw the pillow to the side and stomped out of the bedroom toward the door, throwing it open.

"What?" I demanded, unsurprised to see Cam standing there, showered, clean-shaven, and looking far too yummy. I snarled before I turned away, half-wishing I'd slammed the door right in his face.

Damn him.

"Did I wake you?"

I grunted as I collapsed on the couch, tugging a throw pillow into my lap.

"You want this coffee I brought?"

"I'd rather go back to bed, but you're not going to leave me alone, are you?"

He set the coffee on the table in front of me before sidling around to settle into a deep club chair opposite me.

With a sigh, I picked up of the coffee and took a sip, my eyes never straying from his face.

"Why did you let me believe you were like Kim?"

I set the coffee cup on the table again. "Seriously? You *wanted* to believe that about me."

"You let me leave thinking it was true."

I stood and stepped away, unable to look at him any longer. "No, Cam. See. This is why you should have simply left me alone." I bowed my head. "You believed what you wanted. What you expected. We don't trust each other."

"Kind of hard to do with our histories." He cleared his throat. "My da—uncle dying when he did, without the chance to fix what we both broke between us, but more, in the whole family it's… I don't know how to live with that regret, Jenna. Even knowing he wasn't my father, even knowing he hurt my mother in the process. I loved a woman who never loved me back. She used me. My uncle used us all."

My heart ached at the pain in his eyes, but I lifted my chin. "I don't know what to tell you. I can't change my past or my decisions to fit what you want in a girlfriend. Better to simply end us before we ever really begin."

He rose and came to stand next to me, his eyes sharp but the skin around his mouth pulled tight in worry. "I know I messed up. You're so right. I let past fears destroy my present." He paused, pulling a candy from his pocket with shaking hands.

"How are you feeling, by the way? That should have been my first question."

I raised an eyebrow. Yes, it should have.

"I've missed you, sugar." His voice was soft. "I keep seeing you in my dreams. I keep feeling you snuggled against me like you were that day in the river, but you're gone and I'm empty. I know it's my fault. I know it. But do you want to stop seeing me?"

I went to the table and picked up the coffee there. I needed more of it—I needed time to think.

"This week's been unbearable," he continued. "I—I've missed you, and my mind…it's going a million miles in too many directions. Then I'm in the same room as you again and I can breathe." His eyes held mine, the truth there deep. Resonant. "I can think. I can relax because you're here. Right here, with me."

Why was admitting my desire for Cam so hard? Why did it feel like if I took one more step, the ground would fall out from under me and I'd be in free-fall?

"I care for you, Jenna Marie. And it's scarier now because I know just how much you can hurt me."

"What about you?" I asked.

"Me? Living with my regret?"

I nodded. He shrugged those broad shoulders, but even in doing so, the weight of his mistake settled more tightly there.

"I don't know. But I do know I have to try to fix what I broke with you." He leaned in and pressed a kiss to my forehead. "I've been miserable without you. All I've wanted was to hold you close and talk this through."

"Would it help?"

"To talk it through?"

I nodded against his chest. And he did. He told me the whole story—how he and Kim met, when he fell in love, how she was cheating with his uncle. How his identity shifted when he found out the man he'd called father was his uncle.

As he spoke I settled into his side. His arm slid around me and he hauled me closer so I practically lay on him, his deep voice against my cheek even as it filled my ears. I laid my hand over his heart—that fragile organ so in need of my nearness, of my ability to simply *be* here and listen.

We stayed like that, wrapped together, soaking in each other's heat but also awareness.

"Comparing our pasts is silly, but yours is…"

"Atrocious. I mean, cheating on my mother? That's enough to stomach. But with my wife." He sighed, a heavy, heartfelt sign. "They're both dead. I can't rail at either of them."

"Would it make you feel better?" I lifted my head.

His brows wrinkled in confusion. "What do you mean?"

"To yell at them—to scream all the bad words you can think of. My counselor and I did that after Ben had me ostracized from my classmates and after the miscarriage rumors. That's the only way I was able to show up at that club that night."

"Worked out well. Aren't you glad you did that?" he asked.

I pressed my finger to my lip, considering. "I am."

His body tensed, his arms loosening around my waist.

"No, I am. Hear me out. Up to that point, I thought the worst thing that could happen to me was to no longer be popular, to have people say mean things about me. I'd lost my dream boyfriend and my best friend. I'd lost a baby that I never even had to begin with." I smoothed my hands down his chest. "That night, I reclaimed a piece of me—the part that wasn't Homecoming Queen or Robbie's ex-girlfriend. I was just Jenna Olsen, high school senior. Sure, bad things happened. But I was there. I was alive. I'm still alive. And I've found out who my true friends are in the process."

His arms tightened to tell me he was my friend, hopefully my lover.

"Your coffee's gone cold," he said.

"I don't care."

Our breathing synched, my lids grew heavy and that inexplicable tightening returned to my chest and throat. But this time, I knew. It was out of thankfulness.

"I'm going to spend the day with my friends," I said, my eyes drifting closed.

"All right. May I come?"

Did I want him there? I bit my lip, considering.

"Okay."

———— ★ ————

We didn't leave Kai and Evie's place until late, mainly because I didn't know when I'd get to see them again.

Cam fidgeted for most of the ride back to the hotel.

"What's got into you?" I asked.

"I liked hanging out with your friends."

"Well, you should. They're musicians."

Cam smirked. "That's a huge bonus. But, no, I like them. They're a good group."

I looked out the window, unable to focus on Cam because my throat constricted. Leaving the warmth and acceptance I had here proved harder each time. Yet…my life was in Austin.

I'd chosen to stay there, to help Pop-pop, and as I'd told Nessa many times before, I loved my work.

The silence grew, and Cam squirmed in his seat.

"Can I stay with you tonight?" he blurted.

I yelped, pulled out of my sad thoughts. "What?" I laid my hand over my heart.

"Tonight. I'd like to stay in your room."

His cheeks reddened and his shoulders pulled in. Cam, the big-name country music legend, just practically begged to stay in my room with me.

He pulled out a Werther's and popped it in his mouth. He was *nervous*.

"Um. Sure."

He leaned in close and wrapped his arm around my shoulder. "Thank you."

We pulled up to the hotel and one of the other security guards opened the door, helping me out first. A few photographers swarmed us, their flashes momentarily blinding me until I managed to look away.

Cam tugged me tight into his side in that protective way of his. He led me up the stairs, a bodyguard in front and another behind.

"I'm kind of surprised there were so few," Cam muttered.

"We routed out a bunch earlier when Chuck said you were on your way back," the guy in front of us said. I didn't know his name, but I needed to learn it. He pressed the button on the elevator before looking around to ensure our continued safety.

The elevator dinged and we stepped into the empty car. I yawned. Cam yawned. I leaned my head against his shoulder and he cuddled me closer to his chest.

We stopped off on his floor so he could grab his toothbrush, a change of clothes, and his phone charger.

Once we'd settled into my room, I turned toward him. "I'm surprised you didn't book a suite."

"Most were taken. I had a tough time getting that floor as it was."

"Why the floor?" I asked.

"Privacy," he said with a shrug.

My shoulders knotted. The way he led his life was so different from mine. "Should we go back down? I mean, I don't want the press to bother you anymore."

He set his bag on the floor and cupped my cheeks. "It's not me I'm worried about. Now, what time's your flight out tomorrow?"

"Eight-thirty, I think."

Cam pulled out his phone and sent a text. "I'll be on it with you. So will Chuck and your guards at least."

I blew out a breath, which caused goosebumps to sprout on Cam's neck. Interesting.

"You don't have to coddle me, Cam. I do know how to take care of myself."

He lifted his head and tilted my chin back so I met his eyes.

"That's the thing, sugar. I can't get enough of taking care of you."

He tweaked my nose. "Ready for bed?"

I was. I wanted to push our relationship—seal the emotional with the physical—but I was scared. So, I brushed my teeth and put on my pajamas.

Three hours later, I couldn't stand the gnawing ache between my legs.

I rolled onto my other side so I could face Cam. My fingertips drifted over his bristly cheek, drifting closer to his lips. A soft puff of air hit the sensitive skin there, and I bit my lip to keep in my moan.

Maybe I shouldn't wake him. I pulled my hand back and he caught my fingers, never opening his eyes.

"I like you touching me," he said, his voice raspy.

"I want to do more than just touch."

He opened his eyes and they shone brightly in the darkness.

"You sure about that? I made you a decent proposal."

I scooted forward until my body hugged every inch of his. My breath caught at the feel of him through his boxer briefs. "I want to change our relationship. Make it physical. And very, very indecent."

He rolled so I was pinned under him, his hips pressed against the juncture of mine. "That I can do. With great joy and even more enthusiasm."

His mouth claimed mine. The kiss was scorching—filled with need, longing, and a whopping dose of straight-up lust. I pressed my lips harder to his, our teeth touching, as we devoured each other.

I'd had sex before. Those first fumbling and sweet moments with Robbie. That furtive and soul-destroying moment with Ben, followed, thankfully, by much more empowering moments with a few others. But nothing—not one moment in my past—prepared me for loving Camden Grace.

He was potent. He was attentive. He was responsive. He was in charge.

I reveled in his patient, gentle dominance.

I wanted more. More skin, more kisses, more passion. And he gave that—more—to me.

We kept kissing and the urgency grew. When I wrapped my arms around his neck, he tugged my hands away as he broke the kiss. I whimpered because I needed to touch his warm skin, desperate for him to devour my mouth again.

"You have to let me pace this, sugar. I want you too bad. Too damn bad for you to get all handsy."

With trembling fingers, he pushed up my thin camisole. I hissed out a breath as his warm palms slid up my ribs to cup my breasts. Then he moved on, continuing to push up my top until it was over my head. He dropped it to the side of the bed.

"Lord, you are lovely." His whispered words were buried against my breast as he took one nipple in his mouth. I moaned as the warm suction increased.

He moved to the other side, his dark hair a heady contrast to my pale skin. He pushed the two globes together and nibbled the space between. My hips left the bed, seeking his.

His deep chuckle slid over my skin and I thrust my hips up again, this time in demand.

"All in good time." He nipped his way down my right side only to work his way up my left. My fingers tangled in his hair as I lost myself in his touch.

He continued to kiss each inch of my skin, his warm breath a soft counterpoint to the butterfly-light skim of his lips. I sank further into the sensual haze Cam created.

He worked his way back down to my sleep shorts, placing love bites at the sensitive skin just inside my hip bones. Once again, I writhed under him, searching for the right friction to ease the deep ache inside.

As if he had all the time in the world, he sat back on his heels to ease off my shorts and panties.

"You are, without a doubt, the most delectable treat I have ever seen."

"I'm a woman, Cam."

His hands spanned my hips. "Not likely to forget that. Your

naked body is burned into my mind. So much better than I imagined." He looked up with a wicked grin. "And I've got a good imagination."

He slid his hands behind me, pulling my hips higher as he placed kisses on my thighs. My legs and stomach trembled. He kept moving upward, missing my needy center to instead map my hipbones, the slight give of my stomach, his tongue flicking in to taste my belly button.

"Cam!" I cried in frustration, my fists slamming into the bed.

He slid his lips across to the other hip before pressing his nose between my thighs. With gentle fingers, he parted me and groaned deep in his throat.

"You're ready for me."

"Been there for a while. I think I might explode."

He pressed a kiss against the soft flesh of my lower abdomen. "Oh, you will. Now that I've got you, you will many times."

He rose from the bed in a lithe motion. A slight grimace crossed his face as his weight rested on his injured calf. Before I could ask, he was over me, covering me with his hot, silky skin. I slid my fingers through the sparse hair on his chest, drifting my hand downward toward his navel, which I circled once. He grunted. I circled it again and he pulled my hand away, pinning it above my head. He grabbed the other one and held both my wrists in his one hand, working his way down the inside of my arm, over my chest, nuzzling my breast, down my stomach.

My breath hitched as he kissed my lower lips. He thrust a second finger inside me and my hips rose from the bed as my cry pierced the quiet.

"Shh, sugar. We got neighbors. You have to be quiet."

"Can't," I panted as he thrust in and out of my body. The ache grew, twisting and twirling through my core. "Please."

He lifted himself again and bent down. A small silver packet shone in the minimal light. He tore it open and sheathed himself, then he was once again over me. In me. My back arched and I made some breathy sound.

"You." He kissed my arched throat. "Are." He pressed another to my jaw. "The most." Kiss by my ear. "Incredible woman I've ever known." His mouth covered mine. His tongue pushed past my lips, opening my mouth as he opened my body.

I arched my hips, trying to take more of him as I strained my neck to kiss him harder, deeper.

He pulled back and dropped his hands to my hips. "I got you, sugar. I'll get you there."

"Please." The word sounded like a sob. Too much need, too much emotion. He pulsed inside me, steady, unmoving. I slammed my foot against the bed.

"All right," he crooned. He slid out of me, then slammed back in hard.

"Oh my…"

He did it again. My head hit the headboard.

"Cam." The high, thready sound was almost a scream.

Again, and again and again, he eased from my body only to pound back in. He stripped me raw—my body shuddering, ready for his next thrust.

"You fit me, Jenna Marie."

His fingers gripped the flesh of my hips as he raised up to his knees, changing the angle to get deeper into me.

"Yes," I cried.

My arms dug into his shoulders. He hammered into me. Sweat slicked our bodies. I needed more. I needed release.

He stared down at where we joined. That was *so* hot, knowing all his focus was there, on us, together.

His look of utter concentration, of sheer pleasure, pushed me over the edge and I unwound around him.

Each flutter and gasp seemed to set him off more and he lost his steady rhythm, his hips jerking, before he too tipped his head back and moaned out his release.

———— ★ ————

We didn't sleep much the rest of the night.

"You can sleep on the plane. I can't put my hands on you there. Not like I want to, at least." He nipped at my neck as he slid his warm palms down my body.

I hummed in agreement.

The flight home was uneventful, and I did sleep most of the trip, my head resting on Cam's shoulder, his fingers tangled with mine. We spent the whole of Sunday together. Cam tugged me down at one point to watch a football game—I couldn't even tell you who was playing—before he heaved a great sigh.

"You got something else you want to do?" he asked.

"Just laundry. You finish watching your game."

He settled into the couch, arm thrown across the back, booted feet on the edge of my coffee table. I shook my head, trying to ignore just how much I wanted him there every day.

Going to work the next day proved hard—not just getting

up, made more difficult by Cam, half-naked and begging me to spend another hour with him in bed.

After a long shower that did little to ease the throbbing in my head, neck, or between my thighs, I dressed quickly and bent to press a kiss to his lips.

"I have to finish this rather important client's guitar." I raised my eyebrows. "He needs it in three weeks, and I'm well behind the deadline. And I'm also meeting *your* sister in," I glanced up at the clock and grimaced. "About an hour."

"I'll make you some coffee." Cam swung his legs over the side of the bed. My mouth watered at the sight of him standing, and then stretching, in nothing but tight black cotton.

"You can stay in bed," I whispered. Even my vocal cords were in awe of his sexiness.

He scratched his lower abdomen, and I whimpered a little as my eyes fell to the deep-cut V that slid into the elastic waistband.

"I better get back to my place. I need to make some calls. Work out my strategy to keep you with a constant guard."

"Oh. Okay," I said, my voice still faint. I turned, head muzzy because I wanted to rub my hands, hell, my body, all over his.

He reached out a hand and snagged me around my wrist, pulling me back toward him. I tilted my head up as he grazed his lips over my jaw, moving slowly toward the corner of my mouth.

"You could have gone another round, sugar."

I shook my head but it was almost imperceptible. If he asked again, I'd climb back into bed with him—and never leave.

"We good?" he murmured. "I can't let you leave until I know we're good. Solid. Together."

I panted as I turned my face and caught his lips in a soft, desperate kiss. I pulled back in tiny increments, not wanting to lose our connection.

"I can't resist you."

He ran his hand up my side, over the swell of my breast to the back of my neck. "Don't try. But first I need to know how you're feeling, sugar."

"I…" I met his gaze. He was serious—still worried I was upset with him about how Saturday, or maybe the night before, went down. "We're good. As long as you're not upset with me."

His fingers tightened on my neck, the grip more possessive. "Tell you one thing. I need you. And I want you happy."

He finally kissed me, long and hard and oh-so-hot. Which was why I arrived at the office with only moments to spare before Kate showed up.

Pop-pop hadn't been in the shop much last week, but he and Mom told me they were glad Kate kept me company. She answered the phones and managed annoyed clients better than Pop-pop or I ever had. The few walk-ins we had, Kate handled too, explaining the custom design work and the intricate details of the wood.

She made the days pass more quickly, and I was pleased with her company. Pop-pop seemed happy to take much-needed time off. Even in the last few months he'd slowed down; his hands beginning to shake and swell if he worked for too long. More and more of the design work shifted to my plate. Not that I minded. In fact, that was the main part of the work I enjoyed.

The days of the week and that of the next two thereafter fell into a nice pattern, and I looked forward to spending my time with my grandfather and my new friend.

Cam's guitar came together well. Maybe I'd put more feeling into this one, but even Pop-pop said this instrument was my best work.

"That's a beautiful piece, Jenna-dove. And you finished it. I wasn't sure it was possible."

I wiggled my fingers, trying to get feeling back into the tips. "Me either. Golly gee green jelly beans, that was a *task*. But it's done now."

A hollowness built behind my breastbone. I rubbed the spot absently.

"Want to come to dinner with your parents and me tomorrow? We're going to Swift's Attic," Pop-Pop asked.

I licked my lips, humming. The blistered shishito peppers and the interesting desserts were hard to resist—especially the Earl Grey snickerdoodle one. But I shook my head.

"Cam's concert is tomorrow. I promised him I'd go. And I should come in early in the morning to start on that next guitar. Another rush job," I said with a sigh. If I wasn't careful, I was going to get a reputation for pulling these short-turnarounds and then I would be up a creek when everyone wanted their custom-made guitar in a month.

I wrote on a sticky note: *I want to build an extra week or two into every new contract we sign* and settled it against Kate's sleek, silver iMac. I'd told her to order what she wanted, and that computer showed up two weeks later, causing her to squeal and jump up and down like a toddler on Christmas morning.

If she had any questions, Kate and I would discuss next Monday during our informal meeting—that seemed to always include a large mug of coffee and a pastry or two. Kate paid attention to what made me a happy boss lady.

"You decided to go to Cam's performance?"

"I did." Going to another venue caused my upper lip to sweat and my body to stiffen, but I needed to get past my fears. Mitch, my full-time guard, said I'd be fine. That he'd make sure to keep me safe.

He liked learning about the design process even more than Kate did. I enjoyed their light flirtations, too. He'd promised—as had Chuck and Cam—that I'd be safe.

Trusting Cam tomorrow was important to and for both of us.

"I just have to work most of the morning." Stupid to have taken this project on—but it was a big name. As big as Asher Smith's, and if he liked my work, I was going to have more calls than I could handle. I'd be able to choose which clients I worked with—based on my preferences, not theirs.

That was a nice place to sit, especially in an industry of inflated egos.

"Well, then, you mind if I keep your SUV to drive tomorrow? It's roomier than my Prius, and I know your mom appreciates the leg room."

"Of course." I handed him the key, glad I'd driven myself to work this morning. Now that Cam had claimed me publicly as his girlfriend, I could no longer walk around with the same level of anonymity.

"Speaking of, I'm glad you and Camden worked out your

differences. He's a good man, Jenna."

I smiled at my grandfather. "He said he was going to talk to you."

He leaned in and kissed my cheek. "Came by a couple of weeks ago while you were getting more wood. He looked nervous, which tells me a lot."

"Bet you made him sweat."

Pop-pop grinned. "A bit." He touched my nose with his index finger. "I like you happy. I'm proud of you, mainly for the fine work you've done on this project." Pop-pop packed up his Bento lunch box and his briefcase.

My heart rate kicked up as my face flushed. Not often my grandfather lavished me in praise. I wallowed in the moment. "You're going to spoil me."

Pop-pop laughed. "By telling the truth? Not hardly."

"Well, I've already been brought back down to earth, though I did enjoy the nice tour of inexpressible joy you gave me just now." I scowled, feeling my annoyance build. "My new client needs his instrument in about six weeks. Seven if Kate can sweet-talk him into giving me more time. And you know how long it takes to coat these bad boys to that pristine satin."

"I do. Call me if you change your mind about dinner. Your mother would love to see you." He winked. "I know your father's been off a bit, but maybe it's because he needs to see your beautiful face."

That wasn't why. My father was jealous of my relationship with Pop-pop. Granted, he never wanted to be a guitar-maker, but also didn't want to share his father's fortune with me.

Not that I'd asked for it—or planned to. "Will do. I love you, Pop-pop."

He patted my cheek. "Love you, too, dove."

I sucked in a deep breath and stepped from the shop, locking the door behind me.

I waved at Chuck, who raised his hand in response. The man was quiet, but I could see the caring he shared with Cam, and that was enough for me.

A small squeak left my body as an arm snaked around my waist, pulling my bottom tight against his thighs and my back to his chest. I relaxed as Cam pressed a wet kiss to the side of my neck.

"You scared me."

"I couldn't help it. You're just too cute."

Pop-pop pulled out of the lot and waved.

"Isn't that your car?" Cam asked.

"Yes. Pop-pop needed it for dinner with my parents tomorrow." I turned in his arms and rose on my tiptoes. I sealed my lips over his. Those tingles coursed from my lips up into my chest, swirling, before settling low in my belly.

I pulled back, breathless.

"Now that's a greeting," Cam said with a smile.

"I finished your guitar." I lifted the case in my hand.

Cam's brows rose and he whooped, scooping me up at my hips and twirling me around. He stopped with a grimace, and I knew his leg must be bothering him.

"Hot damn, woman, I'm some excited about trying it out. Just in time for my show."

"Are you coming back to my place?" I asked.

Cam's face fell into lines of contrition. "Can't. My mother called and lit into me. She wants me home for dinner tonight. I haven't seen her since…well, before Seattle, and she needs some reassurance I'm not angry with her for keeping the truth from her."

He frowned as he glared at the shop, no doubt thinking about his sister and the fact his mother didn't want to tell Kate the family secrets.

I agreed with Cam that Kate needed to know, but it wasn't my place to push.

"Plus, I need to get to know this gorgeous girl before I have to play it in front of thousands of people tomorrow."

"All right," I said, and handed him the case.

He pulled me in close to his side and led me over to his large, dark SUV we'd been using since we came back from Seattle.

I stewed during the short drive back to my condo. Something about his willingness to leave me alone for the first time after I completed the guitar left me off-kilter.

"I'll walk you up to your place," Cam offered.

"That's okay. I'm sure you want to get to your mom's."

Cam gave me a strange look before exiting the car and helping me out.

He lingered in the doorway, his lips clinging to mine for a sweet, luxurious moment, before he caressed my cheek with his thumb. After a long look in my eyes, he turned back and strode down the hallway, his legs eating up the distance to the elevator. For the first time since he flew to Seattle, I roamed through my loft, restless and uncertain.

CHAPTER TWENTY | Cam

I hadn't wanted to tell Jenna my brother was in town. Not because I didn't want her to meet my twin, but because I needed to talk to him about Mom's desire to keep Katie Rose in the dark about her father—and to make sure the tail-tucking ass knew Jenna was *mine*.

I met Carter on my porch where he sat, an open beer on his knees and the rest of the six-pack under his chair. He was bigger than I remembered, a slightly rougher version of me. Now that I knew, I could see Jensen, our father, clearly in his features, especially the nose and chin. At least based on the pictures I'd snagged from Mom's attic.

I set down my new guitar with great care just inside the door of my house.

After a long round of back-pounding hugs, Carter offered me a beer, which I gladly accepted.

"Come on in." I motioned him inside.

"What you got there?" Carter asked, tipping his head toward my guitar. I set the beer bottle on the coffee table in the living room and grabbed the guitar case. I opened it with care and my breath caught when I looked at the beautiful designs Jenna created in the wood.

"Holy mother…that's one heckuva guitar," he said. He sucked

on his beer, eyes running over the wood's soft gleam.

"Jenna made it for me."

"The gal you're seeing?" Carter asked. "Saw her picture in the paper with you. Pretty lady. Love all that blond hair."

I nodded. I ran my fingers along the gleaming body, reverently following the line of the silver she'd added there.

With a quick glance up, I met first Carter's eyes. "She matters to me. I couldn't have you meeting her until you promised to treat her right. And as mine."

Carter whistled through his teeth. "Wedding bells in the future, man?"

I shrugged. "Yeah…I could see that, maybe in a few years."

Carter settled back against the sofa, absorbing my words—and what I didn't say. Finally, he set his beer on the coffee table and linked his hands between his knees. "I never would have hurt you like that, Cam. I mean, I thought something was up with Da—er, Laurence. I should have told you of my suspicions before you married Kim."

"Might not have mattered. I wanted her. I knew she'd been around a bit before we married, but if I'd known that piece-of-shit we called our father was one of the ones screwing her… Still, it's over now. Best thing to come out of it was knowing Laurence isn't my real dad. A definite plus in my book."

"Mom won't tell Katie Rose?" Carter asked.

"Mom's flat-out forbidden me to talk to her about it. And it's killing me. Katie Rose deserves the truth." I shook my head. "I got to thinking about the time you and I've lost because of him—how much these secrets hurt us all. I've missed you, man."

Carter's smile flashed with the same pain mine must hold. "You, too, baby bro."

I rolled my eyes. Eleven minutes. He was eleven minutes older.

I placed my booted heel on the edge of my coffee table and settled the guitar more firmly in my lap. I strummed without much thought but the zing from the sound caused the hair all over my body to ripple in excitement.

"Wowee," Carter breathed. "That's some sound."

I launched into my newest tune, one I'd planned to play for Jenna tomorrow. I'd written it for her, and I loved the smooth, easy progression up the fretboard she'd made me.

Carter clapped when I finished. "You've turned into a great performer. Should have known you would be—all that clowning around you did back when we were kids."

With reluctance, I tucked the guitar back in its case and stood. "We should get over to Mom's. She's expecting us. Remember, not a word to Katie Rose."

My brother nodded as we trooped to the door and out into the hot, humid air of mid-summer in Texas.

———— ★ ————

My phone beeped early the next morning with a text from Jenna.

Going into the shop. I have a new commission I need to start on. Kate's going to bring me to the concert later because I lent my car to Pop-pop.

She'd talked to my sister before me? She knew how much I wanted her there, with me, in the Green Room beforehand.

Wait. I hadn't talked to her about that—just assumed

she knew. And with Jenna, assumptions were almost always dangerous. I called her back, but she didn't answer. Because she was angry with me for not spending the night? Because she found out my brother was in town from Katie Rose? Or because she was already lost in the new design?

Hard to say.

I settled for a return text.

Missed you last night. My brother showed up. Can't wait to see your bright face in a couple of hours.

No response.

Even after another few hours when I had to leave for the venue, Jenna hadn't responded.

I called again, probably acting lovesick and stupid. She didn't answer.

I spent enough of my life around women to know I'd hurt or angered Jenna. I didn't know how or why, though, and her lack of response—my inability to fix the problem—angered me.

Today was an important day. I'd planned to close my concert by announcing a big donation to the Service Members Fund, offering the large check with Jenna by my side. The couples picture further solidified the image I was trying to build in the media and my fans hearts.

Unsure what else to do, I called my sister on the way to the venue.

"You know what's gotten into Jenna?" I asked Katie Rose in lieu of a greeting.

"Yes. I caught her just before she planned to go into the shop and she's spent the morning comforting me because my brothers didn't see fit to tell me we're only half-siblings."

My stomach crashed into my guts. I ran my hand through my hair. "Katie Ro—"

"Don't you dare try to placate me. You all lied to me about that man…he cheated on my mama with *your wife*."

And she clicked off.

That was a few hours ago. No further word from either of them. Unfortunately, I had to go through a sound check. There was a prop malfunction and we had to return to the stage after the roadies and the venue staff cleared bits of debris from the destroyed fireworks mount.

Thankfully, no one was hurt.

But I was frazzled by the time I finally entered the green room.

When Carter arrived, I told him about my conversation with our sister.

"Think she overheard us talking at your place last night?"

I tugged on my lip. "Yeah. She didn't come down to dinner, but Mama said she'd been home for a while."

"It's either that or your girlfriend told her and is now afraid to face you."

I swung around toward my brother, hands fisted. "Don't talk about Jenna like that. You don't know her."

Carter held up his hands. "I don't. But you sure are defensive."

"Cam," my assistant Erika said, poking her head into the room. "Time to go."

I rubbed the back of my neck, trying to ease the sore muscles as I strode toward the stage. Accepting my new guitar from the stagehand was bittersweet.

I raised my hands as I stepped out onto the stage, frustrated, too, that not only wasn't I seeing Jenna right now, but my sister hated me and my brother thought I was too fixated on Jenna. But, Jenna had told me she'd be here, and since we were dating, I should matter more than those other customers, more than her parents...shit, I was acting like a selfish rock star. One who put his wants and desires above those he cared about.

Maybe it was time to say goodbye to the limelight. Shania did for fifteen years—she built herself a normal life, loved her man and her kids—before she considered coming back to the grind of touring and the microscope of media attention.

Now wasn't the time for these thoughts, though. I had nearly one hundred thousand active and former military men and women and their spouses to entertain now.

"Hey, there, Fort Bliss! How's your Fourth?"

The roar of the crowd knocked me back on the heels of my boots, but I cupped my ear, wanting to pump them up further. My best concerts came from the crowd's energy, and I was not feeling this one—even with my beautiful instrument.

The crowd didn't disappoint. They yelled and screamed even louder. I smiled, my mood lifting somewhat as I wished them a happy Independence Day.

I nodded to my band and we segued into the first song—one of my faster hits with lots of catchy lyrics. By the fifth song, I was dripping with sweat from the heat of the lights and enjoying the ability to do this with my life.

By the end of the first set I was on one of those rare highs that came from a perfectly-orchestrated concert. The crowd was responsive. My band was so on, we were even amping up the bridge before barreling into another chorus. The lyrics poured out of me, all tight and perfect.

I stepped off stage for a short breather and swiped my face and downed a bottle of water. I glanced around for Katie Rose and my mama, but Carter hugged me hard, rocking me back and forth.

"You're epic, my brother."

My manager called me back onto the stage. The second set was even better than the first. I finished the last encore to the loudest applause of my career.

Heading off stage, my grin was so wide I wasn't sure how it stayed on my face. But it fell as soon as I saw my assistant Erika's tear-streaked and splotchy face.

"What's wrong?" I asked. I yanked out my earplug and whipped my guitar strap over my head. I didn't even know what the problem was and my body hummed with the need to do something.

"Kate called. She's with Jenna, and Jenna didn't want you to stop your concert. Said it was important to your fans. Your sister's still there, I think. At Jenna's. She said to call her."

"Do you know what happened?" I asked.

Erika handed me my phone. I swiped the sweaty towel across my face and the back of my neck. Listening to my voicemail, my heart began to pound and my ears rang.

"Cancel my meet and greet," I said to Erika, already hurrying down the back hall, calling for Chuck.

He materialized nearby—always there when I needed him.

"What's up, chief?"

"We gotta get to Jenna's. Pronto."

Chuck didn't ask more questions. He spoke into his microphone to collect more of my security before pulling the car keys from his pocket, all while hurrying to keep up with my steps.

"Everything okay?" he asked.

I slammed out into the parking lot. "No."

CHAPTER TWENTY-ONE | Jenna

I shut off the shower taps when my phone rang. Might be Cam again. I needed to talk to him, even though I wasn't sure what to say.

Kate was upset—rightly so—but after explaining what I knew about the situation, she'd calmed down some. But gee whiz-bang willikers, I was doing my best to toe the line—kind of like the tomcat who kept trying to sneak into the building.

I slipped and slid across the tile of the bathroom and lunged for my phone where it rested on my nightstand.

"Hello?" I asked, my voice breathless from my naked dash.

At my father's voice, as it cracked on my name, I collapsed onto my bed. Shivering, my wet hair stuck to my neck, tears streamed down my cheeks at my father's words, "Thank god you didn't go with him tonight, Jen. I thought you'd be there because... Your mother is beside herself."

I wanted to deny. My vocal cords refused to cooperate.

"Jenna? Are you there? Did you hear me?"

"Yes." I sucked in much-needed air. My chest hurt more than ever—more than after my stomach was pumped to ensure all the GHB left my system.

"I'm on my way to the hospital." He choked up on the last word.

I gripped the phone tighter, trying to regulate my breathing, but the harsh sound whooshed through the speaker. "Who was hurt, Dad? How...who? I need you to talk to me."

"Pop-pop." His voice cracked. "My father's dead."

No. I shook my head. Mouthed the word. *No.* I saw Pop-pop yesterday. He winked at me. Told me he loved me.

"You sure?" I managed to ask.

"Yeah. Yeah, I'm sure," my father said, his voice rough with regret.

The ache in my chest expanded as I shivered, pulling my damp knees to my wet chest. I tossed my hair over my shoulder, my back arching as wet rivulets slid down my spine. I wished for a towel. I couldn't leave my phone. My legs shook too hard to walk across the room.

He and I breathed into the phone, neither willing to think, let alone speak the words swirling in our heads. I squeezed my eyes shut and pressed my forehead harder against my knees, needing the pain, anything, to help block out this new, awful reality.

Dad would rub his thumbs across his eyes, try to dry the tears there. He'd always done that—for as long as I could remember, anyway.

"Jude and Micah are headed to their respective airports now. To fly in. They'll be here in a few hours."

Dad sniffled. My heart broke because I knew he was crying. My own eyes filled, my nose stung. I slammed my fist against the rumpled sheets. I sucked in a deep breath, sat up straight.

"I'll come there. We can do this together."

"No! You hate hospitals." His voice rose with panic.

I did. The idea of one sent me into a fit of shivers, my stomach twisting with nausea. "This is important. I can deal." I hoped. My drying skin pebbled with gooseflesh.

"No. I don't want to see you right now." He cleared his throat and probably blushed a bit as he always did when he was embarrassed.

"What? Why?"

He made a choked sound and cut off the call. I dropped my phone back on my nightstand and pulled my comforter back over my body, huddling in my bed as memories of the time I spent with my grandfather, how my dad built me a special swing and used to push me on it every evening after work. Those thoughts and myriad others flitted through my mind.

I called my mother.

"Jenna, honey. I'm so sorry for what your father said."

"You heard?"

"Yes."

And she hadn't called me. I had to call her. "Pop-pop's dead?" My teeth began to chatter.

"Jenna, I know you're upset, but so is your father. Just…just give him some time. Some space to deal with this."

"You're telling me you don't want me there, either?" I cried.

My mother made a strange sound. Not a sob, not a growl, but somehow both. "I love you, Jenna." She clicked off.

What the hell just happened? My mother, my savior, my greatest cheerleader, basically told me she didn't want me to be with my family.

"Jenna?" Kate called.

I tried to answer her, but no words came out.

She poked her head around the door. "We need to get going if you want to be on time...why are you in bed?"

"My father called." My voice was raspy from crying. "My grandfather...he's dead. Car accident."

Kate's hands flew to her mouth, her eyes wide. Right. She'd just lost her father a few months ago. She understood.

"Oh! Jenna! What can I do? Wait. I need to call Cam, let him know we're not coming."

She pulled her phone from her pocket, already pressing buttons. I didn't have the heart or the will to argue. I laid my head back down, replaying my father's words, my mother's, over and over again. I didn't understand. When Kate checked on me a while later, I told her I needed some time.

Time floated by and my cheeks grew raw from the tears.

Sometime later, knocking commenced on my bedroom door. I ignored it, just like I ignored the texts from Kate saying she was in my living room, wanting to comfort me. How could they comfort me? I lost my grandfather—the emotional stability of my life. My dad didn't want me. Pop-pop was my go-to, always had been. And now he was gone.

I huddled tighter into my bed, pulling my pillow over my head and bending it around my ears.

A while later the thick down comforter whipped away from my body, bringing me upright with a horrified shriek. I dropped the pillow and scrambled back, reminded in that moment that I was naked.

"I was real worried, sugar."

"Cam."

I pressed my hand to my chest, trying to calm my raging heart. His gaze followed, causing my skin to heat with embarrassment.

"I'm naked!"

Cam's lips flipped up. "I noticed. Good look on you, too."

I sprang to the far side of the bed, tugging at the comforter. Cam dropped the other end from his fist and I busied myself with covering my front.

"Not like you haven't seen me this way before. Where's your sister?" I asked.

"I sent her home with my mother." He rubbed his hand through his hair before sliding his palm down the back of his neck. "They need to talk anyway. Why didn't you call me?"

"Your show…"

Cam cut me off with a sharp look. "Isn't as important as this."

I scrubbed my cheeks with the edge of the comforter, wincing at the ache there. I needed clothes. Lots of them. I was so cold.

I bowed my head, not wanting Cam to see my tears. A moment later, his brown, scuffed motorcycle boots slid into my vision and then his arms wrapped tightly around me, warming me for the first time since I stepped from the shower.

"How do I deal with this?" I whispered against his shoulder.

He pulled my damp, tangled hair from my face and pressed a kiss to my cheek. "I don't know. Except to tell you to breathe."

He thought I meant my grandfather's death. And, yes, that was part of it. But my parents…what had I done? How did I fix it? My heart rate ratcheted up and I couldn't get air in my lungs.

"How?"

My breathing escalated as I clenched my fingers into his T-shirt. I focused on the logistics. Solving that…maybe it would help.

"Pop-pop. I can't…how do I carry on the business without him?"

"None of that matters right this second. Let me hold you tight while you cry this first bit out."

I did. After the last bout of tears, I shouldn't have more in me, but Cam's arms were strong and warm and my heart was too heavy with loss. When my tears subsided, I sighed.

"Feeling a little better?" Cam asked, pressing a kiss to my forehead. I closed my eyes, soaking in the warmth of his breath and skin against my overheated flesh.

"My head aches." My stomach growled loudly.

"And you're hungry. Haven't had a bite to eat, I bet."

I shook my head. "My father called just as I finished my shower."

"That why you're nude? Not that I don't enjoy you in your birthday suit, but you've never been that comfortable in your skin around me." He raised his brows. "Seems like I would have seen some exhibitionism by now if that was the case."

"I'm not. Comfortable naked." My cheeks burned.

"And that's a damn shame."

He tipped my chin up and wiped the last of my tears from my cheeks. He produced a tissue and wiped my leaky nose, much like a mother would for a toddler. Again, my cheeks flamed.

"I'm a mess," I moaned.

"Too right. But you have a reason to be, and I'm content to comfort you. For the moment."

"What does that mean?" I asked. I stepped out of his embrace and wrapped my arms tighter around the comforter. Did he plan to dump me, too? Was I that much of a problem?

I'd thought I was improving. I was more grounded, found my place in the business.

Now, every one of my insecurities swirled through my mind. Cam would leave, too. Or want me to leave him. Why wouldn't he? My parents didn't want me, and I completed his guitar.

I blinked hard, over and over, until this round of tears dissipated.

"Just what I said. Right now, you need a shoulder. I got a nice broad one." He winked. "One's a bit damp from your tears, but that's why I have another."

I growled at him as I spun on my heel and stalked toward my closet, tripping over the ends of my queen-sized bedspread. Once in the closet, I shut the door and turned on the light.

"Jenna?"

"What?" I called as I leaned against the cool wooden door. I shivered as my bare back came in to contact with the cool wood.

"Would you be madder at me if I said you have a mighty fine ass? I've always enjoyed cupping those sweet cheeks while I kiss you silly."

I chuckled before the sorrow once again slammed its fist into my gut.

"Sugar?"

He was closer—just outside the door.

"No. I wouldn't be mad. I'm not mad. Cam?"

"Jenna?"

"Thanks for trying to cheer me up."

"Is it working?"

"Sort of. But I feel a bit strange flirting right now."

Silence stretched for a long moment and I held my breath. Had he left?

"How about I make you some coffee and rustle up a bite? That-a-way, you're ready for whatever you need to do next."

Before I lost my courage, I opened the door and flung my arms around his neck, pressing my lips to his. The comforter slid down, catching between us at my belly button. Just as his hands came up to cup my hips, I pulled back, out of his embrace.

"Thank you." He might leave—he probably would—but he was here now. That was more than I could say for my own family. That meant something.

He raised a brow. "Don't mention it. Just kiss me with that much enthusiasm next time I do something to please you. And, Jenna?"

I met his gaze. He touched my cheek with the pad of his thumb.

"I'd take this pain from you if I could."

I shut the door again, unable to speak past the lump of emotion boiling up my throat. Not for my grandfather as much as knowing Cam had become my go-to person. And…I feared I loved him.

His leaving would hurt more than I already did.

CHAPTER TWENTY-TWO | Cam

Jenna's kitchen had surprised me that first morning I stayed over—the coffee was in the same place I put mine on the counter. Her creamer in the same door compartment. Mugs in the cabinet above, to the right side. Whole wheat English muffins instead of the bagels I preferred, but she couldn't be *perfect*.

That would be too weird. As if the similarities in our thinking and organization strategy didn't freak me out enough.

Jenna walked into the main room, her steps hesitant and her eyes darting about, ten minutes later. Her face was clean and a bit damp, her eyes still puffy and her cheeks red. Her golden hair pulled up into a high ponytail that swished with each step. She'd paired her faded, soft jeans with an embroidered sleeveless top and some low-heeled brown boots. She rocked those boots better any woman I'd ever met—same went for the jeans, which cupped the flare of her hips and her sassy flanks almost as well as my hands would.

I blinked my mind clear of the image of those sweet, naked globes with just the right amount of jiggle. I liked her rump—wanted to squeeze that flesh as I pulled her flush to my body. But she didn't need the distraction of sex.

And it seemed like most of the men in Jenna's life used her for sex then dropped her. Maybe not so much with the ball player ex-boyfriend, Robbie, but for sure his asshole friend Ben. My lips set in a firm line as I considered my newest round of options for *that* little punk. My lawyer said we could get him years in prison, which was something he probably deserved. But, after living in some of the worst hellholes on this dusty earth, I wasn't sure the kid would straighten up his act through punishment. Problem was, he wasn't a first-time offender, which would be the best chance to nip violent behaviors and poor decision making before it had the chance to bloom into full-blown felonies.

His record as a minor related to the incident with Jenna at that concert—I just knew it. Ben was dangerous, especially after he loosed those women on us.

Didn't sit right to let Ben off easy—not after what he'd put Jenna through. My lawyer promised to come up with a list of options. Hopefully they taught humility and empathy, something I'd needed to learn myself—the hard way—during one of the bleakest nights of my life.

Only reason to explain my continued presence—my normal MO, at least since Kim, seemed to be cut and run when emotions passed the surface. But the mere whiff of Jenna hurting, seeing the ravages of grief on her face, ripped at my composure, aching to hold her through this storm. Hell if I knew what to do with those feelings.

So, I handed her a cup of coffee and smacked a kiss on her surprised lips before turning back to the stove, trying to look busy and give my heart and hands a chance to settle.

"What are you making?" she asked as she leaned against the counter, peering over my shoulder.

"Hash. My secret recipe, so don't go getting any ideas, hear?"

She wrinkled her nose. "Hash? Like that old-timey dish of mashed up meat and potatoes?"

"And other bits that'll stick to those ribs." I poked her in her side and then wiggled my finger, eliciting a small, grunting laugh from her. "You need to eat, sugar."

"You calling me too skinny?" She turned away and opened one of the cabinets, pulling down plates before moving to my other side to get flatware. Still surprised me that her stuff was set up just like my kitchen. I shook my head.

"Not calling you any name but sugar. Just pointing out we all need calories." I slid some of the food onto her plate before loading up mine. I added orange sections and half of an English muffin to each plate. "And seeing as how it's after midnight, this seemed like the best option."

"It's that late?" Jenna asked, startled.

"Yep." I put a plate in front of her as she sat at the table and carried mine to the other side where I settled in. "Eat up, then we'll discuss how best to tackle the rest of this."

Jenna picked up her fork but simply moved a potato around. "I'm not good company, Cam. I have to go to the hospital." Her throat seemed to close on the word.

"And I told you I was here for you till we decided we didn't click." I cupped her listless hand in my larger, warmer one.

"Much as I liked the way you looked at me earlier, sex just isn't on my radar right now."

I leaned forward so she had to look me in the eyes. "This may come as a bit of a shocker. One, I don't need to have sex every minute of the day. Two, I happen to like you even without sex. Though I like sex, too. But you're hurting right now, sugar, so let me do that—be here for you."

She nodded, her eyes still too somber, as she finally forked up a bite. Her eyes widened as she chewed and her stomach gurgled.

"This is really good."

I sat back, pleased. "Thanks."

She took another bite and moaned a little as she tipped her head back, exposing her long neck. I shifted, trying to find a more comfortable fit of my jeans. I settled into my meal, and we ate in companionable silence.

A solid relationship—from my family to my comrades-in-arms to my wife and every other romantic relationship—was built on the ability to *be* with each other. To remain silent and comfortable. To trust in those breaks in conversation that once we each regrouped, we'd have more to say—more to share.

I scowled down at my plate. Jenna's grandfather approved of me, actively helping me win over his granddaughter when Jenna got all stubborn and I got scared. I'd popped in to see him after we returned to Seattle to explain what a dick I'd been, and he'd forgiven me that, too. Not sure his faith in me was justified—that's why I'd wanted to lay my feelings out there, let the whole family know what I was thinking long-term.

I'd missed that opportunity.

The driver of the other car that hit Mr. Olsen ran a red light at full speed. I didn't like the direction of my thoughts, but I'd already put in a call to Chuck and another to my lawyer to get me the driver's name.

I had a gut reaction the identity was going to further rip Jenna apart. Which was why Jenna needed me to be strong—the emotional rock I'd struggled to be since Kim and my uncle's deaths.

Once Jenna cleared her plate and finished off her coffee, wiped her hands on the dishrag after washing the dishes she insisted on cleaning, that trickle of unease I'd ignored since I heard the news welled back up.

Her grandfather had been her stability, the one she turned to when she needed comfort or wisdom. Now that she'd mentioned it, I worried what would happen to the guitar store. Because it gave Jenna purpose and a passion, both of which she'd need in the coming weeks as she toiled through the painful work of grieving.

I'd been in her spot too many times.

She turned toward me. The tip of her nose was still red, but the puffiness and redness of her eyes cleared enough for her to look her normal gorgeous self.

Jenna twisted the dishtowel in her hands, tightening it to the point it must by pinching the skin of her palms.

"I don't do well in hospitals. The smell, the sounds…reminds me of bad times there."

"We don't have to go."

Jenna turned an incredulous face toward me. "I do." Her voice turned sharp, and I understood.

She sucked in a big breath and let it trickle out slowly. "I should be there already. My family's there, dealing with this, while I huddled in my bed. I have to go, Cam." The last words turned pleading.

I'd left her once without letting her explain. Now, she needed me as she never had before—or probably would again. Instead of shying away from the emotion, I stood and went to her, pulling her into my arms.

"I'll be with you the whole time. I'll hold your hand. Whatever you need."

She nuzzled her cheek against my shoulder, her arms coming up to span my waist. "You sure you don't mind? I mean, I know you just did this with your own family."

I blew out a breath. "I'm not going to lie. This isn't easy for me either."

She pulled back enough to search my eyes, hers softening when she found whatever it was she was looking for. "Thank you. For being the man I need even though this isn't what you want either. Just let me get my phone and purse."

She darted off.

I finished off the last of the coffee and put my mug and the empty pot in the dishwasher, mulling over her words—and what she hadn't said.

My finger searched my pocket and wrapped around the hard candy there. I pulled it out, unwrapped it and popped it in my mouth.

"Why do you eat those?" she asked.

"They help to calm me."

She sighed, an exasperated sound. "How'd you figure out they kept you calm?"

"In the sandbox. My team was pinned down by enemy fire. Sounds better than the reality. Between us, we had two bags of Werther's candies sent by Chuck's grandma, twenty granola bars and ten bananas. And our water that we carried on us."

"How long were you out there?" Jenna's eyes flared wide.

"Three days. We saved the Werther's for last. Nothing's ever tasted so damn good, especially when two Black Hawk helos sped over us and took out the insurgents." I shrugged. "Good connotations for me and caramels."

Jenna wrinkled her nose as I opened the back door of the SUV for her. "Better than me and hospitals. Thanks for driving, Chuck."

When we arrived, none of Jenna's family was there. Her grandfather had already been moved to the funeral home.

"You want to call your folks?" I asked.

Jenna shook her head, wrapping her arms around her mid-section.

Something was going on—something she hadn't shared with me. Her face paled further though her cheeks remained red from the earlier bout of tears. Her dulled eyes worried me most. Jenna's curiosity—her sharp wit and incisive responses—faded as she eased back inside. Her grandfather told me this retreat was how Jenna behaved whenever she was hurt or overwhelmed, and they'd spent months pulling her back out of the shell she'd encased herself in after the GHB overdose in Seattle.

In fact, according to Mr. Olsen, Jenna had only been like her old self for mere weeks before I stepped into her shop. Now I had to wonder how she'd handle this huge loss. More than I'd ever had to deal with, and I'd dealt with plenty.

I began rearranging my day and the following one so I could be with Jenna, taking care of her as she worked through the initial grief.

I popped another candy as I sent off a final text. I slammed my car door and waited for Jenna to buckle up.

Chuck started the car and eased out of the lot and into the traffic. Jenna paid little attention, eyes on her knees and arms once again crossed over her middle the entire ride back to my place.

———— ★ ————

Something in Jenna's expression remained off—the grief settled there, as it would for many months to come. Jenna watched me as if waiting for…something. Something I feared I couldn't provide.

"Let's go." I grabbed her hand.

"Where?"

"Down to the river."

"I don't have a swimsuit."

I smiled in a way that must have told Jenna I didn't care—didn't want her in a suit—and she balked, digging her heels into my bricked patio.

"I am not skinny dipping with you!"

I raised my eyebrow. "Who asked you to? I bought you a swimsuit. Rather, my assistant did. It's in my bedroom."

"It's the middle of the night."

"And you're not going to sleep till you relax some. So, get a move on."

Jenna walked into my bedroom without another word, head still bowed. I wanted her to turn back and give me a snarky Jenna-type response. She shut the door.

Jenna stepped out on the porch in the tankini Erika purchased earlier. It wasn't overly revealing. Erika didn't approve of the parade of women I'd led through my life these past few years and this was her conservative statement to think with something other than my dick. That's what I deserved when I hired one of my mother's old chums to help me clean up my image and get more organized.

Still, the cornflower blue material clung to Jenna's breasts and slid over her smooth belly. The small bottoms showed off her long, toned legs. I'd never seen a shapelier pair of calves or drooled over trim ankles before. Even her feet in those wedged flip flips turned me on.

"Let me get changed and we can head out."

Jenna's face softened with gratitude. I made the call before I did something stupid—like pull her into my arms and take advantage of her grief and worry.

"If it's all right, I'll need to check in with my mother and sister in the morning. See how they're getting along. Wouldn't mind you meeting my brother now that I'm sure he won't try to steal you away."

"I'm not a pet kitty," she said, voice sharp. "I am more than capable of making my own decisions as far as who I date."

I brushed her hair back from her forehead and cupped her cheek. Before I realized it, I'd leaned down and taken her lips in a kiss. I managed to keep it soft, gentle, but my body raged with need for more.

"I know it. The warning was more for my brother. And how much I'd whup his ass if he laid even a finger on you."

She sighed and shook her head, exasperation radiating from her every pore. Jenna turned back to go through the door and my breath caught. The back was held together by a bow at the neck and another in the middle of her back. One little tug and I'd get the top to drop down to show me those lovely pink-tipped breasts. I loved her breasts. One more tug and I'd have the top off, able to feast on all that lustrous skin.

Damn Erika for letting me think the suit was conservative. It was hot as hell, and I wanted to see the color darken with water, then see Jenna's eyes darken with need as I pulled the bow out.

But now wasn't that moment. I needed to help Jenna relax. Soothe out some of the grief at least enough for her to sleep. Because if Jenna grieved like I did, sleep would be difficult to capture.

CHAPTER TWENTY-THREE | Jenna

I fidgeted on the rock seat carved into the little pool. The night noises were soothing, as Cam predicted. I wondered how to ask Cam for what I needed. Him, touching me, bringing me pleasure so that I could focus on life, on feeling good, not the fear and blackness that tugged at my consciousness.

I half-expected the phone to ring any moment with news of my dismissal from the family.

Unable to take the self-doubt spinning through my head any longer, I slid from Cam's side and straddled his hips. He tilted his head back and met my gaze with a patient understanding.

I wrapped my arms around his neck and slid my wet hands into the short hairs at his nape. "Cam."

"Sweet Jenna Marie."

"I want…"

"To feel good?"

I nodded. Instead, of saying the words, I pressed my breasts against his chest. Cam released a breath and a curse.

"I'm not going to tell you no. You sure about this?"

"Yes. Please, Cam. I need you."

His lips quirked up but his eyes remained watchful.

"I love the feel of your hands on me. How you make me feel when you touch me," I tried to explain again. I slid my palms down his neck, over those broad shoulders and onto his pecs.

"I'll give you what you need," he said against the sensitive skin of my neck. He nipped that warmed flesh. "I'm desperate to be inside you."

I reached up and pulled at the bow on my suit. Cam's eyes burned with appreciation as the suit tumbled down, baring my breasts to his intense gaze. My nipples puckered into painful peaks and a deep throb settled between my thighs.

He raised his hands and palmed my right breast, keeping his other hand on my hip. His eyes fixed on mine, he leaned forward and took the nipple into the warm, wet heat of his mouth. I whimpered as my hips undulated against his, seeking the much-needed friction.

He switched to my other breast, sucking hard enough to hollow out his cheeks, his eyes never leaving mine. The sensation was too great and I threw my head back.

"We're just getting started, sugar." His voice held promises no one else could ever match. Cam proved more sensitive to my needs than any of my previous lovers. My passion seemed to stoke his.

That's why I loved him.

My breath hitched. Was I ready for opening myself up that much to him?

He fingered the bow along my spine. "I wanted to untie this the moment I saw it." With a strong tug, my top fell, floating in the swirling current.

He ran his hands up my ribs back to my aching breasts. My breathing ramped up again as desire pooled, heating my belly.

I took the opportunity to bring my hands back up to his hair, fisting them there as I leaned in and kissed him.

This kiss wasn't gentle. My lips slammed against his as my mouth opened, my tongue already dueling with his. His hips thrust upward against my wet center as his tongue slid over mine. I liked that. A lot. So, I rubbed against his hard erection while my lips sealed to his and my tongue plundered the warmth of his mouth.

On and on I kissed him—I'd nibble, then lick, suckle on his lower lip before thrusting my tongue back into his mouth. And each change was more glorious, bringing me higher and closer to the ultimate pleasure I needed. Each kiss, each touch of his hands against my overheated skin caused the throb between my legs to build.

I tore my mouth from his when his fingertips drifted up my thigh to the edge of my bikini bottoms, liking his slumberous eyes and his red, plumped lips.

"I'm going to touch you now, Jenna."

I leaned back in close enough to take his lips but instead I laid my cheek against his. "Yes."

His fingers dipped under the elastic and he palmed my hot, needy flesh. I moaned as he pressed the heel of his hand against my pubic bone, causing the bundle of nerves hidden there to flash with desire.

"Cam."

"I got you, sugar. Just enjoy."

He slid a finger inside me and I shuddered, my fingernails biting into his shoulders. I was desperate and wet and so close to losing my mind. When he added another finger, I forced my hips down, taking him even deeper into my body, needing him to understand how much I desired his touch.

He grunted. I hoped in appreciation. Then his thumb found my clit and my eyes slammed closed on the sparks shooting behind those lids. One soft pump out with his fingers, then three were in me, pushing in toward that…oh, please, yes, that perfect spot…as his thumb pressed harder, and I brought my head forward on the deep cry that ripped from my lips as my body clenched tight, hard, around his fingers.

Cam rode out each shudder, holding me with his free arm, keeping me as safe as he'd promised. I collapsed, sprawled over his chest as my breathing slowed.

With gentle care, he eased his fingers from my tender flesh as he kissed my temple.

"Cam?"

"Yeah?"

I ran my hand up and over his thick, hard erection. "I want you inside me."

"You can enjoy your…"

"One way or another, I'm going to make you come, and I'd really like to feel you inside me when it happens."

He gritted his teeth even as he looked with sheepish concern at his straining board shorts. "I don't have a condom. That's not why I brought you down here."

I shivered as a softer breeze slid through the thick, humid summer air.

"It's unlikely I'll get pregnant. That time I bled? It was a cyst. When it ruptured, it damaged my ovary." I shrugged like it wasn't a big deal, but it was. Another reason I'd felt so useless and unneeded at the ripe old age of eighteen.

Cam must have heard something in my voice or maybe it was just how well he already knew me. He tipped my head down and forced me to meet his gaze.

"I'm clean. I had my physical a few months ago and haven't been with anyone but you since."

I shuddered, not liking the idea of Cam touching and loving another woman, but then, I'd let Charles use my body, so how could I be upset with him for his past?

"I'm good, too." I didn't want to say I'd gotten a clean sexual bill of health after my last hospitalization, worried it'd kill the mood. So, instead. I ran my hand up and down his erection, my body once again enjoying the idea of more intimacy with Cam.

I leaned in closer and brushed my lips over his in a soft, teasing caress. I followed that with a warm glide of my breasts across his chest. His eyes darkened and his hands dropped to my hips, cupping my bottom.

"You're beautiful, Jenna Marie. The most beautiful water sprite I've ever seen."

I smiled at his words, thankful he was willing to keep us away from the thick, churning uncertainty just on the other side of this moment.

I loosened his shorts. After running my hands over his hard, muscular stomach, I pushed my hand under his trunks and gripped him, hissing as I always did at his heat and girth. His fingers slid back under my bikini bottoms, easing them to the side so he had better access to my flesh.

"Next time is in a bed where I can take my time with you," Cam murmured against my neck. "I don't like doing this too fast." He moved down to my shoulder. "So much of you I like to savor."

He ran his fingers along my lips and my chest slid against his. I squeezed him just as his fingers brushed my inner lips, readying my body.

When I couldn't take the touches anymore, I wiggled out of my bikini bottoms and settled over him, guiding his thick shaft into my body.

Cam's arms tucked me tighter to his chest as his hips thrust upward. I bit my lip at the fullness of him. He was big and oh so hard. Perfect. And mine. Right now, this sexy man had eyes only for me. The crickets sang and the water swished around us as he let me set the pace.

One breath turned to three, then mingled together as we moved, striving for fulfillment. He kissed the side of my neck, working back to my mouth.

When he sealed his lips over mine, he was so gentle, tears formed in my eyes. Much as I wanted to believe he was telling me this moment meant something more than amazing sex of two people who had incredible chemistry, I couldn't.

He thrust into me again, and I let my head fall back, away from the overpowering emotion in that kiss. He followed, pressing his lips to the hollow of my throat as his pace quickened. His fingers found and plucked my nipples and the buzz of need built to a fever pitch.

Faster and harder, he moved in my body. Deep...so deep

inside me—showing me that he could take even as he gave greater pleasure. I loved how he gave, making sure my pleasure exploded before his.

I collapsed against him with an exhausted sigh.

Camden Grace might well be the best man I'd ever met. Too bad he'd never want to keep me and my level of crazy, especially now that my family blew apart.

———————— ★ ————————

He woke me with kisses. I murmured against his mouth, stretching. Then, my eyes popped open. I'd had sex—amazing sex—*outside*. My grandfather was dead. My parents didn't want to see me.

"What time is it?" I asked, the panic snaking up my spine.

"After ten."

I sat up and realized I was naked and in Cam's bed. Heat blasted through my cheeks and chest. Well, that had to be one heck of a photo opportunity—Cam carrying me, asleep, from his river pool.

"Oh, you don't get to go all shy on me now." He leaned down and kissed me again. Long and slow with lots of luscious nips and languid swipes of tongue. I melted in a puddle of need.

Camden Grace's sexuality might be the most potent drug I'd ever ingested. And, damn, if I didn't want another hit.

He looked me in the eyes for a long time before he bent down and placed a soft, sweet kiss on my lips. When he pulled back my eyes fluttered open, meeting his intense gaze.

I edged in closer, my breath breaking on my lips even as my insides squirmed and I wanted to shy away from the big emotions he offered. "Cam—"

I cupped his cheeks as his lips slid over my shoulder, sucking the skin there with gentle insistence.

"I should call my family," I managed to say, unscrambling my hazy brain. I took my phone from Cam's hand. I played with the edge.

"We can pick something up on the way to your folks' place. Then, I'd like you to come back here for the week or whatever."

"You're okay with that?" The butterflies in my stomach took off, sailing with delight.

"I'd like nothing more than to spend more time with you."

I pressed my lips to his in thanks. After another long moment of losing myself in his mouth, I pulled back and picked up my phone.

"Hey, Micah. How are Dad and Mom doing?"

"Driving Jude and me crazy."

His sadness slid into the phone and wrapped around my skin. I blinked down, shocked to realize I was talking to my brother while sitting in Cam's bed, naked. When I caught Cam's gaze, he raised his eyebrow as if he knew what I was thinking.

I gripped the phone tighter and breathed through the rush of emotion. "Thank you. Is Dad...is he still mad at me?"

"Yeah." Jude practically snarled the word. "Won't say why, just that he doesn't want to see you."

My body curved in on itself. Crap on a stick—these emotions tearing through my chest *hurt*. "Oh."

He sighed. "Maybe...maybe it's best if you wait it out, Jen. I don't know what's going on."

"Okay."

"Jude and I can come out to see you."

My brother always had an olive branch. I loved him for it. "I'll see what Cam says."

I tossed my phone onto the bedside table and stared at it, wondering what I did to anger my father so much.

Cam tugged me up and into the bathroom. He turned on the shower. Stepping into the shower, I started when he wrapped his arms around me.

"I don't think…" I stopped, unsure how to tell him that while I wanted him, the desire right now seemed wrong.

"I'm just going to hold you, Jenna. Then, we're going to get cleaned up and meet your family."

I tipped my head back, squinting as the fine mist caught in my lashes, a few droplets hitting me in the eye. "My dad doesn't want to see me."

Cam narrowed his eyes, his mouth pulling in to a pinched line.

"My brothers said they'd come to me. If…if that's okay?"

"I'd love to meet them." He pressed a kiss to the tip of my nose. "Now, let's wash your hair."

CHAPTER TWENTY-FOUR | Cam

While Jenna finished getting ready, I called my brother, thrilling a little to be able to do so. Our relationship would take a while to rebuild—too many years passed for the ease we once had—but for the first time, confidence surged through me when I thought of my brother.

"You had a bad night," Carter said without preamble. "Bet it was worse than mine here, and the fireworks between Mom and Katie Rose lit the sky."

"Sorry to leave you with that." I rubbed the back of my neck, chagrined.

"Nah. Don't be. I'm part of this family, whether I've been good about participating or not."

My heart warmed at the conviction in his words. "Thanks, C. What, exactly, is Katie Rose so mad about?"

"The cheating. You know she thought her father hung the moon and the stars. Oh, and she's upset for you, too, that Laurence stepped out with your wife. That's really stuck in her craw." He sighed. "But worst of it is she's upset with Mama for lying."

"So'm I, if I'm honest."

"I'd be, too, but I lied to you as well. I thought I was helping. Now I see I just messed it up more."

"I'll come down, see if I can diffuse the situation."

"If anyone can, it's you, Cam. Cuz, damn, baby brother, you're a bona fide rock star."

Heat crept up my cheeks. I wanted to shrug it off, but it felt good to have my twin complimenting me, especially with all that sincerity in his voice.

"I'll come down in a bit. I'd like you to meet Jenna."

"I'll be here." His voice was laconic but the words spread happiness through my chest.

Jenna and I finished getting ready in an easy synchronicity we'd established over the last few weeks at her place. Jenna met me at the front door, her wet hair combed back from her face, in a pair of white cut-offs and a gauzy, oversized top. A tunic, Katie Rose called them. She liked that style, too.

Chuck had the car out front, idling. We slid into the air-conditioned comfort of the back seat and Jenna and I buckled in before I took her hand in mine. Not far up the road, but we'd head to get some food after and I didn't want Jenna to wilt in this heat wave.

The front door opened and my mother stepped out onto the porch. She waved just as another figure darkened the door.

"I can't do this," Jenna mumbled. Her breath escalated to harsh bursts.

"It's just my mom and sister."

She turned to look at me, eyes wild and lids red. She reminded me of a raging bull.

"You don't get to spring this on me!"

"What's got you in such a lather?"

Jenna's face crumpled, tears streaming down her cheeks, and

my stomach iced over at the harsh sobs.

"What's wrong, sugar?"

"I can't meet your mother. My own father seems to hate me."

I cupped her cheek. "My mom won't hate you."

She swiped at her runny nose, her eyes meeting mine through the deluge of tears. "I can't deal with rejection right now," she whispered.

"She won't. She and Katie Rose already love you. Promise."

Navigating Jenna's mercurial mood switches might prove more difficult than I'd anticipated. And I wanted to get hold of her father to find out why he shut out his only daughter during such a rough time for her.

Carter smiled and shook Jenna's hand—sure not to touch her in any inappropriate manner. I appreciated his reticence though Jenna seemed concerned. No matter. I could tell Carter liked her. A lot.

My mama did, too, just as I'd predicted. She even wrapped Jenna up in one of her big hugs that had Jenna sighing and snuggling in tighter. That made me happy.

We decided to meet Jenna's brothers at her condo since they'd asked to meet us there.

Jenna's silence on the way was a small price to pay for getting the meet-and-greet of her brothers out of the way.

We'd picked up dinner from Torchy's Tacos, which Jenna said was her brothers' comfort food. Chuck and I carried it in while Jenna hugged her brothers.

"You doing okay?" Chuck asked me.

I considered his question, unwilling to give him anything less than the truth. "Not really. This whole situation blows."

Chuck thumped his fist on my shoulder. "Life can be a cruel, fickle beast." He crossed his arms over his chest. "You going to mess this up with her cuz your head isn't on straight?"

I dropped my hands to the granite counter top and let my head fall forward between my raised shoulders. "I'm not sure she's going to help me screw it on any better. And, anyway, she's as messed up as I am."

At the slight gasp, I turned to see Jenna paused in the doorway, on her tiptoes as if she'd been about to step further into the room.

Well, shit.

———————— ★ ————————

The rest of the night fell apart from there.

Micah, Jenna's oldest brother, took her by the hands and led her over to the couch. My heart rate slowed and a thick heaviness lingered in the air.

Micah edged his butt onto Jenna's coffee table, keeping her small, pale hands in his. Jude came to sit next to her, his arm wrapped protectively around her shoulders.

Micah sucked in a big breath, his entire chest heaving. He must have drawn the short straw, the one who had to tell Jenna the reason her father was being such a dick. My fingers flicked against my jeans as the dread built in my chest. I moved toward Jenna, instinct telling me these next words would shatter her.

"Dad told us who hit Pop-pop," Micah began.

I settled onto the couch, my thigh touching Jenna's.

"It was Ben."

CHAPTER TWENTY-FIVE | Jenna

I'd known. Some part of me guessed. When Dad hung up on me. Pop-pop had borrowed my car. *My* car. Ben knew it—I'd bet. I stood, the rush of emotion too big to hold in while I sat there.

Cam stood, too.

I tried to move around Jude, tried to get out, get to my room, shut the door. To process what my dad believed…what my brothers just told.

I killed my grandfather.

The best man I'd ever known was dead. Because of me.

Cam met me before I reached my bedroom door. He locked his hands on my biceps. I shook my head. I needed space. I needed time. I needed to be alone.

"No, you don't," Cam said, making me realize I'd spoken aloud. "You don't. You need to breathe, sugar. Breathe through this blow. You can. Come on. Look at me and breathe."

As with any other time he used that tone, I obeyed. My eyes met his and I took a breath. I didn't want him to have this power over me. At the same time, some of the tightness in my chest eased. My lips began to tremble.

Cam settled me against his chest. The steady beat of his heart against my cheek soothed me.

I stayed there for a long minute, maybe five. Finally, I raised my head. I looked at my silent brothers.

"Do you believe that?" I asked, my voice choppy and clogged with emotion. If they did, I might not be able to hold in the sobs that kept trying to build in my throat.

"Believe what?" Jude asked.

"That I k-killed Pop-pop?" Those words were hard to speak but they needed to be said. Each tiny movement they made, I studied. If they believed that, then I had no family. *No one.* I wrapped my arms around my waist and Cam stepped back, giving me space. Leaving me in this moment when I desperately needed his warmth, his shoulder. His support.

The world spun. I was alone. I didn't want to be alone.

Jude and Micah walked to me. Jude placed his hands on my shoulders. Micah took my hands.

"No," Micah said, his voice firm yet quiet.

"No," Jude echoed. "You didn't cause that accident—which probably wasn't an accident at all. That's on Ben. Not you."

"But Pop-pop had my car," I whispered.

"And Ben plowed into it," Micah said. "Seems like, from what Dad said anyway, that this was intentional, Jen."

I flinched. Jude tightened his hold on me. Cam stepped back in—close enough for me to feel the heat of his body. These wonderful men protected me now, but would it be enough? Should they even be here?

My grandfather was *dead* because of me.

"What happened to him?" Cam asked. "Ben."

Micah shrugged, crossing his arms over his chest and scowling. "He's in the hospital. Don't know which one and don't know how extensive his injuries are."

I twisted to face Cam. "You didn't know?"

He cupped my cheek as he shook his head. "I would have told you, sugar."

His eyes gleamed with sincerity.

"Jen," Micah said, his voice gentle.

I closed my eyes before I turned to look at him.

"Dad's really upset. Mom's doing her best, but you have to understand something else."

I waited, breath baited.

Jude's mouth tightened into a grim line. Uh oh. That was Jude's I'm-really-pissed face.

"Mom and Dad have gotten lots of phone calls about the accident. Rather, Ben hitting Pop-pop." Micah's eyes flicked over to Cam, offering an apology.

"We're betting a story will come out tomorrow," Micah said. Each word dropped, staccato and harsh, like a bomb on my heart.

CHAPTER TWENTY-SIX | Cam

My head ached from the stiffness in my shoulders. Jenna didn't say much on the way back to my place, letting me hold her curled form against my side.

I'd made calls to Brenda and to my label. I'd gotten as far ahead of the story as I could. Might not be enough, especially since I had no idea what Jenna's father told reporters.

I waited until we were settled in bed before I brought up the conversation she'd overheard. I played with strands of her long hair. "Remember that first dinner we had at your place? When you told me you were messed up, too?"

"I don't want to talk about this," she said, her voice catching.

"I need you to understand, that wasn't a dig at you tonight, sugar. More at me. I'm the one that bashed apart my guitar because I couldn't take all the emotions building in me."

"Cam. Please, don't." With that, she walked into the bathroom and shut the door.

Everyone handled grief differently. I knew that—I'd witnessed it in the sandbox and again, here, within my own family.

But Jenna shutting down worried me.

Because she wasn't just dealing with grief. Right now, from where she stood, her father betrayed her, and I knew just how hard it was to come back from that type of hurt.

I hadn't. My childhood, no matter how happy, was forever tainted by Laurence's deeds with Kim. Nothing—not one thing—could ever make me see past those choices.

"I'm sleepy," Jenna murmured, eyes still downcast, when she walked out of the bathroom a few minutes later. She climbed into bed, rolled away from me and tucked herself into a ball. I opened my mouth to try to talk to her but then I closed it. What could I say?

———— ★ ————

The story hit the next morning with the strength of a ten-foot tsunami. My fans were not happy. Many threatened to boycott my albums and my label if I didn't dump Jenna—the reason a sweet old man, a legend in the music world was dead—immediately.

Yep, the media reports spun this the worst way they could. Nothing Jenna's parents said seemed damaging to their daughter outright, but the overall impact was a family torn apart by grief. Salacious—the perfect click-bait that had my fans in a lather within minutes.

I held firm in my belief Jenna did no wrong. My mother, Carter, and Katie Rose were hounded by reporters each time they left the house.

Jenna slid further into herself. No matter where I took her or what we did, her mind wandered away from the present.

She didn't cry. She didn't call her parents, either, which I understood. But I ached for her.

The third morning, over coffee, I asked her what she'd like to do that day.

"I need to work on a client's guitar."

That was the worst idea. No way I was letting her back into the space she worked each day with her grandfather without someone to take her mind off the empty desk across the room. An idea wormed its way forward and I smiled, liking that scheme as it'd fix another ongoing problem I'd struggled to solve. But that was for later. Right now, I needed to get some light back in Jenna's eyes. And, if I was honest, I wanted to hold her close to me. I always wanted to do that, but right now it seemed especially important.

I took her horseback riding. She thanked me with another passionate round of lovemaking out-of-doors. Much as I enjoyed that treat, I worried about the wake the next day.

This goodbye proved as difficult to get through as any other. Driving to the funeral parlor, I held her hand as Jenna turned her wan face, cheekbones more prominent, toward the window. She didn't speak and her fingers lay cold and too still in my hand. The media met us at the entrance, their shouted questions horrific.

"Did you lend your grandfather your car because you knew Ben was after you?"

"Ben's supposed to make a full recovery. Do you have a statement?"

"Are you looking forward to another trial, Jenna?"

"Do you enjoy the spotlight that much?"

Angry as I was, I stared straight ahead and pulled Jenna through the throng, holding her tighter to my side as I mentally damned the press, my fans, the entire world who'd found Jenna guilty without a shred of evidence.

Chuck stepped in behind us, arms crossed over his chest, the scowl deeper and uglier than I'd ever seen it.

I couldn't take away her grief, and the more I tried to shoulder it for her, the more my mind revved into overdrive.

I felt the cracks form in my composure, and I detested this place we were in. I watched Jenna throughout the service. She seemed to fold into herself—becoming the tired, scared young woman her grandfather mentioned when I used to come into his shop years before.

I stopped to shake hands with Jenna's brother Jude.

"You doing all right?" I asked.

He shrugged. "Dad made everything a million times worse with that interview. I can't leave the house. We had to unplug the home phone, stop checking our emails. I'll be glad to go back to San Francisco."

"Don't blame you, man."

"How's Jen doing?" Micah asked, joining us.

"Not good. I'm really worried about her."

Micah tugged at his short, neat beard. "I don't know if this'll help…"

I tensed and didn't hear the rest of Micah's words because Jenna's father grabbed her arm and pulled her aside. Before I could make my way through the crowd—which included many musicians I would have enjoyed talking to any other day—Jenna's mother joined her father and cut him off mid-sentence.

Jenna wouldn't look at her mother. She turned her back on her father and walked directly to me.

"I'm ready to go," she said, still unable to look at me.

"All right." I clasped her hand and pulled her from the large, crowded room.

I caught Micah's eye and dipped my head toward Jenna. He nodded, a frown building across his face. Jude stood next to him, eyes narrowed as he turned from us to glare at his father, who still scowled at Jenna's bowed head.

What the hell was going on here?

She didn't speak as we waited in the vestibule while the media yelled questions through the door. Chuck called for the vehicle, which two of my staff brought around. Chuck stood in front of us, blasting a path for Jenna, mainly, who still didn't speak once we settled into the SUV. I leaned my head back against the supple leather of the seat, thankful we'd made it through this tangible step of saying goodbye.

The afternoon sun warmed the interior, making me shift uncomfortably. I was ready to get this suit off and put on something comfortable. Maybe haul Jenna down to the river for some relaxation.

We both needed it.

As soon as Chuck parked the SUV, she tore up the porch like ants lit up her pants. Whoa. Not what I expected. Whatever went down with her father upset her.

I caught her as she hurried into my bedroom. I turned her stiff frame, unsurprised by her rigid posture.

"What's wrong? Please talk to me, sugar."

Her lips twisted and she dropped her chin, a sure sign she was about to move away. Not happening. I cupped her jaw and tugged her gently around to face me. She kept her lids lowered as I waited.

"Nothing," she finally mumbled.

I unwrapped a candy and shoved it in my mouth, trying to ignore my shaking hands. "Oh, it's something."

She stepped back, trying to retreat. I couldn't let her. Not this time.

"Jenna."

She stilled. Her shoulders dropped.

"What happened with your parents?" I asked.

"I don't want to talk about that." Her voice rang with finality. She refused to turn around and look at me.

"Are you angry with me?"

A quick shake of that bright blond head.

"Are you sick?"

Another negation.

"Hurt?"

A pause before the shake.

"I want to help you."

"You can't." The words burst from her lips as if they'd been hovering there, right there, waiting for the chance.

"Why's that, sugar?"

"B-because."

"You're a grown woman, Jenna Marie. Don't devolve down to grade schooler now because you're scared to talk to me."

That brought those bright blue eyes flashing up to mine. They burned with just the right amount of temper.

"Going to try to deny it?" I taunted. My heart rate escalated and my nose twitched, but I held her gaze with mine, steady and firm like she needed.

"I'm late."

I paused, shut my mouth, sucked the candy. "You're late? As in your period."

She nodded, eyes wide and deep shadows building within.

"And you've known for how long?" I asked, trying to keep my voice neutral.

"Since we went horseback riding. Yesterday," she said to clarify.

Not long. And not what I'd wanted to talk about, but we'd deal with this first. "All right. Well, should we get a test?"

She sank to the edge of the bed and bowed her head. For the first time in days, emotion seemed to waft from her.

"I was afraid to tell you," she murmured.

"Why?"

She stood and paced. I let her go, understanding the need to burn off that excess energy. Finally, she turned back toward me. "Because of the questions tossed at me like I'm such an evil person of course they won't hurt me. About hurting your image, your brand. Your career. My life."

Each word came out faster, sharper, until they piled on top of each other.

"That's a lot of worries. Have I given you a reason to think I'd leave you alone?"

Jenna tugged at her skirt, gripping the material and twisting it in her hand. "What you said the other night. At my condo."

I absorbed that. Not that she meant it as a blow, but I'd known then I'd have to pay for those words she misconstrued. Now was that time. "You think I meant what I said then as a slight against you?"

She shook her head, slower this time. I stepped in closer, using my legs to bracket hers before I lowered my forehead down. The first brush of her silky hair against my skin brought a sigh of pleasure to my lips. My heart rate settled and the quivering in my hands stilled.

Her breath puffed across my chin, warm and sweet. Like Jenna when she wasn't so caught up in her head.

Keeping her out of there was more challenging than my last tour outside the perimeter. Her demons were every bit as real to me as the sand-colored-camo monsters who killed my buddies. I closed my eyes, took a deep, slow breath. Not the time to fall back into that nightmare.

Not when I was trying to build a future. Here. Now.

CHAPTER TWENTY-SEVEN | Jenna

My father pulled me aside at the funeral. "I'm sorry, Jenna. I didn't know how this story would turn out."

I cleared my throat and forced my gaze up to his. "Do you think I'd do that? Get Pop-pop killed to protect myself?" My heart raced and I clenched my hands into fists, trying hard to keep it together.

Dad opened his mouth, shut it. He and Pop-pop, together, were my rock. My reason I was standing here—alive today.

"I don't know what to think," Dad finally said. His eyes filled with tears. "I miss my dad. Why couldn't that boy leave you alone? That's the stem of all this. If he'd just left you alone, I'd be able to call my dad tonight and watch the game with him."

"David," my mother said, coming up beside him.

I couldn't look at her. Maybe she thought I was responsible, too. I ducked away, asking Cam to take me home. To his home.

But I wanted to run.

To bury my head under my pillow and just give up.

Some people had a knack for living—found joy in every nuance of their days. I could barely cobble together two words to form a coherent sentence, let alone pick a reasonable outfit or trust myself out in public.

———— ★ ————

Cam must have seen the panic rising as it clawed its way up my throat because he wrapped me back up in those thick, warm arms and drew me close against his chest as soon as we settled into his SUV, moving away from my family, from the funeral home—from my last glimpse of my grandfather.

Cam was my home. The only place I wanted to rest my head. I told him I was a day late, needing to steer clear of my parents' strange behavior. I was closer to a week late, but that wasn't uncommon, especially when I was stressed.

Cam's calm acceptance of the possibility of a baby made me fall even deeper in love with him. He knew just what to say to me, just how to soothe. He was the only man I'd ever yearned for, ever wanted to tuck into.

Which was exactly why I needed to get away. In a minute. After my legs quit shaking and my breathing regulated.

"Better?" he asked.

I wasn't. So I waited for a long moment before I nodded.

"You able to listen with those ears and your head now? I got a few words to say back about what you think I said and what I meant."

No. I did not want to hear him gently let me down, explain while he was looking for companionship, he never planned to love another woman—wouldn't let himself after the way Kim busted his dreams. And I was simply too much work to deal with.

I slammed my eyes shut, willing my heart to calm again.

"Cam—"

"Before you get fussier than a wet cat, hear me out." He lifted his arm from my back and used his thumb and forefinger to tip my chin up. Much as I resisted, my eyes rose to meet his.

Those beautiful depths held patience, a hint of humor and a whole lot of passion. I frowned, trying to step back, but Cam tightened his arm around my waist and his thumb against my chin.

He nuzzled into my neck before pressing tiny kisses to my throat and down to the skin available above the scoop neck of my blouse. I shivered as his warm breath drifted over my skin, overheating me further. He chuckled, a deep, dark sound. Like dark chocolate and rumpled satin sheets.

"Damn, sugar. We need to talk but I get so caught up… You're my sugar-laced addiction."

Cue internal destruction. My chest ached as my body roared with need only to collapse with a whimper of rejected ash.

"I'm not an addiction." I twisted away, stumbling back from his feel-good hands as I tried to regulate my breathing, to keep the tears from pouring out of my eyes.

"Jen—"

I dropped my hands and wrapped them around my waist, eyes darting every which way but landing on his again.

"What if I…" I sucked in a breath. "What if I just need you to hold me?"

"That's all I've *been* doing, sugar. Through this media storm, with my fans clamoring for me to cut you lose."

Frustration bit through his words.

My shoulders hunched and I nodded once. Not so much in acceptance because Cam crushed me even further with words like my father's.

I stood, my chest heaving. "I didn't do *anything* wrong." I slashed my hand, negating my father's words, but Cam's still swam through my head. "I just…for one minute I wanted something more than sex."

"Jenna." He said my name, softly, sweetly. I heard the melody of it, what I thought was caring in the timbre of it, but I'd already turned and began to stumble away. "I don't want—"

There was nothing more I wanted to say or hear from him right now. Not one damn thing. His phone chimed.

"Dammit, Jenna, I don't like you walking out on me," he called.

I whirled back to face him. "What *do* you want, Camden?"

He opened his mouth but slowly shut it, looking pensive. I slammed the heels of my hands to my eyes.

"You want your other guitar."

"Well, sure. But I want to spend time with you, too."

Those awful words. Spend time. Pass the time. None meant anything too serious. Even after I'd told him I might be pregnant.

"Where do you see us going?" I rasped out, dropping my hands to meet his gaze.

He stepped back, his eyes shuttering. "You're focused on your career. You don't want to come live here and live off me."

"She did a real number on you, Cam. You're right, I don't want that. I don't even know if I want kids. I'm so messed up."

He nodded. "You are."

I cleared my throat. "If we weren't sleeping together, would you have gone with me to Pop-pop's funeral?"

His brow creased with consternation. "I…I don't like them."

"Fine," I said, my anger draining from my body, leaving it achy, old. "What do you like?"

His phone chimed again. He pulled it from his pocket. His scowl intensified.

"Shit."

What?

"I have to take Carter to the airport."

Now? As in, right in the middle of this conversation?

"Fine," I said.

"Jenna… I'll see you later."

I turned my back, unwilling to agree.

CHAPTER TWENTY-EIGHT | Cam

Maybe it was a good thing I promised to take Carter to the airport. Didn't feel like it, not with the fear in Jenna's eyes. She needed reassurance now that I wouldn't leave her or the baby. If there was a baby.

Hot damn, I hoped there was. A tiny version of Jenna with all that blond hair and big blue eyes. Jenna could make her a tiny guitar and we'd jam on our patio.

More images immediately filled my head. Of us in a little brick house, sitting on the porch swing as the sun set over Lake Travis, the whine of mosquitos and the hum of the whippoor-will filling the soft, humid night air. Jenna curled into my side, watching our kids run through the grass, her glass of sweet tea clutched in her work-roughened hands. I loved those hands and what they produced. I loved that she was willing to use them, to show the world that a woman was just as capable—more capable—than the men who'd come before.

But I needed space to figure out how to deal with her fear— about us, about how to move us forward instead of wallowing in the guilt and grief of her grandfather's death.

Carter and I talked of inconsequential details, mostly sports and the ranches. I heaved out a sigh, enjoying the lessening tension in my body.

Carter promised to come down for the holidays. We hugged for a long minute, but I already missed my twin and the closeness we still worked to repair.

"Jenna's a great gal," Carter murmured.

I grunted.

He stepped back and narrowed his eyes. "What did you do?"

"Not a thing."

"Camden. You forget I know you."

Jenna wasn't here at the airport, but that didn't mean ears weren't listening. The downside of fame was the lack of anonymity. If people realized who I was and what we were talking about, the press and my fans would know my plans before Jenna did. That didn't sit well with me, especially because Jenna hadn't ever been romanced properly before.

"I don't like how we left it today." Understatement of the decade. "She might be…" Nope I didn't want to say the words. Might jinx it somehow. I wanted Jenna to be pregnant. I wanted her to be tied to me forever.

Carter raised his eyebrow.

"She just lost an important person in her life. She needs time to deal with that."

Carter caught the handle of his carry-on even as his face morphed into disappointment. "Seems like more of an excuse you're throwing out there, Ace."

I narrowed my eyes and crossed my arms over my chest. "What are you saying?"

"Think about what you did after Da—Laurence died. You broke stuff. As much of it as you could."

"So?"

"You really think Jenna feels any different than you did? She's hurting and has a right to be. Those comments going 'round are harsh."

"She wants to get back to her shop."

"Does she? Or does she not know how to handle all the emotion from the media shitstorm and is looking to you for support? Except because she cares about you, she's also trying to distance herself so that you can make the smartest move for your career. At least I'd guess that based on the few of your phone conversations I've overheard since this story broke." He squinted at me, tugging at his lip. "I bet you're telling her you have to go out and tour?"

I rubbed the back of my neck. "I do. I have a series of shows starting next week."

Carter made a disgusted sound low in his throat. "Is that what Jenna needs? Space from you?"

I drew myself up, tall as I could. "I made commitments to my men, Carter."

He laid his hand on my shoulder, a heavy weight of responsibility I couldn't shrug off. "You got a gal that needs you more right now, Camden."

CHAPTER TWENTY-NINE | Jenna

He'd said his fans didn't want him with me. I waited for him to leave before I opened my laptop—something I'd avoided for days.

My mouth fell open and my eyes watered at the horrendous comments people made.

They didn't just want him to stop seeing me. They said they'd stop buying his records, going to his concerts if he didn't cut me loose.

I slammed the laptop lid shut and began to pace.

This was bad.

So bad.

My shoulders slumped as I wrapped my arms around my waist.

I glanced around Cam's house. I'd felt safe here. Happy as I could ever be.

But each day I did so, each day I settled into the protective nest Cam built me, he came closer to losing his livelihood.

I sucked in a breath. I needed to think. I needed space. *We* needed space.

I called Kate. "Can you lend me your car?"

"Um, sure. Where are you going?"

"Home."

I didn't know where that was. Seattle maybe.

"I don't know, Jenna. I mean, I don't mind you borrowing

my car, but I get the sense from your voice Cam's going to be mad at me."

"I just realized how bad the situation here is, Kate." I bit the knuckle on my free hand to keep the sobs inside, where they belonged. That wasn't the worst of it, but I couldn't get out those other words. The ones that broke my heart.

Silence pervaded the space between us. Considering her loyalties and her options, no doubt. "Why don't you let me drive you somewhere?"

The best I could hope for right now. Fine. "Take me to my place? Please."

Kate pulled up in her car a few minutes later with a scowl, wearing a dark tank top and cutoffs, her thick mass of ringlets tied up in a messy bun. I chucked my suitcase in the trunk and settled into the seat next to her, feeling formal and frumpy.

"I won't have the shop open this week," I told her when I climbed in. "You'll still get paid, but I need to spend time with my family." A total lie, but I didn't want Kate to worry about her income. She'd found a cute little apartment not too far from downtown that she wanted to rent. Getting out from under the constant supervision of her family meant a level of freedom she deserved—one I'd help facilitate. Every woman needed to find her own feet.

Once she dropped me off, I shot out of the car and bolted into the building past the few loitering paparazzi, who clearly weren't expecting me. I fell through the door to my apartment and chucked my suitcase in the corner. Then I curled up on my bed.

I turned off my phone. When the shadows lengthened, I

finally rose and changed into my oldest sweats. I pulled my hair up into a tight braid and pulled a beanie over the mass, grabbed my phone and shoved it into the hoodie's pocket.

I went to the shop.

The low nighttime lights were on. I paused out front, feeling furtive and tentative.

Finally, I opened the door and walked in, inhaling the scents of raw wood and varnish. I shut and locked the door behind me.

Then I headed back to the workshop where I lost myself in the new project I'd been paid a lot of money to complete. Here, at least, I could stop thinking about whether Cam loved me, if he wanted the baby we might have created. How to change my media image and make Cam's fans like me.

Nothing came except bleary-eyed fatigue.

When my eyes refused to focus, I closed them and laid my folded hands on the table, wishing I'd made better choices somewhere along the line. Choices that meant Pop-pop was alive, my father didn't hate me, and Cam wanted me as his lover and partner.

Raised voices woke me. I sat up in a rush, wincing as sharp pain slashed down my neck and into my shoulders.

What was going on? The voices seemed louder.

I stood, grabbing Gerald, my bat, and peeking around the corner just as Kate slammed the door on the raised voices of what had to be probably twenty or more reporters outside the door.

She turned the lock with a grunt and yanked down the twill skirt that had bunched around her thighs while she wrestled with the door.

"Good. You are here."

"What's going on?"

Kate studied me. "You look like crap."

I shrugged. "Feel like it. I spent most of the night working on the new guitar."

"So…you haven't checked the news?" she asked, her voice hesitant.

I shook my head even as I clutched the bat tighter to my chest. My heart slammed against it, causing me to wince.

"What happened now?" I asked.

Kate bit her lip. She looked from the floor to me and back again. "I don't know how to tell you this, so I'm just going to say it. Ben was hit by a car late last night."

I fell against the wall. "What?"

Kate pulled her phone from her purse and fiddled with the settings. She handed it to me, and I stared at the headline: *Hit-and-run suspect in his own hit-and-run.*

I closed my eyes. "Oh, shit."

"It's actually a lot worse in the article."

I scanned it, my heart thrumming hard as my stomach dropped away. Ben was released yesterday from the hospital, only to be readmitted late last night after he was hit not far from his parents' house…or mine, for that matter. His parents' house sat around the corner from my parents', less than a quarter of a mile.

"Jen…I hate to ask you this…but, do you have any kind of an alibi?"

My stomach dropped further as I shook my head.

"I was here. All night. And, as you know, I don't currently have a car."

"You didn't call anyone? There's no way to prove that, right?"

I shook my head again as I sucked in a breath. "They think… people think I did that?"

Kate closed her eyes and tilted her head back. "You're a person of interest, thanks to the shit Ben's pulled against you, but I have no idea if the police think you smashed him with a car." She sighed. "Cam's out of his mind with worry and the press is really hounding him hard."

I twisted my hands together, faster and harder than before. "He thinks…he thinks I did that?"

Kate opened her eyes but they were dark. The skin around them pulled tight. "I don't know, but, Jen…I'd suggest you get a lawyer. Pronto."

"Where's Cam?" I asked, wishing I'd stayed yesterday. Wishing he was holding me.

Kate's face crumpled—as if this, more than anything else hurt her to say. "He's at a meeting with his label. The executives flew in this morning, after the news broke about Ben."

"He called you to check on me."

She nodded.

I pressed a hand to my stomach. "They—the executives—want Cam to stop seeing me. To publicly denounce me. Because of the bad press."

Kate cleared her throat as tears pooled in her eyes. The tip of her nose turned bright red as she struggled to control her trembling chin.

"That's what they want. They said they'd blacklist him not just from their label but from the entire industry if he doesn't."

——————— ★ ———————

I called my lawyer after Kate's comments. She met me at my shop and drove me to the police station—since I still didn't have a car. There, I spent the next few hours being interrogated about my whereabouts last night. After hours upon hours and re-hashing my relationship with Ben, his visits to my shop and the subsequent death of my grandfather, my lawyer requested a break.

I cradled a Styrofoam cup of thick black sludge, also known as coffee, in my hands. I closed my tired eyes, wincing as my lids scraped against the bloodshot mess.

"This is ridiculous," Karen, my lawyer, griped. "I don't know why we're still here. You can't tell them anything, but that one cop wants you to be the driver that hit Ben. It has to be the location they've keyed in on." She scowled. "They *know* you don't have a car. They *know* you left your apartment on foot, thanks to the cameras in the lobby and the closed-circuit surveillance cameras on Sixth Street."

I lifted my head, my mouth dropping open. "We have cameras in the shop. At both doors, in the front room and in the workshop where I spent the night."

Karen scowled even as her eyes began to dance. "You're just mentioning this now?" she grumbled but her lips twisted upward.

"I just remembered them now," I said on a sigh. "I've been a bit distracted, seeing as how I was accused of a felony and my boyfriend's decided to dump me to save his career."

Not that I knew what Cam planned to do—he hadn't contacted me today. Rather, I hadn't heard from him in the brief time I had between calling Karen Whitby and arriving at the police station, when my phone died. Not that I would have taken it out of my purse anyway. Not with all the questions thrown at me the past few hours.

"What's the name of the company that handles your security?" Karen asked.

She wrote it down and then looked up the number on her phone. Within two minutes, she had the company's manager on the line, and he promised to pull all the video from our shop and send it to both Karen and the detective assigned to Ben's hit-and-run.

I waited on that hard chair for another hour before the police dismissed me.

As I walked out, free to go, two officers tugged my father into the station, his hands cuffed behind his back. My mother trailed behind him, face wet with tears.

I rushed toward him. "What's going on?"

I laid my hand on my dad's chest.

"I did it for you, baby girl," he said on a sigh. He dropped his head forward so I could no longer see his haggard face.

"That's enough, David," my mother said, her voice sharp. She looked to the police on either side of my father. "Please take him back. I'd like to speak to my daughter."

The officers hustled my father down the hallway, even as he struggled and continued to yell.

"That's why they held you," Karen muttered. "They were trying to flush him out. Get him to come here to defend you." She shook her head, but her eyes gleamed with new respect when they lifted toward the closed door that led to the interrogation rooms where I'd spent most of the day.

Mom turned toward me, her shoulders stooped with fatigue. "None of this is on you, Jenna. Your father made his choices, just as Ben made his."

"What—what's going on?" I asked, sounding as small and scared as I felt.

"Your dad tried to kill that boy," my mother whispered, her eyes pooling with tears. "I-I didn't want him to say so in front of the police." She pressed her lips together until she had better control of her voice. "I can't believe this. Any of it. But the Suburban shows the damage. I expect the police will collect enough samples off the front to build a case against your father. And...and he'll go to jail."

"Dad?" I asked, swallowing hard.

Mom placed her hands on my shoulders. "He's not handled his father's death well. I'm... I think he's quite lost his mind."

I stared at her, horror washing over me in a thick, cold wave. Mom cupped my chin and tried to smile.

"What's going to happen to him?" I asked. I clenched my jaw together to keep my teeth from chattering.

Mom pursed her lips. "I don't know. Maybe..." Her voice broke. "Maybe this will be the wake-up call he needs to realize he's acting as badly, if not worse, than Ben has."

"Mom..." I stared at her for a long moment. "What can I do?"

She smoothed my hair with shaky hands. "Help me find a good lawyer."

Karen stepped forward. "I can suggest the names of a colleague if you need one. And I'll stay here with you until he arrives."

Mom smiled but it was filled with sadness. "Thank you."

Karen pulled out her phone again and dialed a number. Within seconds, she was talking to a man named Vincent.

Mom touched my cheek once more. "I'm serious, Jen. None of this is your fault."

I stared at her, sure she must be wrong.

"I should go sit with your father," Mom said with a sigh. "What are you going to do? Where's Cam?"

I dropped my gaze, not wanting to add to her pain. "He had a show tonight. I'm sure he's there preparing."

Karen walked back over, already talking to my mother. I broke in to wish them goodbye before all but running from the police station.

I trudged down the street, ignoring all the other pedestrians. Within moments I began to sweat, but I continued, needing to move, trying to outpace the anger and desolation building within me. My father…Ben…Cam…the label…the press… The huge cauldron of problems ate at me as I tried to breathe through the issues, find a solution.

Three miles later, my body quivered with the need for water but no solutions came. I pushed into the air-conditioned coolness of my building's lobby, ignoring the questions yelled at me by the reporters who seemed to camp out here now.

Hurrying down my hallway from the elevator, I opened my front door and dropped my purse. I pulled out my phone and plugged it in, hoping for a message from Cam. There were multiple from my brothers and even my mom and Kate. Cam's one text was terse: *In meetings. Need to talk to you.*

I sucked in a breath and stared at those words. Written almost six hours ago now. I glanced up, taking in my kitchen, living room, the dark windows beyond where the city glowed.

They said they'd blacklist him not just from their label but from the entire industry if he doesn't.

Cam would be at his show now.

I picked up my keys, grabbed my suitcase, and threw it on the bed. Only to sit next to it, realizing I didn't know where to go. Or what to do next.

They said they'd blacklist him not just from their label but from the entire industry if he doesn't.

Cam would lose not just his position as a country music star, he'd have to disband his crew—the men he'd fought with all those years ago, who trusted him to provide them with a livelihood. I knew Cam well enough that he'd want to remain loyal, especially if I were pregnant.

I placed my hand over my stomach, hoping, wishing, I was. But, at the same time, my life grew more complicated by the hour.

The best thing I could do for Cam, for his family, for Chuck and even my parents, was leave.

I started to laugh. The hysterical, ugly, broken laugh that I'd heard once before—during my "psychotic break."

I forced my mouth shut and stiffened my spine.

Time to leave. Yes, leaving, finding something I could focus my attention, my energy on…that was smart. I packed quickly, trying to ignore my shaking hands.

I made phone calls as I packed, swallowing down the bitter pill of regret that once again, my life was not mine to lead.

"No time like the present for a little road trip!" I sing-songed into the empty, quiet space just before I began to tremble from the weight of the terrible choice I'd been forced to make.

CHAPTER THIRTY | Cam

I finished my set and bowed off the stage. Time for my encore. I rolled my head, trying to ease the tension that built there as the day progressed. I really needed to talk to Jenna.

Much as I wanted to be there with her, for her, my label made that impossible. Which left me only one choice.

I stepped back on the stage to a great cheer. I smiled, my heart warming at the adulation. Time to see where the fans' loyalty lay.

I glanced over at Chuck and Erika as the roadie handed me my guitar, my nerves making my guts turn molten. Man, I hoped I'd made the right decision because both their paychecks—and many others—depended on me to do right.

I stepped up to the mic. Time to man up.

"You like my guitar?" I asked.

The crowd roared.

"Couldn't quite tell if you approved."

The volume went up a lot of decibels. I waited for the noise to die down.

"My gal Jenna Olsen made it for me."

The yelling all but stopped. My stomach cramped, but I maintained my smile as I began to stroke out a few chords to a well-loved song.

"From all the posts on social media, I get the sense some of y'all don't like Jen all that much."

Some boos filled the room, along with words I'd never say about a woman. I gritted my teeth.

"And that's too bad. She's not only an amazing artisan, she's also one of the best people I've ever met."

No more boos but the crowd remained stubbornly silent.

"Had a meeting with my record label today," I said, keeping it conversational. "They told me if I kept seeing Jenna, they'd cut me loose. Make sure I never made music again."

This time the crowd grumbled, some gasped. Others hissed.

"But, see here. I didn't serve my country for years to be told what I can and cannot do in my free time."

People shifted their feet. I picked up the pace of my tune and the band behind me joined in.

"I happen to love Jenna. She's what makes me happier than I've ever been. So, I told the record label they can keep their fancy contract, fancy tour, and fancy bus. I'd rather sit on a porch swing with my gal, drinking sweet tea as we watch our tots in the yard than kowtow to a bunch of suits." I stopped playing as did the band behind me. "So, I guess, I'm announcing my retirement. Y'all have been great. Thanks for supporting me in the past. Too bad we had to end it here."

I slid my guitar down, my hand still around the neck as I walked off the stage, my footfalls loud in the stunned silence.

Chuck kept his arms crossed, but a hint of a smile played around his mouth. "Best speech you ever gave, chief."

"Too bad Jenna couldn't be here to hear it delivered in

person." I laid my guitar in its case, snapped the locks and picked up the handle. "Can you drive me over to her place now? I have a hankering to kiss her pretty lips."

Chuck's smile bloomed. "Sure hope I find a nice lady I'm that in love with someday. Seems a pretty good place to be."

"Will be. Once I hold her in my arms."

———— ★ ————

I tossed Chuck my truck keys as I pulled out my phone. Jenna didn't pick up her phone when I called her again.

A twinge hit my loosening neck muscles. Jenna always answered her phone.

I called Katie Rose.

"You heard from Jenna?" I asked as soon as she picked up.

"Not since she and her lawyer headed to the police station."

"What? When was that?"

"Y-you didn't know about that?" Katie Rose stammered.

"Hell, no. I got no idea what you're talking about."

"Umm…"

"Spit it out. I'm on my way over to her place now, and I don't know what I'll be walking into."

"You're going to be so mad at me," Katie murmured on a hiccup.

Probably I was. I sighed, running my hand through the short hairs on the back of my neck. "Lay it on me."

She did. I tried to stay calm and breathe through her recitation, but I couldn't help cursing a time or two. Damn Jenna's father for acting so rash and damn Ben, too. These men were mucking up my selfless gesture.

Could have told her you loved her when you had the chance, one of the voices in my head whispered. I tried to ignore it.

Katie Rose said, the first bit of panic threading through her voice, "You haven't seen her all day? She was upset earlier, like really."

"Like, how really?" Now the panic began to seep into my chest.

"I don't know. She shut me down. Said she was closing the shop next week—"

"And you're just telling me this *now*?"

"Well, yeah. I mean. I didn't think it was weird. Now I'm…I'm scared."

Not as terrified as me. My chest ached and my guts iced, just like they used to before a serious firefight.

Shit.

Why hadn't I thought about how deep the loss of her grandfather immediately followed by her father would cut her?

I'd told her I was there for her. But when she needed me most, I wasn't.

Last night I thought she needed the space, but I started today in meetings that didn't let out until I was already late for sound check at The Moody Theater. I hoped I'd been smart to lay my relationship with Jenna on the line during my first—and likely last—Austin City Limits performance.

Time would tell if my fans stuck by me or were swayed by Ben's craziness and tabloid headlines. Right now, I couldn't worry about that because all my head space was taken up with worry about my gal.

Why hadn't I pressed harder after the funeral? Her eyes held such desolation.

Because pushing her then meant accepting her broken bits, helping her find a way to heal them. She'd warned me. From the beginning, that first dinner together, she attempted to explain. I just didn't want to see…didn't *want* that kind of responsibility again.

"Is Mitch with Jenna?" I asked Chuck as we pulled onto her street.

"No. She told him to go home a couple of hours ago."

I cursed and Chuck dipped his head, lips pressed together in a grim line.

I tore into the building, probably looking at least half-crazed. I beat on her door until my hand throbbed, but she didn't answer.

I took the stairs two at a time and my leg burned even more than my hand when I returned to the lobby.

"You seen Jenna?" I asked the concierge.

"I'm sorry, Mr. Grace. Ms. Olsen left a little while ago."

"Did she leave a message? *Anything?*"

Chuck started and turned to stare at me, mouth gaping. Yeah, that bad, my friend.

The younger man blinked, his mouth twisting as he clutched at his papers. "No, sir. She didn't. She just said she wouldn't be back for a while."

"No." The words tore up my throat, ripped from my chest, already leaving a deep, primal, unquenchable ache. I should have told her I loved her. I should have got up and walked out on the label earlier instead of trying to pacify them.

But I didn't. I'd wanted Jenna on *my* terms—with my career

intact and my fans adoring. When I finally had to choose, I waited too long.

And Jenna was gone.

Unsure what else to do, I called Jenna's brother, Jude.

"Have you heard from your sister?"

"No. I assumed she was with you."

"She's not at her place."

"You hear that, Mom? Jen's missing."

I heard a scuffle, a choked sob. Not that I cared. Mrs. Olsen played a part in this, too.

"Micah's calling her now."

We waited in strained silence. "She's not picking up," Jude said.

"She doesn't have a car. It's totaled," I heard Mrs. Olsen say.

"Where could she be?" Micah rumbled in the background. "We'll go out, start looking."

"I'm on it," I said.

"This is my fault," Mrs. Olsen sobbed. "I didn't think. I didn't *think* about how she'd react to her father's actions. I told her today…at the station none of this was her fault… She has to know that."

No, she didn't. Everyone in her life said they cared about her but then slashed her with carelessness—me included. She ran away to Seattle but was forced back here by more cruelty. She buried herself in work, a clear attempt to eliminate the need for relationships, for emotion.

Why was I just seeing this now?

After hanging up the call, I slammed my hands on the clerk's desk.

Damn me nine times over for a complete fool.

He started, but he'd paid attention to my call.

"How did Jenna leave?"

"By courtesy shuttle."

"To the airport or a car dealership?" I asked.

"I don't know. I didn't see anything other than the front of the vehicle and the man's shirt. Ms. Olsen had a suitcase with her."

"She could be anywhere," Chuck muttered.

I headed toward the door, intent to get out there, do something. Find my gal before...

"What are you doing?" Chuck grunted, finally catching up.

I ignored him, turning in a circle on the busy downtown street instead. I headed back toward the parking lot, planning to get in my truck and...do something. Where would she go? Seattle. To Nessa and Abbi. Seemed likely. Chuck scrambled around people, cursing me in more creative speech than I'd heard even in the military.

I glared at my phone, willing Jenna to call me, to let me know where she was, how she was. I stumbled to a stop. "Find a goddamn phone." I pulled up the application on my phone.

The benefit of spending days together was I'd learned her passwords. I tried the first and it failed. Without stopping to think, I slammed my fist straight into the side of the building in front of me, barely registering the pain in my knuckles and whole hand.

After thinking for a moment, I typed in a second.

Fail.

I sucked in a breath and blinked back the tears threatening to fall from my eyes. "I can't lose you, sugar. You're my everything."

Of course. I typed in the first two words of the song I'd sung for her that first night at her guitar shop, and then the 00 she put at the end of every password I'd ever seen her use.

My breath trickled out slow, just this side of a sob. She'd turned me into a blubbery fool, and I couldn't care less if people thought I was insane. I was crazy about that crazy girl I'd managed to let slip away.

I clicked on the locate button and jumped up with a fist bump, landing with a hiss and tucking my injured hand into my armpit.

"Chuck, can you find me some ice? I need to get to Luckenbach. Now."

Chuck hurried off, returning as I hitched myself into the driver's seat of my truck. "Thanks, man. I'm pretty sure I broke it."

"Better get it looked at, then."

"After Jenna's safe."

He walked around toward the other side of the vehicle and opened the door while I settled in and turned on the ignition with my one good hand.

"What are you doing?" I asked.

"Coming with you since you won't let me drive. To guard you. You know, what you *pay* me to do."

"Not this time." Chuck glared, hauling himself upward. "No, Chuck. Follow in another car if you need to but no way. Close the door. I have a lot of speeding to do."

"Cam, I can't let you..."

"Shut the goddamn door!" I yelled, revving the engine.

Chuck glared but did as I said. He jumped back with a curse as I peeled from the spot.

CHAPTER THIRTY-ONE | Jenna

I had no plan, just the knowledge I needed to leave before I pulled Cam and the rest of my family down any further.

Needing a distraction, I turned on the car stereo and out blared an Old 97s song, one of Cam's favorite bands. How unfair that the first song the Bluetooth picked up was *that* one. I whimpered as the lyrics to "Streets of Where I'm From."

"Hearts paving streets. Country music is the *best* at break-up songs."

I fumbled with the buttons until Eminem's "The Monster" roared from the speakers.

"I really love you, Camden Grace. I wanted to be happy." I gripped the wheel harder and I screamed it again, then again, until my throat raged raw. Still I screamed.

That's when I had to pull over. Out in the middle of nowhere with nothing but prairie and too much night pressing in, pressing down on me.

I hated the dark. I leaned my head back against the seat and frowned up at my sunroof, trying to make out a star through the thick blanket of clouds.

Rain, maybe a thunderstorm. And I was out in it. Alone.

Because Cam didn't love me. Not enough to tell his label to take a hike. Not enough to even call me today to check in.

I blinked back the tears.

"All right. Now's not the time to throw that pity party."

Actually, it totally was. I hated to drive in storms. Hated the way the thunder boomed like a gun.

I glanced over at my pills. Twenty-three of each. I could dump them in my mouth, take them all right now and end my misery.

I picked up the bottles. My hands shook with longing—with the need to just *do* it—put myself out of this miserable loop.

Cam's words to me last month flowed through my mind, over my skin, heating me from the inside as my skin contracted with the shiver of rejection. "Skin to skin with you is better than anything I've ever felt. Better than any heaven could be." He'd kissed me so softly, and I'd believed him.

I set the pills down and covered my belly with my palm. Until my body betrayed my deepest wish, I wouldn't put the tiny sliver of hope at risk.

"We're in this together, baby," I said, trying not to choke on the words Cam had said to me so many times.

Probably nothing was there, but I needed the reason to keep driving, keep breathing. Just keep going.

I pulled back onto the highway, finally paying attention to where I was. Not too far from Luckenbach. I snorted, cutting off the next round of hysterical giggles that threatened to burst forth. Stupid of me to fall so hard for a country singer. Every city or town in the humongous state was listed in some country song— and had to do with a lost love or broken-down pickups.

"Don't you die on me, car." I tightened my hands on the wheel of the brand-new sedan. "You're not a truck, the rainstorm hasn't hit yet, so this isn't an actual reenactment, got it?"

Lightning flashed, thunder rolled, and I realized, just like that Garth Brooks song, fate still hated my guts.

I checked into a motel, mainly for the novelty. I'd never stayed in a tiny place like this. It was the first option I'd come to with a vacancy sign and the lightning struck so close to my car I freaked out and ended up in the parking lot before I had time to blink.

Now that I was settled into my room, showered and still so damn achy from the long interrogation today, I settled a notepad on my lap and chewed on a pen cap.

I had plenty of money, thanks to Pop-pop leaving me the shop. If I sold my chic condo, I'd turn a tidy profit.

I picked up my phone and dialed Nes's number.

"I can't go back to Austin. That town's jinxed for me. Can I…"

"Jump the first plane and get your ass here *now*. We've got the extra space, and you know I want you here with me. Who else am I going to have ramen with?"

Tears pooled in my eyes. Nes said what I needed to hear.

Lightning slashed across the sky and Nes's voice grew tinny.

"I didn't catch that, Nes."

"…when you're here…Dane said…" Too much static.

The ache in my heart seemed to expand. I wanted that—what Nes and Dane had. What Abbi and Clay built. The loving family Kai created with Evie. The ache turned into a searing pain that ripped through my stomach.

"No," I moaned.

"What's wrong?" Nessa's words were clear and scared.

"Stomach. Ouch!" I sat up with a gush of fluid wetting my

legs. No. No! Blood. Everywhere.

"Nessa. I'm bleeding."

"Where? How?"

"I think… I must be miscarrying." The last word was a keening wail that Nessa matched with a shriek of my name.

I dropped my phone to the bed, holding my stomach as the next deep, terrible ache bit into me.

"No," I moaned. "No."

"Jenna!" Nessa's scream filled the room and my head, but I couldn't do more than sob and gasp as the last tiny dream, my tiny tendril of hope, slipped from my body.

Lightning flashed, thunder drummed closer than before. I flinched, moaning as the sharp, stabbing ache intensified.

Another thud. Wait. Not thunder. A fist to the door. Like Ben all those weeks ago. But Ben was in the hospital again. The detective today told me so.

Another round of pounding, followed by curses.

No one knew where I was.

I wanted Cam. I needed him *right now*.

Nessa screamed my name again. She sobbed for me to pick up, but I simply grunted as the next wave of agony ripped through my abdomen.

The pounding on the door stopped. I gasped for breath as the tears threatened to choke me. My arms tightened around my waist as I pulled my knees up even tighter to my chest.

"Dane's calling 9-1-1, Jen. Can you hear me? Talk to me. Please," she begged, nearly as hysterical as I was.

"Someone's trying to break into my room," I whispered.

"What the hell, girl! Can't you have one crisis at a time!" Nessa's shriek was drowned out by the crashing wood of the frame. Nessa's scream was louder than mine because the pain cut mine off mid-holler.

Cam tripped into the room, cradling his right hand to his heaving chest. His damp hair stuck up in crazy whorls. His eyes roamed wild around the room before settling on me.

"What have you done to yourself?" he whispered, eyes wide with disbelief.

"I didn't do this on purpose."

He picked me up, grunting as I jostled into his arms. I writhed as another stabbing pain lanced through my middle. "Stopping wiggling, sugar. My hand's broke and hurts like the devil. My shoulder's not much better since I used it on the door."

"Put me down. Stop it, Camden! I can't go anywhere with you."

"Cam's there?" Nessa's voice blared through the speaker. "I can't keep up with the drama." She sounded exhausted, maybe winded.

"I don't want to go with him!" I yelled at the phone. "Don't let him take me!"

"How am I supposed to stop him?" Nes yelled back. "I'm in Seattle!"

"We're going to the hospital, you loon. You're obviously hemorrhaging."

He hoisted me into his truck, grunting either because of his hand or his calf.

Another spasm hit and I bit my lip, whimpering. "I'll mess up your truck."

"Christ and all the saints, woman! I don't care about the

upholstery. I care about *you*."

The pain that hit this time caused lights to flash in front of my eyes and my ears to ring.

I must have passed out because next thing I knew I was in a hospital bed, two IVs in my arm. I turned my aching head to see Cam sitting beside the bed, his dark head bowed and his right hand splinted and wrapped in gauze.

He lifted his head and stared at me, his face haggard and his eyes red.

"Before you say one damn thing, hear me: I love you, Jenna Marie Olsen. I. Love. You."

I bit my lip. "I lost the baby."

Cam shook his head, his eyes never leaving mine. "Didn't."

I scowled. "I hemorrhaged." I shifted my legs. "I still have blood on my thighs."

"True, but you had a cyst pop. You didn't lose the baby." He closed those beautiful eyes, his lashes brushing his cheek. "You were never pregnant. And that's a damn shame."

"I wasn't pregnant?" That loss hit me as hard as the thought of miscarrying.

Cam shook his head. "Why am I so sad over a baby we never even created?" He opened his eyes and stared hard at me. "I want that with you. Babies. The ring, wedding, whole white-and-lace enchilada."

"Wait." My breathing escalated. "I'm still on the not-pregnant-but-hemorrhaging part."

His lip flipped up for a millisecond. "Only you, sugar. Damn good thing I'm so good in pressure situations. Because a lifetime with you would kill an average man. In his grave by forty."

"You love me. I'm not pregnant. I hemorrhaged. You broke your hand."

Cam looked down at his bandaged wrist. "Yep. Hurts like a son of a gun."

"So, I'm not the only one who had trauma tonight?"

"You're almost always the only one with trauma. And I love you."

I wrinkled my nose. "Neither of us is broken?"

Cam shook his head. "Not too bad, anyway."

"And you love me?"

He nodded.

"Anything else to add to that?"

"Yep. I laid out the issue to my fans at the ACL performance last night. Told 'em I planned to retire completely if they didn't accept us, together."

"Cam—"

"I'll show you the clip later. It's got over five million views on YouTube. Not bad for less than four hours."

"Cam, you can't give up your career. I don't want you to do that."

He leaned in again, his fingertips lingering on my cheek. "I don't have to. My fans have been snatching up songs, albums, merch, you name it. I'm hotter than I was yesterday, mainly thanks to you."

"Me?"

Maybe I was still dehydrated or low on blood or whatever. But I was struggling to keep up with Cam's revelations.

"Yes, you. My fans love how much I love you—what I'm willing to give up for you. And they think you make one helluva guitar."

"Um."

"But they're also willing to forgive now that the rest of Ben's crazy came out. Jesus, Jenna. You have to keep me in the loop."

"What are you talking about?" I whispered.

"Right. It's been all over the news the past couple of hours. Ben was walking toward your parents' house just as your dad was driving home. Ben had a gun."

I nodded. The police had told us before he had a concealed-carry permit.

"Anyway, Ben and your dad got in an argument. Ben shot at the car or your dad—it's unclear—and your dad mowed Ben down. Stopped the vehicle soon as he hit him, took his gun, and called the cops."

"Wow." I stared up at Cam, stunned. "What does that mean?"

"Means your dad isn't going to be charged with attempted murder. It was clearly self-defense. And Ben is being charged with hitting your Pop-pop with his car and with assault with a deadly weapon. He's going to jail, sugar. For a long time."

"Really?" I asked. "But…I don't understand. Why did they hold me all day, then?"

"Because your father didn't stick around to wait for the ambulance. Based on Ben's injuries, they assumed a hit-and-run. But Ben's story matched your father's."

I did my best to wrap my head around all this new information. "Ben admitted it?"

Cam nodded.

"And Dad's not in trouble?" I asked.

Cam hesitated. "Not as much trouble, anyway. Him leaving's a sticking point with the police."

I swallowed, trying to process the situation. "What did my dad mean, he did it for me?"

Cam's face contorted with rage. "Seems like Ben was still planning something nasty."

"He wanted to kill me," I said on a sigh.

"Yeah."

"What caused him to lose it like that?" I asked.

Cam pressed his lips together. "Don't know. Not really. Seems like his getting cut from the ballclub and his wife cheating with another player—the star player—didn't sit too well. Maybe you were just the target of all that rage."

"That's…" Words failed me because this whole situation was *messed up*. "Shit on sugar toast."

Cam cracked a smile at my muttered words. "Enough about him. Your dad's got some more legal stuff to work through, but I've got my people on it now, too. And just so we're clear: I plan to marry you, Jenna Marie. Soon's I can. I need to take care of you, see."

My mouth fell open. "What? But you said…" I slammed my lips together. "I'm not a good bet."

Cam chuckled. "Sugar, you are many, *many* things, and a good bet has never been one of them. And still I love you. So much I couldn't breathe when you disappeared on me." He tilted his head forward and stared straight into my eyes. "Don't pull that stunt again."

"But your label…"

"Doesn't get to tell me what to do. And while I can still make music without a label contract, there's only one you. Now, I'll tell you one more time. I love you, Jenna. Got anything to say back?"

I stared into his eyes for a long minute. "I love you, Camden Grace."

This time, his smile lit up his eyes. "'Bout time you got with the show." He gestured to my left hand. "Ring's already on and I posted pictures to Instagram and Facebook. The world gave us their blessing. And that was *before* the whole story with Ben came out."

I narrowed my eyes. "Were you planning to actually ask me?"

"I did ask you. And you said yes."

"Was I drugged?"

"Heavily," he said in a cheerful voice.

"Cam. I cannot deal with joking. I'm in a hospital bed. Again."

He sat up straight. "All right. I didn't ask you yet. But I will, and I plan to do it properly." His fingers shook as he touched the ring. "I bought this ring weeks ago." His voice softened to a near-whisper.

Galloping cane toads. This man.

"You did?" I stuttered.

"Before I met you in Seattle."

I was surprised the machines didn't start beeping a warning because my heart melted into goo.

"I put the ring on your finger to remind us both of perma-nence. Of accepting each other's best and worst. You're grieving and I… I love you. So damn much you make my teeth ache and my guts crawl. I love you so much I can't think of anything but keeping you happy and safe. I love you, sugar, because you're kind and thoughtful, sensitive and hardworking. I love you because you always think about my feelings first."

He paused for breath. "I didn't want you to make that choice, Cam." I raised a shaky hand and laid it against his cheek. "I never wanted you to be forced into something. Not because of me."

He pressed a kiss to my palm before he clasped it in his good one, lowering both our hands to the bed.

"I want to marry you and raise some hell-raising, crazy kids with you. Many as you want. I want to see your hands nicked and scarred from your work. I want to hold you all night, every night. I want to kiss you at five a.m. and five p.m. I just plain need you much as I need air. Jenna, will you marry me?"

I nodded because the words wouldn't come. Then I launched myself at him, wrapping my arms around his shoulders with a gasp as the tears streamed down my face.

"You sure I didn't miscarry?" I said into his shoulder.

"I'm sure. The doctor said you're just fine. Healthy as a horse and ten times as pretty."

"I love you, Cam. I…I thought the best thing I could do was get out of your life, and that hurt."

He rocked me back and forth. "I need to do a better job showing you that you don't need to worry." He dropped a kiss on my forehead. "You going to look at your ring?"

"Later." I pressed my lips to his. Cam growled, his tongue

stroking mine in long, leisurely swipes that said we had all day, all year—a lifetime.

I answered him, clung to him. Loved him.

Until the nurse came into the room and yelped, "What do you think you're doing?"

CHAPTER THIRTY-TWO | Cam

I pulled back just enough to look in Jenna's red, puffy, luminous eyes. "Kissing my bride-to-be."

"Oh," the nurse whispered, her voice all breathy. "That's so sweet." She turned to Jenna, and as she checked Jenna's vitals, the nurse leaned in closer to whisper, "What he did for you was real romantic."

"I haven't seen it," Jenna whispered back.

"If I were you, I'd keep it on repeat," the nurse said, her cheeks staining bright red as she peeked at me.

I leaned back and winked at the petite brunette. I chuckled when Jenna's grip tightened. Like I was ever going to get anything better from another gal. Nope, this one here—even as sickly as she was with that rat's nest hair—was my everything.

I settled into the chair and let Jenna chat with her nurse. She had a lot of questions, some of which the nurse couldn't answer. That was all right. I understood her prognosis—best as a non-medical person could, I expect.

Her mama would be here soon to talk it all over, and we'd visit with Jenna's dad once she was able to travel.

"Nessa's called at least five hundred times."

"Okay," Jenna said.

"She's happy you agreed to marry me. Said it should cut back on the drama."

Jenna settled back into her pillows.

"I talked to my manager. We're going to take a trip up to Seattle soon as you're ready. I'll have to do the shows he's lined up. That'll take us through the fall. But then we're going to do something nice and relaxing. Just us. And I talked to Katie Rose. She's already put it on your schedule in red indelible marker."

"You two okay?" Jenna asked with a yawn. "How's she taking her dad's changed role?"

"We're working on it. Just like you and I need to work on some details."

Jenna smiled—that bright, white, All-American cheerleader grin I'd missed. "Promise?"

"Yep."

I cupped her hand gently, my thumb resting on her pulse, steadying my own heart rate as I ticked off each beat of hers.

I loved the comfort of her skin against mine. Of us, taking on the world.

Of knowing, this time, I'd chosen a woman who would love me as I loved her: with all my heart and every bit of my broken, piecemeal soul.

"I'm still a lava-monster mess, Cam."

"So am I. A right hot one that almost lost you forever because of it. Not a lesson I'll forget. Ever."

"Because you love me."

"I do." I bent down to press my lips to hers again.

"So, we'll be okay."

"We will."

I clasped her hand tighter in mine, admiring the sparkle of the large diamond I'd shoved unceremoniously on her finger earlier. No way I wasn't getting all the information I could from the hospital staff and only way to do that was as her fiancé. Good thing I'd taken to carrying the damn thing with me.

I rubbed my fingers over her knuckles, loving her white, rough hands. I turned her palm over and pressed a kiss there.

I'd propose again—with tons of romance to knock Jenna on her butt. I'd hold her and help her, just as I wanted, not as I'd fought with myself to do before. I kissed her soft, red lips before staring into her blue eyes.

"We'll be okay," I murmured. "That I can promise you."

ACKNOWLEDGEMENTS

Daqri Bernardo of Covers by Combs created the delightful cover for this book and this series. You made something special, Daqri, and I thank you!

Thank you, Sarah Allan, for your military expertise as well as your detailed comments in the manuscript. I really enjoy working with you.

To Deborah Nemeth, thank you for helping me take this manuscript from a decent premise to a novel I'm proud to have written.

Thanks to Charity Chimni for her time and amazing proofreading skills.

And, as always, to Chris. You help me in so many ways. Thank you for all that you do (and for putting up with my crazy all these years).

ABOUT THE AUTHOR

With a degree in international marketing and a varied career path that includes content management for a web firm, marketing direction for a high-profile sports agency, and a two-year stint with a renowned literary agency, Alexa Padgett has returned to her first love: writing fiction.

Alexa spent a good part of her youth traveling. From Budapest to Belize, Calgary to Coober Pedy, she soaked in the myriad smells, sounds, and feels of these gorgeous places, wishing she could live in them all—at least for a while. And she does in her books.

She lives in New Mexico with her husband, children, and Great Pyrenees pup, Ash. When not writing, schlepping, or volunteering, she can be found in her tiny kitchen, channeling her inner Barefoot Contessa.

The next page is an excerpt of Broken Rose of Texas, Book 2 of the Austin After Dark series.

CHAPTER ONE | Regan

I glared at the shimmering neon rocket with building trepidation. My body hummed with a restless energy that shimmied through my nerve-endings, making me jumpy.

"You sure about this?" I asked.

I mean, I'd heard of The Blue Bar and wanted to attend a live show here for ages, but the crowded parking lot and long entrance line worried me. So did the clench low in my gut.

That feeling I hadn't been able to shake since my father's message two days earlier. The one I ignored—just like the message before and the message before that.

"You said you wanted to kick back with some great tunes. This is the place to do that in Denver."

I turned my head to study Mindy. Her short, dark ringlets rioted around her head in that sexy, I-just-got-out-of-bed look men adored. Her large hazel eyes popped more than usual, thanks to the smoky shadow, and her glossed lips turned up in happiness.

Mindy deserved happy. I sighed, knowing I was going to end up wishing I'd stayed in the hotel room. Not even the lure of fantastic music could allay the fear that something…something terrible would happen tonight.

We walked in, getting the typical VIP treatment that made me cringe even as it made Mindy preen. Sometimes I wondered why she couldn't be the performer and I the assistant.

But Mindy didn't have the compulsion to lay all her pain out in lyrics, set to throbbing beats. No, that was my way of handling my formative years.

Not sure my form of therapy was healthy, but there you go. And lots of people were willing to pay to hear more about my pre-pop-queen life.

I smiled and posed for about twenty selfies before we made it into the actual bar. A waitress met us and led the way to a nice table stationed off to one side. Yeah, The Blue Bar staff were professionals when it came to the glitterati.

I hated my tiny space in the group.

But I did want to see the act. Not an easy feat—going to live shows. I nodded to Darryl and John, my bodyguards, who stood off to the side but near enough to intervene if necessary.

I would have preferred my guards to sit with me, but they refused. While I loved the guys, they tended to be a bit gruff and standoffish. I wasn't sure if that was because of my age—all twenty-five years of it—or the fact I'd overheard Darryl and John talking about my smokin' hotness. When I called them out on it, they both clammed up and backed off.

I glanced down, as unimpressed as I normally was by myself. Sure, I kept in shape. I liked to do Krav Maga. It gave me a sense of independence, and I spent at least two hours working out in the discipline each day. That didn't count the time I did yoga, which I also loved. But that was for relaxation and focus, not strength and kicking booty.

I understood my features classified me as pretty, but people got caught up in my stardom and forgot I was a person who liked to veg out in sweats and watch movies, same as the next gal. Maybe more so because it was such a rare occurrence anymore.

Not that my short jean skirt and scuffed, ten-year-old cowboy boots screamed sexy, but I did like looking nice. For myself, sure, but also because any time I left the security of my hotel room or house, someone was going to take a picture, and it was easier to look put together rather than face the rumors about my impending drug overdose or pregnancy.

I settled into my chair and took in the stage. A rich red light slashed across The Blue Bar's coat of arms at the back, giving the space an eerie, cold feel. The stage was shallower than most of the ones I performed on and raised only a couple feet off the ground.

While I liked the intimacy of the space, I did not like the red lights. Those reminded me of the night my mother died.

Deep breath in, then out. Again, just as I did each day in yoga. Okay, so not the stage on which I wanted to perform, but then, the world considered me a pop princess. Everyone assumed I loved synchronized, heavy beats, not the light instrumental touch and intimate space of tonight's singer-songwriter.

Fact was, I liked both. After this tour ended, I planned to end my relationship with my current label and strike out in a more artistic fashion. Sure, I knew that was a risk. But it was one I felt compelled to take.

That's part of why I was there tonight. I wanted to see Janie Thorpe in action. If we got along as well as I hoped we would in our lunch meeting scheduled in Austin later in the week, I hoped to talk with her about a collaboration for my next EP. If she chose to see me as anything other than the airhead sex-pot so many of my fans regarded me as, anyway. An image my own father helped create.

The waitress waited patiently at my elbow, and I realized she wanted to take my drink order. I flushed, thankful I'd picked up the menu during my zoning out.

"Sad Panda Coffee Stout," I murmured because I just had to try a beer with a name like that. I wasn't much of a beer drinker—drinker at all—so I added, "And a water, please."

The waitress must have already taken Mindy's order because she scurried off.

I blew out a breath.

"Well, I hope tonight's fun," I said.

"Relax, Regan. It will be. I have a good feeling about this."

At least one of us did.

———————— ★ ————————

I was bored and had heard enough to know that Janie Thorpe's studio albums would always be her bestsellers. This was why she played small clubs. I grimaced as she hit another flat note.

I caught him staring at me sometime during Janie's second set. My head and his eyes penetrated my every pore, even from across the room, heating me up and making my skin plump.

Whoa. I'd never had that kind of a reaction, especially from a man's look.

But there was something about him. Sexy, of course, and, well…hmmm. Predatory. Primal. Yeah, that was the right word. His desire was primal, and his face was stamped with sex and sin.

I wanted him to keep looking. Wanted him to touch me.

That freaked me out.

Maybe that's why I paused, beer raised halfway to my mouth, as I gawped like an idiot.

"What are you looking at?" Mindy asked, craning her head. She couldn't see him from her angle, thanks to the people milling between us and his table.

"N-nothing," I managed to stutter. "I just need to use the restroom. Be right back."

I hurried off before Mindy managed to open her mouth. Either John or Darryl would follow—that's just how my life worked, and no, it wasn't all due to my fame.

After using the facilities, I washed my hands and let the cold water run over my wrists, cooling me further. I shut off the tap and looked in the mirror.

I shook my head, thankful for the momentary quiet to calm myself. I dried my hands and opened the door, nodding to Darryl who stood off to the left. I stepped forward, but then immediately darted into a small alcove when a herd of women scuttled past me.

A large hand gripped my waist as one of the women nearly mowed me down, pulling me snug against a muscular chest. I craned my head back to look up into clear gray-blue eyes. A gasp fell from my lips. It was him. He'd been potent across the room, but up close and this personal, my pulse quickened and my body hummed to life.

My reaction baffled me. I wasn't one to take undue risks—I knew the pain and fear that could swiftly come because of them. So why was my body, my freaking heart, so interested in this man?

"Hope you didn't get trampled."

Dear puppies in heaven, the man had an accent. Softly Southern. Combined with that deep voice washing over my sensitized skin and holy cow!

"No. I'm fine."

"Glad to hear that, sweetheart. Wouldn't want anything to muss such a special package. My name's Carter. What's yours?"

Oh. He didn't recognize me. I blinked up at him, waiting for him to laugh at the joke. But I tended to be most popular with the under-thirty female crowd, so it was possible Carter didn't recognize me without my stage costumes and big hair.

"Regan," I said. I gave him my real name because I liked him and wanted to keep the energy between us even.

"Regan. Lovely name for a lovely face."

His lips turned up but his eyes remained firmly trained on mine.

Something clicked—that stranger danger my mother warned me about way back in first grade.

"Wait. Did you follow me back here?" I asked.

He nodded.

I stepped away. "All right. Well, thanks for the save from the ladies. Bye."

"You're just going to walk away?" he asked, surprise flaring in his eyes.

"Yep." Keep it simple, hope Darryl was nearby. Get out fast.

"May I ask why?"

The gaggle of women shuffled out of the bathroom en masse. As I'd turned to face him, this time my chest pressed to his. My pulse slammed in my neck. His gaze dropped there and he chuckled lightly.

"I don't bite," he whispered. "Not unless you want me to."

"I don't." But the words came out breathy. Like I did. Except I didn't. I didn't.

The music started up again, the crowd louder now that they had some drinks in them, and Janie was into her dance hall blues tunes.

"I have to go," I said.

"What if I took you somewhere quieter? Offered you a night-cap? Coffee?"

My brow wrinkled. "Why?"

He reached up and gently brushed a dark brown curl from my cheek. "Because I like looking at you, and I think I'll like talking to you even more. Can't really do that here."

Even though he'd leaned down toward me, his voice was loud—almost a yell. Speaking here would be difficult.

But did that mean I wanted to go somewhere with him?

I kept my gaze locked on his as I analyzed my body's reaction. I trusted it more than my mind. Unlike my mind, the prey buried deep within my genetics still knew when to run. But right now, all my inner prey wanted to do was rub against this man's hard chest and purr.

I glanced over at the entrance to the dance hall and considered my options: sitting at the table while Mindy continued to flirt; take a million more selfies; maybe get asked to come up on stage to perform. Janie had noticed me earlier and winked. That was usually code for "I'll call on you to entertain my crowd later."

I didn't want to after listening to the last hour of missed cues and notes. Janie missed a note, and her voice shrilled. I winced. No way I could let my reputation get mixed up in this hot mess.

"Okay," I said. "Just let me tell my friend where I'm going."

"What about your bodyguard?" he asked.

Observant. I liked that. I also liked the fact that he didn't seem overly fazed by my personal protection.

I wanted to get to know him better, but I wasn't sure going anywhere with him was smart.

He must have seen my hesitation. "Live a little, Regan," his voice was low, soft. His eyes held mine.

I bit my lip.

A couple of women stumbled back into the hallway, laughing as they fell against each other. One stopped to blink at me, her mouth opening as recognition dawned. I turned away quickly, that sick feeling in my gut lingering as tension built in my shoulders and neck.

I didn't want to have to play the part. Not tonight. My head began to ache as tension coiled up my spine. Carter held touched my cheek and my good sense crumbled.

"If you promise to play nice, Darryl can have the rest of the evening off."

Carter smiled, his eyes dancing with pleasure.

He rubbed his callused thumb down my cheek to the edge of my lip. My breathing stopped. He dropped his hand and I shivered, thankful he hadn't pushed me for more. Because, much as I was attracted to him, there was no way I could offer him more than my company.

"I'd be honored to get you home later."

I smiled more brightly than I had in months. After texting Mindy, I faced Carter, thankful for the chance to get to know him better.

"I'm ready."

"So am I," Carter said, his voice softer than spun sugar and twice as yummy.

CHAPTER TWO | Carter

We spoke about bits and pieces in the car. I told her I lived in Wyoming most of the year on the vast ranch I'd purchased there after completing my computer science degree at the University of Texas. I didn't mention I owned another place near San Francisco for when I needed to geek out with the biggest names in the industry, or that I'd just decided to move back to Austin to spend time with my family now that my twin and I had mended our relationship.

Until Cam and I hashed out the issues that led to me cutting off contact, I hadn't realized how much I'd missed him—like one misses a lost limb, I'd expect. Cam would understand that metaphor better than I, having some army buddies who'd been through horrific accidents and firefights that cost them arms, legs, eyes. Sanity.

I shook off that melancholy, trying to once again focus on the lovely young woman next to me. But that proved hard—for years, I'd second-guessed my decision to get a degree and not follow my brother into the military.

I didn't want glory or have the warrior mentality; I'd let Cam go because I was pissed he'd dropped out of college and married Kim. I was even more pissed off when he left the succubus Kim on our family's ranch and decided to become a badass Army Ranger.

Then, Kim died in an unspeakable disaster. Cam's injury a

few months later led to his medical discharge and an extra pile of guilt because I hadn't saved my brother from any of the demons that tried to take him down.

They'd nearly succeeded, and that was on me.

Going back home proved hard, but I'd found I enjoyed Austin's charm more than San Francisco's tech-heavy charisma, or even the vast openness of Wyoming's ranch land—the place I'd needed so desperately in order to heal.

Just something about the vibe in Austin—the cross between frenetic and easy-going, eclectic and cutting edge, appealed to me. That's why I'd built a tech empire based on independent authors who sold me the rights to construct choose-your-own-adventure stories in a fun little app I put together over a three-year span.

That "side business" had already overtaken my ranching ventures. Thankfully, I enjoyed the work and already had a few other apps in the works to further my portfolio.

"How long are you in town?" I asked to be polite, but also to get out of my head.

"Um. A few days."

"For work."

"Yes."

"Me, too. Where are you off to next?"

Regan hesitated, nibbling at that luscious lower lip. I wouldn't mind biting it myself.

"A few places. My calendar's booked solid through the end of the year."

"Oh? You headed out to, I don't know, San Francisco or Austin any time soon?"

Again, Regan hesitated. The street lamps flashed light into the car, casting her face into sharp relief. She reminded me of that new American/British princess. The one my sister was so gaga over. Meghan something.

Except Regan's hair was curlier and longer and she was an inch, maybe two, taller. In her heels, she came to my chin, and I stood over six feet tall. And her eyes. They were a rare, deep sky-blue. Arresting, especially against the warm skin tone and surrounded by her long dark lashes.

The light slid past and we were cast in shadow. I didn't get the sense she needed to consult her calendar to give me details, simply that she chose not to share with me.

"I'd need to check with my assistant about the exact timing."

"She handles your travel?"

"Among other things," Regan said.

I frowned, not liking how evasive she was being. With two bodyguards and an assistant, Regan was rich, probably famous. While she looked familiar enough to tickle a memory, I'd clearly buried myself way too deep in my tech company if I couldn't place a woman as beautiful as Regan.

We parked in the underground garage, and I led her to the elevator, both of us ignoring the heat of the Colorado evening.

I inserted my keycard and pressed the floor to the penthouse. Regan didn't even raise an eyebrow.

I always got a response when I pressed the penthouse button.

I shifted, starting to wonder just who Regan was. She turned toward me, raising those striking eyes to mine, and I decided who she was didn't matter. She was beautiful and the chemistry sizzling between us was undeniable.

Anticipation began a slow, steady drip through my tightening body.

Once the doors opened and I led her into the suite's large living room, she glanced around. I let my own gaze roam over the large, airy space. After a long moment, her bright, clear gaze landed back on me.

"What do you want to drink?" I asked, moving closer and running my hands over her hips. The denim skirt she wore was short enough to give me a good idea of the suppleness of her tanned thighs. I wanted to drag my fingers up the inner side to see if they were as soft as I imagined.

She stepped back, out of my embrace.

"You brought me here to seduce me," she said, her voice hinting at a huskiness that made my pants less comfortable.

"And if I did?" I asked, once again shifting closer to her, but I didn't touch her again. Not yet. Just let the heat between us build, swirl, intoxicate.

She smiled. Not the smile of a sultry witch I wanted under me. Hell, over me worked, too. No, this smile was sad—as if she were disappointed in me.

The last woman to look at me like that broke my heart.

"May I ask you something?" Regan asked.

I blinked, shoving the hot anger in those brown eyes and stiff lips from my memory. I was alive, standing next to a beautiful woman.

All was right in my world.

"Sure." I didn't lean back, but I didn't lean in closer. Something told me now wasn't the time to push her.

"Is this an every night experience?"

I rolled back on my heels, nonplussed and unsure how to answer.

"What do you mean?" I hedged.

But I knew what she was asking. And, dammit, my erection died because any answer I gave her now would destroy my evening plans.

Her lips flipped up again. "Every night. You bring a different woman back here and screw them, don't you?"

"No, not every night," I mumbled. Not often right now when I'd spent weeks on this newest update to my software. "Not here." Because I didn't actually live in this city. This was a stopover on my way home, to Austin.

Wait. Why was me wanting companionship—wanting a chance to forget—wrong?

She turned her back toward me, and I swallowed the groan working its way through my gut, up my chest. The skirt slithered over her hips, cupping her ass. I wanted my hands there, fingers digging into the supple flesh, as I pounded into her body. And forget…

Whoa. Not going there. Especially twice in under five minutes.

Thankfully, she spoke, breaking my near-trance.

"I'm going to have to pass," she said over her shoulder.

I crowded her a little. Her pupils dilated and her delicate nostrils flared. I lifted my hands, prepared to run my palms down her bare arms.

She walked back in clear dismissal.

"There's one thing you didn't ask me," she snapped.

I dropped my hands. "Fine. I'll bite. What's that?"

"If I was interested in a one-night stand."

"Who doesn't like pleasure?" I growled. She was as into me down at the bar as I was into her.

She cocked her head, all that long, luscious dark hair spilling across her neck and down her back. "You're sexy. You're charismatic. Unfortunately, your reasoning that I would fall into bed with you after having a fifteen-minute conversation is unacceptable."

A live wire zipping up my spine wouldn't have hurt any more. "Unacceptable?"

She slid her purse strap back on her shoulder but continued to face me, her eyes filled with such disappointment—in me—that my gaze slid to the floor.

"You use sex. For pleasure. Nothing wrong with that, I guess, if both people are okay with it." Her tone said there was a lot wrong with my choices. She stepped in closer, her rich voice caressing my skin, causing a ripple over my flesh. "But, see, I'm not okay with that."

My chest ached at the weary sadness that filtered into her eyes.

"Did someone…" I didn't know how to ask—what I wanted to ask—but it was evident from her bleak expression that she'd seen sex used as a weapon. That realization made my heart stutter.

She brushed off my question with a flip of her hair. That silky, shiny hair I really wanted to pet. Not in a sexual way, not now. I just…shit. I wanted to hold her close and tell her everything would be okay.

We both knew that was a lie.

"You want to do intimate things to my body without understanding my mind, my feelings."

"What does sex have to do with feelings?" I asked, my voice harsh because these emotions she'd churned up inside me hurt.

Her smile held no amusement and her eyes cut me with their sharpness. What had happened to her?

"For many men and women, but most importantly, for me, everything."

"You're saying you've never fucked for the sake of the release?" I asked. No, I couldn't have heard her response right.

"I don't fuck." Her voice was as flat as her expression.

The word fell, hard and ugly between us. I shivered. When she said it, it sounded…well, bad. Everything about this evening had taken a nose-dive into unfamiliar and painful territory. I didn't know how to respond.

"I'll take you home."

She pursed her plump lips. "No."

"No?" I asked. I was so out of my depth.

"No. Me coming here was insanity." Her delicate throat convulsed and her eyes filled with tears that she blinked back with a ruthlessness of long practice.

She was ripping my heart out. Bringing her here had been an epic level mistake.

"I have one very simple rule." Her voice broke but she kept her gaze locked on mine and her back straighter than a flagpole. "You don't get in here without getting in here first." She tapped her chest then her temple.

Her words settled against my skin like acid rain.

"You expect me to…what? Love you? I don't even know you."

And this time she didn't even smile. Her gaze remained steady, true as I met it.

"Exactly."

My eyes narrowed, but her next words, spoken in that rich voice that wrapped around me like a mug of hot chocolate stopped both my heart and my desire to comfort her.

"I don't think you can love a woman."

With effort, I managed not to stagger. My body turned stiff as I shut each emotion down. She was right—I didn't. Well, not the kind of relationship she meant. I mean, I loved my mama and my sister, but not wanting emotional entanglements with other women? That was a choice. One I'd made because…I shook my head, hard, trying to force the memories from my mind.

She turned on her cowboy boots walked to the door. Hand on the knob, she turned back and looked at me. The light set her hair aglow.

"Good luck with the seducing."